RAPTURE

or,

SATAN WINS AGAIN

A Contemporary Novel

BY

W. JASON PETRUZZI

ISBN: 978-1-7338804-3-5 (paperback)
ISBN: 978-1-7338804-2-8 (eBook)

Abstract Cover Art: Graffiti—painted by: Michelle Delgado
Cover & Interior Book Design by www.TeaBerryCreative.com

CONTENTS

INTRODUCTION

Rapture: Or, Satan Wins Again is a sarcastic, irreverent riff on the Christian concept of an end-time event, where all believers will rise into heaven; this event precedes the Second Coming.

This contemporary thriller begins in Manhattan, with the NYC Police and FBI investigating a rash of murders. Meanwhile, a retired CEO, and Romania's UN Ambassador (and a generous contributor to the US president's reelection campaigns), was on his way to a critical meeting. At the same time, people begin disappearing. The Nation is in ruin, buildings are shuttered, and NYC is bombed.

In the midst of this chaos, the Ambassador delivers a stirring speech at the UN; he then moves to Washington, D.C. as the President's confidant, and they travel to Jerusalem and Rome in search of answers. As it turns out, the UN Ambassador is actually the Antichrist. Once his full life-history is revealed, the quick-paced events will keep the reader glued to the book until the surprise conclusion.

And I stood upon the sand of the sea, and saw a beast rise up out of the sea, having seven heads and ten horns, or maybe it was ten heads and seven horns, or three heads and twelve legs and twenty-eight tails, I don't remember, it was a pretty trippy vision, man. But with all those limbs, man, that beast could sure dance.

—CHARLES MANSON

had a propensity to cut the throats of wealthy investment bankers. There were three running theories among the police concerning this puzzle. The first was that the killer was someone who had lost his life savings in a market correction or corporate scandal or some such trifle, and was out for revenge. The second theory was that he was your usual cherry-bright random psycho who realized that killing super-rich white men will get you on the front page faster than anything else, even killing blond coeds. The third theory, and this view was held by a minority, mainly the man alone, was that these killings were a small but integral part of a grand, diabolical scheme to take over the world.

As the man stepped under the tape, one of the cops said, "Hey, you can't come in here." Without saying a word, or even turning to acknowledge the officer, he handed him the card he was already holding, which read "Lucious D. Griffin, PsyD, Forensic Psychologist." "Oh, sure," the cop said, "Dr. Griffin, right, they're waiting for you, right over there." He motioned to the crime scene.

Griffin turned his head to face him. "Yes, thank you," he said slowly, his face expressionless. "I can see they're over there." He turned back and walked over to the three detectives, one woman and two men, standing in a cluster over the body.

"Here he comes," one said to another, in a hushed and exasperated one. "*Que tal*, Doc," he said, putting on a smile.

"Marcel," nodded Griffin.

Still smiling, Detective Marcel Fuentes motioned to the woman, a tall red-head, and went on, "Yes, and this is Detective Tenney and her partner, Detective Haversham. Tenney's the primary on this one." Griffin gave each of them a brief, polite handshake, barely glancing at them as his eyes took in the scene.

Haversham, a bespeckled, slightly pudgy man with wispy, thinning hair who looked like he should have been teaching history somewhere, not walking a beat, said, motioning as he spoke, "The vic came out to get his paper, and we think the perp was just standing right there on the porch, waiting for him. That's where the spatter is, all over the porch and the wall. The perp grabs him from behind and cuts his throat, he falls down the stairs to die here. We think the perp hopped over the railing and ran off; that's because there's no footprints in the blood. Nobody heard or saw anything. But then somebody mentions he's a stockbroker, and so we figure it must be the Slasher, and call it in."

For a long moment there was silence. The three watched Griffin, who stared down at the body, then up at the porch and examined the steps. There were three of them, each with little clusters of blood droplets. Them he looked back down at the body again. He did nothing else. Finally, after several minutes passed, Fuentes said, "Well? What do you think?"

Griffin stirred from his brooding, letting the voice carry him back to the present. He looked up at Fuentes, his eyes shining, intense.

"What do I think? I'll tell you what I think." He spoke in a voice low and rumbling. "I think that we are on the verge, that's what I think. With all the filth occupying the minds of men, the garbage and pornography that spews from the television and radio and internet, with all the catastrophes occurring in the world, with its plagues and famines and global warming and wars and so on, it seems self-evident that we are heading for the end, the great Armageddon in which the twisted wrongheadedness of the gape-mouthed fools of this corrupted, overfattened nation we live in will leave us in the hands of the black-souled avatar of evil and sickness who is fast coming upon this wretched earth. Oh, yes, the millennium may have come and gone, but his putrid, decaying world is dying, and you can smell the stench of death as the soul of the very nation is rotting away and the sulfuric burning stink of hell creeps ever closer. Our fragile peace and prosperity will soon be blown away like the fall of a leaf, you can count on it." His eyes were wide and focused, as though he could see it happening before him in vivid color.

Fuentes was not the least bit flummoxed by this display of freakishness. "Um, yes. No, I meant about Mr. Stockbroker here." He motioned to the corpse. "Don't you think this is the work of the Slasher?"

"This? No. Don't be ridiculous," said Griffin, snapping back to himself. "I can't believe you made me get up early on a Sunday for this nonsense."

"What makes you think it's nonsense? It clearly fits the pattern."

"Please. Just because he works on Wall Street and his throat was slashed doesn't mean he was necessarily killed by the Wall Street Slasher. I don't know who this guy is, and the Slasher's victims have all been high-profile, top-tier people. There's no connection. This guy was clearly killed by one of his neighbors, who's probably hated him for years because of his barking dog or loud parties or whatever it is people kill each other over these days, and decided he could do it and idiots like you would just chalk it up to this month's side-show freak."

"Yeah, but what—"

"Look," said Griffin, holding up his hand. "The Slasher victims were cut on the right side of their necks, indicating a left-handed killer. This guy," he pointed to the knife wound, "was cut on the left side of the neck, indicating a right-handed killer. Clearly someone totally different."

Detective Tenney spoke up. "Well, he might be ambidextrous."

Griffin looked over at her with disgust, which is not an expression a gorgeous red-head like Tenney often sees on people looking at her. "No," he said. "Don't be stupid."

"Well, why not? How do you know?" She did not like his pretentiousness, nor did she like it that her partner was failing to defend her.

"Because he's not. It's never something that clever. Anyway, I already know who the killer is."

"Yeah?" said Fuentes, grinning. "Who?"

Griffin pointed into the crowd of bystanders. "That guy over there. In the yellow bathrobe."

"What, you're kidding?" Fuentes glanced over at the yellow-bathrobe man, who was a stooping, gray-haired geezer, way too old to be committing murders. "Why in God's name would you say that?" He wondered if he was even looking at the right man. There wasn't anyone with a pure yellow bathrobe; the man he had seen was wearing a yellow bathrobe with orange polkadots.

"Because he's wearing sneakers with his pajamas."

The three detectives looked over at the geezer, who probably had trouble opening his mail with a knife, never mind someone's throat. "Um, so what?" asked Fuentes. "Everybody's wearing sneakers with their pajamas. What, do you expect them to stand around barefoot?"

Griffin sighed. "Nobody pays attention. I hint and hint, but nobody ever gets it. His sneakers have blood on them."

The detectives looked closer and noticed that there were, indeed, red splotches on the sneakers, pants, and the hem of the bathrobe. Actually, more than the hem, and they clearly weren't orange polkadots.

"Um, right. Excuse me." Fuentes broke away and ran off towards the crowd, pointing at the man and shouting. "That guy! Stop him!" Soon he and a number of cops were chasing the man down the street, and you'd never have guessed that such an old coot could run so fast.

"Wow," said Haversham. "How'd the hell'd you do that?"

"I'm going back to my hotel. Call me when there's a real crime." Griffin sauntered off, back to his car.

Looking after him, Haversham said, "Who the fuck is that guy? He's insane."

"He's a genius," said Tenney, laughing. "A real freak of nature."

At about the same time, deep in the heart of the city, twelve men, all middle-aged or older, and all dressed in expensive tailored black suits, sat around the long sides of a mahogany table in an enormous fortieth-floor office, waiting. The office had a picture window that took up the entire far wall, giving a fantastic view of the surrounding Manhattan skyline, yet none of the men were looking at it. They all watched the suite's large double doors. Slowly they opened, and in stepped the man of the hour—the *other* man of the hour.

Mr. Shahse had an interesting résumé. He had grown up in poverty and anonymity in a post-communist Obscure Eastern European Country (OEEC), got into Sorbonne University on a scholarship, then immediately upon graduation had gotten a management position with Q-Com, the giant European telcom company, and within seven years, while still in his twenties, had worked his way up to being appointed its CEO. Nobody thought there was anything suspicious in this. Three years later, he retired with his millions and returned to the OEEC that was his home. After donating a fairly large sum of money to the president's re-re-reelection campaign, he was appointed his country's United Nations ambassador, which is how he came to be in New York, wearing a tailored suit that was every bit as expensive and fashionable and black as the suits worn by the twelve powerful men before him.

The click of his shoes on the floor echoed off the walls as he approached the table. "Gentleman!" he said, grinning broadly. He was handsome in an aristocratic way, tall, with an angular face and thick wavy black hair. As he reached the table, the man seated at its head stood up. "Mr. Cohen, a pleasure," Shahse said, vigorously shaking his hand and inclining his head slightly. He spoke perfect

English with a slight Romanian accent. Cohen motioned him to the empty chair at the other end of the table, where Shahse gracefully seated himself.

"Mr. Shahse, welcome," Cohen said gravely, resuming his seat. He spoke with a proper British accent. "We have been following your career with great interest, and have invited you here to offer you a proposal. But first, we must dispense with the secrecy with which we have guarded our previous communications, and reveal to you our identity. Be aware though, that whatever is spoken of in this room is never to leave it!"

"Fear not, Mr. Cohen. You have my word."

"Good. Then allow me to introduce you to the Zionist Committee." He motioned around the table at the other eleven men. Shahse looked them over carefully for the first time, and recognized a number of them. There was that big-shot Hollywood producer who made all those big-budget blockbusters…there was the scion of that famous European banking clan…there was a fellow who was one of the biggest dealers in the international diamond trade…and there! He couldn't believe it! Sitting right here in at this table in New York, the former Prime Minister of Israel! All these rich and powerful people, and every one of them a Jew!

"Wait a minute!" he cried in astonishment. "The Zionist Committee? Is this what I think it is?"

"Yes!" said Mr. Cohen triumphantly. "Throughout history we have been known by many names: The Knights Templar, the Illuminati, the Freemasons, the Rosicurians, the Trilateral Commission, Dreamworks SKG, and so on. But always we were the same, remaining behind the scenes, secretly controlling the world!"

Shahse gasped. "So it's true! All those wild conspiricist fantasies are real! The world actually *is* run by Jews!"

"Exactly! For centuries, our organization has ruled the world through the secret manipulation of governments, markets, businesses, and individuals. We have orchestrated nearly every major event in world history. Wars, assignations, scandals, even who gets voted off each week on all those reality shows!" He laughed, and the others joined in.

"So, everything?"

"Everything! From the Crusades to Columbus's voyage to the New World to the French Revolution to both World Wars to the Internet. We've had our hand in everything!"

Shahse furrowed his brow. "Um, so the Holocaust...?"

"Pure fiction! There never was any Holocaust! I would have thought, growing up in Eastern Europe, you would have known that. Every child in Arabia does, unfortunately. Only the gullible Westerners are so easily manipulated. But it was necessary to fabricate in order to cast off suspicion after our Protocols were stolen by the Czar and revealed to the world. Plus, now the nations of the West feel they owe us some enormous debt, and have not only given us our own state, but supplied us with all the weapons and wealth we asked for. Ha-ha!"

"Okay," said Shahse, feeling disturbed but hiding it well. And disappointed; he had believed. What a softie he was! "So...what do you want with me?"

Cohen smiled. "Well, Mr. Shahse, let me explain. The people of the world would never stand being ruled by us. If they ever found out...well, not even our enormous power could, shall we say, ensure continued stability. And of course, our plans and machinations necessitate stealth. Therefore, occasionally, we choose some Gentile through whom we may operate. The supposed great people of history, people like Napoleon, Lenin, Hitler, Bush, and so on, were only the public figures through which we controlled everything from behind the scenes. And now, we have chosen you to be our next agent. As I said, we've been watching you, and you seem the perfect patsy for our newest scheme. And a glorious scheme it is! You will be the vessel through which we shall finally consummate our global rule!"

"Well, I'm honored," said Shahse, not missing a beat. "But, if I may be so bold as to ask...."

"By all means."

"What exactly is your newest scheme?"

Cohen steepled his hands before him. "Well, you see, Mr. Shahse, we have determined that the time of the Rapture is at hand."

"The Rapture?" he said blankly. "The Christian doctrine wherein all the devout will be taken bodily into heaven before the Second Coming, to escape God's judgment upon the earth?" In saying this he was only mechanically quoting something he'd read. He couldn't grasp his mind around what Cohen was saying, because it lacked any connection to what was going on, it was a complete and absolute *non sequitor.*

"The very same. Once it occurs, there shall be mass chaos and confusion. In the midst of this chaos we shall claim total global power through simple blackmail, by implying that we are responsible for this event, and will do it again if our demands are not met. In such a manner we shall gain absolute power. We have already laid the groundwork. Into the chaos we shall bring order and peace. Our order, our peace!"

"Okay, hold on." Shahse held up his finger. "Back up one tiny second here. Let me just see if I've got this straight. You think the *Rapture* is about to happen?"

"Within a matter of days. All the signs point to it."

"No, no, wait just a second." He waved his hands. His accent had mysteriously disappeared, and he now spoke in a plain, vulgar,

PROLOGUE

The beginning of the end of the world was on a Sunday (remember that, there'll be a test later). This was to be expected—you can never trust a Sunday. Like it says in the Book of Ephesians, "the days are evil," and no day is more evil that Sunday. Sure, it seems harmless, being the Lord's Day and all, a day off work, a day to sleep in and eat brunch and go to a matinee or sit home with an extra-big newspaper with color comics. But don't be fooled! It's all a clever ploy, a carefully designed deception to keep people off their guard, to lull them into a false sense of security so it can sneak up on them, and then, wham!

This particular Sunday would prove to be the most whamiest of them all.

Before the fireworks, though, the beginning of this Sunday was like any other Sunday—bloody (there's a song about that, it must be true). A young man in blue silk pajamas and a red silk bathrobe stepped out of his Upper Manhattan townhouse, to pick up his *Wall Street Journal* off the front steps, and was assaulted by someone from behind. That somebody had been waiting on the porch next to the door, crouching down with his back pressed up against the wall. That somebody sprang up, grabbed the man in silk from behind, and slashed his throat with a Bowie knife, pushed him away so that he fell down the steps, jumped over the railing, and ran off. The man in the pajamas slowly lifted himself up with his hands, and then collapsed back down again, making a gurgling sound as his blood drained out.

No one saw anything until ten minutes later when, a neighbor, also in his pajamas, stepped out to get his paper (which coincidentally enough, was also a *Wall Street Journal*), found the dead man splayed out on the sidewalk, and ran back in, horrified, to call the police. Another ten minutes later, two cops in a squad car pulled up, took a glance around, and set up the tape. More cops in more squad cars came. A city coroner showed up. Then two detectives arrived. After taking a look and talking to the neighbor, they made a call which brought another detective. He too made a quick assessment upon arriving and then another call. Then finally, two hours after the murder, amidst the crowd of cops searching for any tiny clue, photographers taking pictures, reporters talking in front of cameras, and onlookers looking on, the man of the hour appeared on the scene.

A black Lincoln Town car drove up slowly, through the gawkers, right up to the yellow tape, and the man stepped out. He was a sinewy fellow with a face that was hard and creased, dressed in corduroy pants and an old suede blazer, his gray hair in a neat buzz cut. A former FBI Behavioral Scientist, he had left the force after the tragic death of his partner and a resulting Incident, which I'm sure you'll get to hear all about later in the story, lucky you, to work as a private consultant, helping local police to hunt down serial killers and solve sundry other high profile cases. His eyes were cold and dark, eyes that had seen too many scenes of shocking violence, peered too deep into the dark chasms of the diseased souls of the most wretched, vile humans alive, and seen far, far too many bad horror movies.

He was here in New York City to assist in the case of a killer who had become known as the Wall Street Slasher, a fellow who

American tone. "Let's just pretend for a moment that you're right about that."

"Which we are," Cohen scoffed.

"Wouldn't that mean that Christianity was *true*?"

"Well, of course it's true. That's why we hate it."

"Seriously?" said Shahse, completely blown away by this revelation.

"Very," said Cohen. "Two thousand years ago our predecessors murdered Christ, and ever since we have waged a war against him and his followers for total domination. And finally we shall have it!"

Shahse sat wide-eyed with amazement, a joyful smile spreading over his face. They were probably just feeding him tall tales because they still weren't sure that they could trust him, which was understandable. On the other hand, they might be speaking the truth, or what they believed to be the truth, in which case they were totally bonkers. And yet…everything made more sense that way. Everything. A light of understanding shown within him. Either way, he suddenly felt enamored with the Committee. This was definitely the place for him.

"Wow, that really clears things up," he said, his Romanian accent returned. "I definitely want to be a part of this. Gentlemen, I offer myself as your humble servant, and pledge myself to the attainment of all your goals."

"Thank you." Mr. Cohen extended his hands. "Now, gentlemen," he declared, "our thirteenth member, Mr. Sei Shest Shahse!" (Try to say that three times fast!) They all began to applaud, and Shahse, who could not say his own full name three times fast, nodded around, his face beaming.

CHAPTER 1

In a 747, flying above the clouds at 40,000 feet, Captain Hiram Manly leaned back in his chair and sipped his coffee. It had been a pleasant, uneventful, boring flight, just like every single flight he'd ever flown as the captain of a major carrier. "How are we doing?"

"Everything's steady," said his co-pilot, yawing with his own boredom.

"Good." The captain tipped his head back, emptying his cup, then stood up. "I think I'm going to check on the passengers." He opened the steel cockpit door and stepped out. He found his favorite buxom stewardess standing just inside the curtain separating the front area from first class. "Hey there," he said, coming up behind her.

"Oh, hello, Captain," she said, glancing at him.

"And what might you be doing?"

"I'm looking for celebrities."

"Really. How charming. Find any?"

"No. There's usually a couple in first class on every flight, but I can't seem to find any this time."

"That's too bad," Manly said smoothly, placing his hand on her shoulder.

"There is one guy. I wouldn't really consider him a celebrity, but he was on the news last night." She pointed to a balding man sitting near the back. He seemed to be quietly arguing with the woman seated next to him.

"That's Anton 'Tony' LeVay," the stewardess said. "He's a minister. He wrote all those *Rapture* books." (High Priest, Anton 'Tony' LeVay's philosophy was that man, unfettered by fear, should just live naturally for himself. He admits proudly that true Satanism is a "selfish" religion, loaded with hedonism and self-indulgence; it is also honest, in that it doesn't cover up what it's all about. LeVay views other religions, especially Christianity, as hypocritical, guilt-driven, and devoid of any real enjoyment).

"*Rapture* books?"

"Yeah. It's a series of Christian novels about the end of the world."

The captain made a face behind her back. "Christian novels? You read those things?"

The stewardess glanced back at him, frowning. "No, of course not. I told you, he was on the news last night. Apparently his new book broke some sales record."

"Humph. Sounds pretty useless to me."

She turned around to face him fully, and looked straight into his eyes. "Oh yes. Me too." She let the curtain drop, hiding them from the view of the passengers. Captain Manley wrapped his arms around the stewardess and kissed her hard, pushing her back against the wall.

"My, my," she breathed. "What will your wife say?"

"My what?" he said, kissing her again.

Suddenly, the plane shook, and a bright light came filtering through the curtain. People behind it cried out. The Captain pushed the Stewardess away and stepped through the curtain into first class. The whole plane was filled with an intense bright light, which not only shone in through all the widows, on both sides of the plane, but seemed to be coming from within the plane as well. Manly's eyes settled on Tony LeVay just as he seemed to dissolve into thin air. It happened in an instant. He was sitting there one moment, then gone the next. He had blinked into nonexistence like a television picture when the set's turned off. The passengers started screaming, as apparently other people had blinked out as well.

The captain rushed back to the cockpit, knocking the stewardess, who was crying, to the ground. He jumped inside, slamming the steel door shut. He turned around, and—the co-pilot was missing, too!

Manly panicked. No, scratch that. He totally, completely freaked. He had no idea what was happening, and worse, he had no idea how to fly the plane. He had never actually flown the plane! The autopilot always did that, and the co-pilot always took off and landed. He'd learned his flying skills on those jets in the Air Force, but while he had taken lessons, he'd never quite got the hang of all those buttons and dials on the 747s. He'd never needed to, with all the actual flying being done by others. His job, really, was to be suave and reassuring to the paying customers. But he didn't think he could cope with an actual emergency. What little he did know had gone right out of his head.

His terror increasing astronomically! Manly grabbed the emergency parachute, of which there were only three, put it on, and opened the steel door again. He ran out, smack into the stewardess.

"What's going on?" she screamed.

He shoved her aside, and ran to the air hatch. He kicked it open, and jumped out into the atmosphere. He fell thousands of feet, until his parachute opened, and then drifted slowly down into a cornfield in the Heartland, while aboard the plane, the cabin depressurized, suffocating everyone.

The autopilot kept the plane flying steadily for another thousand miles or so, until it finally ran out of fuel and fell into the ocean.

CHAPTER 2

Shahse stepped out onto the balcony of his penthouse suite, drawn by the brilliant light that filled the sky, only a few hours after he'd returned from his meeting with the Zionist Committee. The intense light was as bright as the sun, as though you were staring directly at it, (which as we all know is something you should never do), only it emanated from everywhere. Shielding his eyes, he looked around, confused, blinking, then glanced down at the ground. His gaze fixed on a woman holding a baby just as they seemed to evaporate into thin air. Shahse jerked back in surprise, then rushed to the edge of the balcony to look again. People everywhere were running about, screaming. This was quickly followed by crashes and explosions as suddenly driverless cars careened into each other, nobody having grabbed their steering wheels.

"Oh, sweet!" he exclaimed, his eyes wide in awe. He instantly understood what was going on. The Rapture! The Rapture had really occurred! Those whack-jobs in the Committee had actually been right! "This is so freaking cool!" he said breathlessly, feeling so overwhelmed he almost fell to his knees. "Thank you, God!" Then the light vanished just as suddenly as it had come.

A young blond woman, dressed in a miniskirt, came up behind him on the balcony; "What's going on?" she said nervously. Her words were slurred and her breath smelled strongly of alcohol. She was a cursory acquaintance of his, some minor functionary who worked at the UN and had a crush on him, flirting with him often. She had met with him after lunch, bumping into him accidentally right outside his building. They went up to his penthouse, where she blatantly propositioned him, determined to finally get into bed with him, but he was too wound up by the morning's bombshell, so after giving her a cursory tout, they ended up in the living room where he paced and talked while she kicked off her shoes and sat on his sofa drinking glass after glass of sparkling California champagne, the only alcoholic beverage he had. He kept a few bottles in the kitchen for guests, and she found them on her own during the tour. Disappointingly, the whole penthouse was sparsely decorated; the only thing of interest was the sword collection Shahse displayed in his office. He was a fencer, but he also collected a few more traditional swords, which were hung up on the wall: a scimitar, a double-edged long sword, a rapier, and a *wakizashi*, a samurai short sword.

"Sweetie, you missed the whole thing!"

"What? What happened?"

"The world is ending," he said with an excitement that verged on triumph, as though it was all his doing.

"What?"

Shahse turned to her, grinning ebulliently. "It's the Rapture!"

"The what?"

"The Rapture! You know, when all the good Christians of the world are snatched up into heaven, and everybody else is left on earth to suffer a time of unspeakable horrors known as the Tribulation!"

"What?" she said for the fourth time, shrieking now.

"Just before the Second Coming of Christ, when he brings about the Last Judgment and the end of the world. Haven't you ever heard of any of that? Haven't you read the books?"

"The books?" Poor woman, she was not following things at all.

"Yes, the *Rapture* books! By Tony LeVay. They tell about—" He was interrupted by another explosion, not to far off. The young woman jumped, but he went on smoothly. "They're about how the Bible predicts the world will end, about how the Antichrist appears before the end of the world, and will take over, and there'll be plagues and disasters and curses and Armageddon and all that before the Second Coming. It all starts with the Rapture! Haven't you ever heard of them? They're best sellers." He laughed. "I admit, I can't get enough of them. And here it is! It's all happening for real!"

"The world is ending?" the young woman asked, whimpering.

"And how! And you know what else? You know what the best part is? Since only the good, heaven-bound Christians get raptured, everybody that's left, like us, we're all still here because we're all wretched ungodly sinners!" Shahse was talking fast. He was very excited, giddy even, and his eyes were bouncing around and glowing with brightness almost as intense as the light a moment ago. "If we died right now, we'd go straight to hell!"

By now, the woman was no longer paying attention, she was crying so violently.

"Mmm! It's all so scary, isn't it? It's chilling, it's positively tingling!"

The woman leaned far over the railing to better see what was going on. Unfortunately, with all the alcohol in her system, and all the surging emotions, she lost her balance and fell over the edge.

Shahse froze completely startled as her shrieking faded away. Shoot! Nobody was going to believe that had been an accident. But then there was another explosion, along with the sound of gunshots going off somewhere nearby, and he realized that nobody would probably even notice. He peered over the railing, and saw her body laying out on the sidewalk far below, blood pooling around her. He was suddenly overwhelmed by the reality of what he'd just said.

Right this very moment, her soul was speeding along on its way to hell! He could just imagine the scenario, and hear that lovely piercing wail of hers going on forever and ever and ever!

It was a horrible, horrible thought, too perverse and hideous to even begin contemplating. Yet it was undeniably also very, very exciting. Here was someone he actually knew, who had been alive one moment and was now dead and in hell, and he was certain of that, that she was in hell, burning in hell, right this very moment. Wow. It was so mind-blowing, so spine-tingling. "Positively tingling!" he said again, smacking the railing for emphasis. "Mmm!"

CHAPTER 3

Lucious Griffin sat at his hotel room table, a dozen-plus files and stacks of paper spread out before him. He had spent his day pouring over various bits of evidence in the Wall Street Slasher case, in complete absorption. His drapes were drawn shut, and anyway his back was to the window, so he hadn't noticed the amazing light that had flooded the world. The vague sound of car crashes and sirens in the distance, and people shouting in the other rooms and halls of the hotel had only barely penetrated his single-minded concentration.

This case presented one of the most impenetrable mysteries he'd ever encountered. The killer was proficient and prolific enough to have already claimed six victims, but these were no ordinary people. They were high-level investment bankers. Four of them ran their own firms. They controlled the wealth that propelled entire industries. Not a single one of them had a net worth of less than a hundred million dollars. These were the big dogs.

So really, it was easy to see why he thought there was some larger conspiracy at work in their deaths. Especially considering the expertise in which they had been carried out. The killer had caught each of them at a vulnerable moment, when they were alone, away from the tight security of their offices and homes, and away from prying witnesses. No one had seen a single killing take place.

Griffin wondered if the killer followed each one around for days before finding the perfect opportunity. It all seemed excruciatingly professional.

And yet, that fact that the killings were committed with a knife, instead of a gun, was perplexing. A gun, after all, would be far more efficient. And it's wasn't like the murders were taking place inside airports or some such place where security screening would keep all firearms out. So why go to the trouble? Why risk getting your clothes all bloody, like yellow-bathrobe man?

It was the most important clue he had. Fuck, it was the only clue he had. The Slasher never left any DNA, or a fingerprint, a shoeprint, a hair, or a fiber, or even a wad of spit. Nothing. The whole case was psychological. There wasn't a shred of evidence otherwise. This guy knew how to beat all the forensic tricks. He'd obviously seen a lot of episodes of CSI.

But what did it mean? The use of the knife indicated something about the killer's personality, and his motives. A gun would be too impersonal, too mechanical. A knife, on the other hand, was more, say, expressive. It was an instrument of aggression, of anger, of vengeance. It made a statement. It showed how much he hated his victim—jealous of them, possibly?—and it indicated his prowess in killing. There was an element of ego to this.

Or maybe it was the exact opposite. Perhaps the Slasher thought these bankers were too rich and powerful, too greedy and corrupt. That they were immoral, a blight on the nation, and he was motivated by religious fervor to punish them, and to do so he used the more primitive, symbolic blade. The sword of heaven.

Griffin had no idea. All he knew for certain was that with the deaths of these six people—all men—the global financial picture had been thrown for a loop. The stock market had taken a dive recently that was almost directly attributable to the uncertainty and panic that were the result of these deaths. Perhaps that was the whole aim? Perhaps the murders were a form of economic terrorism? But there was still the knife to consider. Most terrorists, even the religious ones, had no qualms using modern weapons.

As astute as he was, he still couldn't figure it out. He needed more evidence before he could make any judgment.

The TV was on, but tuned to static. There were three video tapes that he had been watching on the table. These tapes were copies of recordings made by security cameras at three of the building where murders and occurred, around the time the crimes took place. He had watched them over and over again. They showed people occasionally walking past, and cars doing the same in the background. After several hours, he realized that there was one car, and only one car, that appeared on all three tapes only minutes after each of the murders.

That was it—the break he'd been looking for.

After sitting right up close to the screen, looking at different angles, and squinting a lot, he finally made out the plate number. It would have to be rechecked, of course, using digital magnification, but there was one thing absolutely, undisputedly clear.

The car had a diplomatic plate.

There was a rapid pounding on the door. "Open up, man!" said the voice of Detective Fuentes. Even that took a moment to break Griffin's focus. He got up and opened the door.

"Hey, Marcel," he said calmly. "How'd it go? That guy confess?"

"What?" Fuentes barked as he stepped in and slammed the door shut, then locked it and put the chain on. His face was very red and his hands were shaking. He was sweating and breathing hard, like he'd run the whole way here from the police station.

Griffin frowned, quizzically. "Something wrong?" he asked.

"Something wrong?" shouted Fuentes. "Something wrong? Where the fuck have you been all day?" He was practically screaming.

Griffin let a moment pass, then said calmly, "I've been right here going through the files. I think I've found something interesting."

"You found something interesting!" Fuentes's voice had not been softened by the pause, nor by Griffin's calm demeanor, but he was suddenly wearing a large, exaggerated grin. "By all means tell me!"

"Um, sure. I think we found a way to identify our guy's car."

"Really! Isn't that great! *Muy simpatico!*" Besides shouting and grinning, Fuentes's eyes had become wide, almost popping out. It was extremely disconcerting.

"Stop it. Look, what's going on?" Briefly he considered the possibility that another murder had occurred, but that wouldn't warrant this kind of odd behavior. Even if they'd caught the guy red-handed and gotten a signed confession, this wasn't appropriate.

Fuentes laughed, a short barking laugh, and Griffin decided he had gone insane. "You don't know! That ridiculous speech you gave us this morning, and you don't even know!"

"Don't know what?"

He took a slow step closer and peered straight into Griffin's eyes, his own aflame and wild. Baring his teeth, he whispered harshly, "The world is ending."

"So soon?" said Griffin. There was no mockery in his voice. He instantly accepted the truth of what Fuentes had said. They had not known each other very long, only since Griffin had been hired to consult on the Slasher case, three weeks past. Yet this temperament clearly did not fit with what he knew of Fuentes. He was an affable enough fellow, and would indulge in the morbid humor of homicide detectives, but he would not make jokes like this. If he'd suddenly lost his mind, there would be just cause for it. Griffin didn't need to ask anything else. Slowly and carefully he moved to the window and pulled the cord to open the curtains. The room's view was a lousy one, of the building across a narrow street, and little else, but when he leaned forward at a right angle he could see bits of the rest of the city beyond it. Off in the distance, the sky was cloudy with smoke.

Unnerved in a deep, profound way he couldn't recall having ever felt before, he moved across the room to the TV, and switched the channel. He stole a glance at Fuentes's still intense gaze, then turned to the screen, and was suddenly sickened with dismay.

The camera showed the station's news desk, but the angle was tilted. At the edge, the dark metalwork of the studio could be seen. The desk itself was empty. Nothing at all was moving. And it was silent. It might have been nothing but a broadcast of a photo, everything was so still.

Everything about it was wrong, fundamentally wrong, and the two men stared at it with a kind of awe. Several moments went by before Griffin could bring himself to switch to a new channel.

"...chaos everywhere," the anchor was saying, and Griffin felt minutely relieved that at least *something* was still working the way it was supposed to. This was a news program where the newsroom was behind the desk, so you could see the efficient newsgathering bustle. But while there were people in the background, it was only a very few, and they were running back and forth from one desk to another. There was a bar at the bottom of the screen where normally the title of the tragedy being covered would appear, but it was blank.

The anchor bravely kept his usual steady, detached demeanor as he spoke. "The world has been rocked by a massive number of sudden disappearances. All over the world, there are reports of a powerful light causing people to vanish. Thousands of people, possibly tens of thousands or more, including thousands of children. Mothers have reported their children vanishing right out of their arms in a catastrophe that defies explanation. Joining me now is Dr. Eugene

Efflebert, Nobel-prize winning professor of physics at UCLA." The camera panned to the right to reveal a man with frizzy white hair sitting next the anchor, who turned to face him. "Dr. Efflebert, thank you for being here, on this terrible, terrible day."

"You're welcome, Bob," said the professor with studied seriousness.

"Dr. Efflebert, what is your explanation as to this mysterious mass vanishing?"

"Bob, I think we finally have proof of extra-terrestrial intelligence. I believe this is the start of an alien invasion. Right now the world's most powerful telescopes are sweeping the sky—"Griffin snapped the set off.

Trembling ever so slightly, he took a deep breath to calm down. He turned back to Fuentes and said, "You know, I always knew it was coming, but I never thought I'd actually see it."

"See what?" said Fuentes sharply.

"I suppose it could be an alien invasion, but to me it seems clear that this is the Rapture."

"The what?"

"The Rapture of the Church," he sigh, frustrated that he was having to explain it again, after it's been explained three times *already* in this novel. So instead he focused on the other part of the story. "It's the last days, when the Antichrist comes to power and rules the world with violence and terror."

Loudly, Fuentes said, "You're kidding, right?"

"It's in the Bible. First Thessalonians Four, verses 16-17." He looked up at the ceiling in concentration, and recited. "'For the Lord himself will descend from heaven with a shout, with the archangel's call, and with the sound of the trumpets of God. And the dead in Christ shall rise first; then we who are alive who are left, shall be caught up together with them in the clouds to meet the Lord in the air, and so we shall always be with the Lord.'"

Fuentes was staring hard at him, his incredulity having apparently put him back into a more reasonable state of mind. "*¡Esto es insano!* You want me to believe God did this?"

"It's prophecy. People have been waiting for this for centuries. Haven't you ever heard of the Rapture before?"

Fuentes stepped closer and stared intently into his eye. With an effort he said, "My children are gone. Right in front of my eyes! *Mis niños.* And you tell me it's prophecy! What the fuck is going on here?"

Griffin continued in a calm manner, hoping his demeanor would rub off. "All true believers as well as all innocents are taken up into heaven. All children are innocent. You don't need to fear for them."

Fuentes smiled a strained smile that looked painful, baring his teeth. "So if you know all this shit what are you still doing here?"

"Well, you know me. I'm a morbid, death-obsessed freak." He was going to say more, but he stopped when he noticed that Fuentes had taken out his pistol. "What are you doing?" he said, following it with his eyes as Fuentes lifted it up and placed the barrel squarely against his right temple. Then he took a step back.

Griffin held up his hands to show that he was unarmed, a standard procedure in tense situations with a hostage-taker or a suicidal person. "Don't do it," he said. "We're still here because we're not good enough for heaven. There's still time to repent, but if you die now, you'll go straight to hell, and you don't want that, right? Then you'll never get to see your children again. Please, just listen to me." But Fuentes was no longer paying him any mind. He was staring off into the distance when he pulled the trigger. Griffin jumped back at the explosion, and quickly spun around to see the body hit the floor.

"Well that was stupid," he said, shaking his head.

CHAPTER 4

Don't worry, it's not the aliens, I promise. Although I certainly did toy with that idea, of having the Rapture occur and then it turns out it's just the aliens come to obliterate us, ha-ha, but I decided against it because, let's just be honest, that doesn't make a lick of sense, dose it now? Nor will this turn out to be one of those stories with a gimmicky, twisty, "gotcha" ending that totally takes everyone by surprise, wherein it turns out that everybody was just at the mall for a giant half-off sale. It really and truly is the Rapture, because this is a Rapture story, where Rapture happens.

So there was panic, and chaos, and looting, and shooting, and people running around in circles screaming their heads off, which sounds kind of fun, actually. Martial law was declared everywhere in the world, except in the United States, where because there were so many good, decent, devout people in the military there was hardly any military left. The president had to beg Canada to send some Mounties in.

So almost nobody was paying attention when Ambassador Sei Shahse of an OEEC took the General Assembly podium at the UN to deliver a stirringly emotional and inspiring speech about the need for the whole world to take action and come together amidst these difficult circumstances and finally achieve the great long-sought dream of global unity, putting aside their long-standing differences to pool their resources to improve the lot of humankind and erect the foundation for a beautiful and shining tomorrow, et cetera. The delegates, having already heard about a hundred stirringly emotional and inspiring speeches that all sounded exactly the same, could barely stay awake.

When he finished, he stood waiting expectantly for the cheers, but there was only scattered applause, as the delegates waited with resigned boredom for the next ambassador to appear and deliver his or her stirringly emotional and inspiring speech.

Disturbed by this lack of response, Shahse remained at the podium and went directly to Plan B. He declared that he is the front man for a group of international terrorists whose mysterious superweapon, utilizing some form of radiation or neutrino rays, or some such thing of which he hasn't the foggiest clue, has caused this global cataclysm by randomly and instantaneously killing by means of vaporization millions of people. They demand the nations of the world surrender to them and grant them absolute control, or else the next time they'll just kill everybody.

That got people on their feet.

Afterwards his phone rang off the hook, an expected but very pleasing development, as world leaders call him nonstop, beseeching him to reveal who the terrorists are, or cursing him out and threatening his life—useless, he promised all of them, since he is only their spokesperson. But lo and behold, soon enough a number of smaller nations have indeed offered to surrender!

And when he wasn't answering his phone, he stood in front of his plasma TV, practicing his swordsmanship while watching, amused to no end that anyone is actually taking him seriously. He almost never heard the word "Rapture" bandied about. Of course, that's because all the people who believed in it are now gone, but surely there were plenty who knew about it. But of course, nobody wants to think of the Rapture, because of what it means for them personally. It means they missed it because their spiritual life is out of whack. They're not right with God. They have the wrong beliefs, or they're not morally clean, or something, and who wants to believe that? Everybody thinks they're right, and everybody thinks they are, while perhaps not perfect, certainly better than most and certainly good enough to get into heaven. They could not stomach thinking otherwise. In fact, the only mention of the word Rapture he heard is when certain self-righteous religious leaders appear to assure their flocks that there was no Rapture, and that this whole terrorist superweapon thing is absolutely genuine, and probably a plot by secular, God-hating liberals.

Shahse only laughed.

He couldn't wait until he got all the power and was free to tell them the *real* truth. He didn't know what strings the Committee was pulling behind the scenes, but things were coming together, and it wouldn't be long now.

His phone rang again. After the first day he got people to screen his calls, so he wouldn't be bombarded having to listen to any insignificant world leaders, so he knew that whoever this was, it was someone of importance, and he was right.

Setting down his saber he picked up the receiver and answered, "Ambassador Shahse."

"It is Mr. Cohen," responded an oily British voice.

"Yes, Mr. Cohen. What can I do for you?"

"Things are not going as well as they might."

Shahse wondered momentarily if that was supposed to be a threat, or what. "Things are going splendidly, sir. A lot of people actually believe this 'superweapon' nonsense."

"But not the right people."

He shifted uncomfortably in his seat. What is the point of this? Hadn't everything been planned out perfectly in advance?

"Sir," he said, "I'm flying to Washington tomorrow for a secret meeting with President Ruben. I'm confident I can persuade him, and once I have him, everyone else will line up in place."

"I am not as assured as you seem to be."

Shahse was dumbstruck for a moment, then he giggled, child-ishly. "I'm sorry, sir," he said quickly, "but why are you laying this on me? This was your plan."

"Yes, but your execution has not been as compelling as we had hoped."

Shahse felt personally offended, and almost told Cohen off, but decided that would not be prudent. Besides, things weren't going exactly as he had hoped, either. In *Volume 1* of LeVay's *Rapture* books, there had been a few pages of confused characters trying to arrange international flights on short notice, which as we all know can seem like the end of the world, but in the book all that seemed to take place over the course of a only a few hours, and then things instantly coalesced into the evil New World Order, with the Antichrist char-acter being unanimously voted dictator-for-life because he was such a nice guy. Shahse considered himself a pretty nice guy, too, but obviously it was silly to expect reality to follow fiction exactly. Still, he'd started off with the cheerful speech because he'd held onto the hope that as soon as he stepped up to that podium, all the how and why details would simply vanish and everyone would just shut up about everything else and hand over all their power to him.

And to the Zionist Committee, of course.

The nerve of them, he thought, hanging up after promising Mr. Cohen he would get results more in line with the Committee's expec-tations. He would be so very glad when they were gone, which would be soon enough. They must not have read LeVay's books, otherwise they would know they were going to drop out of the picture pretty quickly, "evil Jewish conspiracist" not being a favorite character of modern literature. But even if they hadn't, surely the Committee realized what they were getting themselves into. After all, they were the ones who had told him, in advance, that the Rapture was coming. They must have had at least some knowledge of what happens after that.

CHAPTER 5

Captain Manly was heroically recuperating in the town of Corny, Iowa. (A real place!) He had been taken in by the small town's devout, kind-hearted minister, Reverend Lars Trenton, and his sweet, obedient, just-eighteen-year-old daughter Sarah. Of course, the Reverend was only devout *now*, now that he realized he hadn't been taken up to heaven in the Rapture, and thus wasn't saved, despite having been a Jesus-loving, peace-preaching, small-town reverend, and set about to fix his wayward ways. He wasn't sure what those ways were, exactly, except possibly that he didn't love the right Jesus. You had to be sure you had the right Jesus! Not just any Jesus would do. So he was busy at work, feverishly reading his Bible and a whole bunch of scholarly texts, trying to pierce together the Right Jesus, grateful in spite of everything that he'd had this wake-up call, before he had died, otherwise he'd have gone straight to hell.

People had come pouring into his church, distraught over their personal losses, looking to God for answers, as people always do in times of trouble. He bluntly told everyone the hard, degrading truth that they needed to hear, that the right Jesus had come and gone, and left them here to suffer because they weren't good enough; but now they had a second chance, if only they would repent and believe even harder than they had before. This being the home of good old-fashioned real Americans, everybody had always been good and never did anything worse than drink an occasional beer and vote Democratic, and had certainly always believed, so they were as stunned as the good Reverend and as confused as to what they were supposed to believe now. Those who accepted his dire warnings filled his church as it had never been filled before, worshiping and praising Jesus, trying to get on his good side.

The sanctuary space was your classic 19th century church design, beautiful in its simplicity, a white clapboard building with two rows of pews lined up beside a center aisle, leading to the unadorned wooden alter two steps up from the floor, with a bell tower above it all.

Manly, who had wandered in lost, telling of a horrific wreck that he had barely escaped, had been staying at the church, along with a few other lost and desperate people, sleeping on the floor and eating handouts, and seeking some means of returning home to Virginia, where he lived, just outside of Washington. He was eager to get back and reunite with his family, to see that they were all alive and well, and not in heaven.

"Come with me," he pleaded with Trenton one day, as they spoke in the reverend's office, a simple affair with two chairs, a desk, and a single filing cabinets in which he kept all the church's records. "The people out east will need you."

"I can't. My flock needs me here. I can't abandon them now. I feel bad enough just having been a minister and yet believing in the wrong Jesus. And poor Sarah! She's such a good girl, and believed everything just as I had taught her, so she wasn't saved either. I feel partly responsible for that."

"But now you've come to see the truth! Your story will inspire people and bring them to the Lord!"

"Then I will have to trust you to take it to them."

"I will," he stood up to go and offered his hand. "It's been a real pleasure."

"It sure has," said Trenton, grasping it and shaking hard. "Sarah and I will both be very sorry to see you go. But don't fret. Your own story is very inspiring as well."

"Yes. I've done bad things, but God has forgiven me and loves me."

"God can forgive anyone of anything, except being gay. Go and tell everyone you came across the gospel, the good news of Christ!" They walked together out a side door, and into the sunny, humid day.

"I believe," Trenton said, laying a hand on Manly's shoulder, "that God has spared you for some great purpose."

"As do I," agreed Manly.

"We are all privileged to be living in these exciting final days, but I believe God has a special assignment in mind for you. For soon the Antichrist will arise, and will try to kill all Christians, but I am confident you will be a great leader among the resistance that will stand against his tyranny, even though it may require you to sacrifice your life in the service of Christ!"

Manly stopped cold, and looked at the Reverend, his forehead creased with worry. "Wait. Hold on just a second. *Sacrifice my life?* Nobody said anything about that!"

CHAPTER 6

I suppose I ought to briefly tell you what's happened with Dr. Griffin since we last saw him, before going on to join Shahse at that important, secret meeting with the president, but unfortunately, nothing much has happened. So at least it won't take long.

With Fuentes dead, the Slasher case was reassigned to Detective Tenney, along with a whole bunch of other cases, being that most of the honest, hard-working police force of New York City had vanished in the Rapture. Of course, with all the other confusion and rioting and whatnot, nothing much was going to happen with it, or really with any case, for years at the very least. The remaining police were too busying trying to ward off total chaos in the city to have time for anything involving paperwork. These days they mostly just shot suspects and moved on. Even pre-Rapture cases that had been solved were left to die in some file drawer. In fact, yellow-bathrobe man was found dead a week later in a cell among an enormous group of inmates who had been packed into a single holding cell, having starved to death, because nobody had any time for him. When the other inmates' shouts finally caught someone's attention, and it was discovered what had happened, all the other inmates were released with a stern warning, because nobody could do anything else for them or with them.

So Griffin was on his way home. He also lived in Virginia, outside of Washington. (Notice the pattern of convergence.) Tenney liked him enough to take a moment of her time to wish him goodbye and good luck, and promised to call him if anything every happened with the Slasher case.

"What about that license number on that plate?" he asked gruffly. He did not like abandoning cases when he was in hot pursuit, extenuating circumstances notwithstanding. "Can't you at least find out who it's registered to?"

"Sure," she said breezily, "I'll check if the computers ever get fixed. Nothing works anymore, remember? Besides, don't you have more pressing things to worry about now?"

"Not really," he said. "I don't have a family; my job is my life."

"Poor guy. I'm sure you must be very lonely and miserable."

"Not really."

"Of course you are! And I'd love to help, but I just don't have any time anymore." Just then she checked her watch, as though to prove it, and gave him a quick kiss goodbye.

He was traveling to Virginia by bus, because he had no car (the Lincoln was a rental, and even in the midst of the chaos he had dutifully returned it), and it was too risky to fly at this particular moment, even if there had been any airlines providing service, which there weren't, because planes require a lot of service and upkeep, and there was currently a total breakdown of service and upkeep, even for those who were very rich, which he was not, because people simply had far too much else to deal with to worry about things they had never much liked to begin with, such as airplanes, so Captain Manly is going to be very disappointed when he gets back, if he's expecting to still have a job. And even if Griffin did have a car, it was too risky to drive, with roads filled with abandoned vehicles and other detritus of our recently upended pedestrian-hating culture. Even the buses weren't very safe, as they had to use a lot of alternative back-road routes, where there was a risk of thievery, overpriced gasoline, and bad food. In his travels he passed by a nation in ruin. Often the buildings and homes of entire towns were shuttered, the residents too scared to come out and face who knows what evil might lurk about, and possibly be driven mad by the all that had happened, which would be a great boon for him if he ever decided to go into private psychiatric practice.

He lived in a townhouse a few miles from the FBI's headquarters at Quantico, Virginia. His house had been looted, which he expected, and all the good stuff was gone, such as his television, his stereo, his recliner, and his collection of autographed mug-shot photos of serial killers. Fortunately, nothing of the house's structure was broken beyond the bounds of his own handy-man skills. He set to work boarding up windows where the glass had been smashed in, thinking that perhaps the FBI would be extremely short-staffed, as were all agencies, and would be perfectly willing to overlook a certain long-ago 'Incident', and welcome him and his expertise back. He was still young and fit enough, only in his early fifties and still able to run a marathon, should that ever be required.

But it wasn't his own employment which concerned him most. He had his eyes set towards the future, not his in particular, but humanity's. He was painstakingly familiar with the Book of Revelations (it's a requirement of his work, practically in the job description—you can't imagine how many killers and other assorted crazies quote from it), so he knew all too well what horrors were about to be visited upon the earth. Wars and plagues and famines, resulting in the death of billions, and that was only the beginning. Soon there would arise the Antichrist, the Beast, the Man Whose Name Is The Number Six-Six-Six, who would conquer the earth, and once he does, rule it with a rod of iron. No, wait, scratch that last part, it's Jesus who's described as ruling with a rod of iron. In any case, the Antichrist is a truly evil person, the ultimate fascist, whose aim is not mere control, or oppression, or even bodily destruction. He will go after the immortal souls of those people who don't worship and obey him, enacting the cruelest revenge, destroying them by throwing them into the horrendous abyss of hell known as the Lake of Fire. No, wait, sorry again, that's Jesus who will throw the immortal souls of people who don't worship and obey him into the Lake of Fire. But anyway, the Antichrist is a really bad guy.

And his coming, prophesied for millennia, was now at hand.

And Griffin already had a pretty good idea of who it was.

As did anybody else paying even the slightest bit of attention. I mean, this isn't exactly the Riddle of the Sphinx here.

CHAPTER 7

Ambassador Shahse sat in his hotel room in Washington, DC, lying on the bed, watching the news, his important, secret meeting with President Ruben cancelled for the time being.

There had been a nuclear attack on the United States.

In particular, New York City had been destroyed by a nuclear missile, launched by, of all nations, China. With the United States so weakened by the mass disappearances, they clearly rationalized that this was the ideal moment to launch an invasion intended to unseat America from its place as world leader. America was already ruined, basically, so all they had to do was deliver the finishing blow, and then they could just step up and take its place. Once conquering the US, presuming they survived or even avoided the expected counterattack, it would be a simple matter to bully the rest of the nations of the world into subservience.

To avoid the counterattack, once they fired their missile, they immediately announced to the world that they had done it to annihilate the terrorist group that had caused the vaporizations of millions of random people around the globe. And they were sure this group was in New York City, because that's where they were making their announcements, through Ambassador Shahse.

Shahse himself, sitting in his hotel room, found it quite amusing that they had killed millions and risked an annihilating conflagration to assassinate him, and he wasn't even there. Nay, they launched just at the very moment he had left the city. It was providence, to be sure. Of course, now he was in Washington, another major American city, and if they learned of it they might just easily attack here, too, but then that would be guaranteed to provoke a response, not just from America but from the other nuclear nations around the globe. But if they kept their attack limited to New York, everyone might buy into their reasoning, deciding that the loss of the city was worth it to get rid of Shahse and those terrorists, and so they'd avoided a counter strike while having set America upon a path of decline and certain collapse. The fact that the US hadn't struck back immediately proved their gambit was working. But Shahse wasn't worried. President Ruben knew where he was, and if he thought along those lines, the ambassador would already be under arrest.

He watch the images of carnage playing on his television, the crumpled buildings, the metal frames that was all that remained of untold cars and steel skyscrapers, the thousands of bodies burned beyond recognition, and in the midst of his shock and outrage, a realization suddenly came upon him, and he laughed. Don't get me wrong, he wasn't laughing at the destruction, which he honestly thought was atrocious, just absolutely tragic, and which completely devastated him as it had everybody else. No, what made him laugh was the thought that, while he had escaped, the Zionist Committee had remained there, in New York City. And now all the members of this centuries-old group were dead, just as he, and his good buddy Tony LeVay, had predicted. Guess they couldn't control everything, after all.

He watched the scenes of dirt-smeared, burned, and bleeding people crying and screaming at the devastation and the loss of loved ones, of everything they had in the world, their homes and their jobs and absolutely everything, and how wasn't this so unfair, one monstrous catastrophe after another, waiting patiently for President Ruben to appear and give a stirringly emotional and inspiring speech about how sad this tragedy was for everybody, and how they had to remain steadfast, and prevail against their enemies, and work towards a brighter, more hopeful future, and goodnight and God bless.

But as Shahse waited, he got a phone call from the White House, telling him there was a car waiting for him downstairs. It seemed that in the midst of the world coming apart at the seams the president had time to see him after all.

He went down cheerfully enough, and got in the car without hesitation. It was certainly possible that this was all a trap of some sort, but he didn't believe that. There were bigger things in store for him. Besides, it was hardly necessary for them to arrange some elaborate deception if all they wanted to do was to arrest him. He would go quietly enough. So he felt confident that there was a genuine meeting planned, and he was not disappointed.

He was led into the White House, disappointedly through a side door, though at least they didn't do him the dishonor of making him go through security, and down a hall and up some stairs and through another hall, until finally he found himself in the esteemed Oval Office, shaking hands with President Ruben.

President Lawrence H. Ruben, or "President Rube," as his critics sometimes liked to call him, was a heavy-set man with a very down-home, country-boy persona, but this image was belied by the enormous dynastical advantages he had. He was in reality, as well bred as any of the political royalty. He had held the same congressional seat that his father held before him, and his grandfather before that. Of course, they had been content enough with their lifetime appointments to Congress, but Ruben himself was far more ambitious, in the limited sense of being driven to prove himself better than his forbearers. He abandoned his safely held position to run for Senate, and the electorate, sick and tired of him and his family hogging their seat, were only too glad to send him up and on his way. And then, after marrying a rich heiress, and spending a gazillion dollars while pretending to care about "average Americans," he became President.

Shahse sat down on an upholstered green chair, and Ruben sat in a second one across from him. Everyone else was ordered out, and the two sat alone, with glasses of bourbon.

"So why haven't you launched a counter strike?" asked Shahse, to inaugurate the conversation.

"Because I need to speak with you first," said Ruben. He looked very downbeat, not his usually cheerfully optimistic self, a man who seemed to take pride in being blissfully unaware of the distressed condition of most of the world. This in spite of his bright yellow tie. "I don't know what's going on anymore."

"Well, I can tell you what's going on. The Chinese have attacked your country with a nuclear missile. What else do you need to know?"

"They say they did it to kill you."

Shahse shrugged nonchalantly. "Me and my associates. They succeeded with regards to said associates, but failed with me. 'Associates?' Listen to me, I'm starting to sound like a mob boss!" he laughed. "But anyway, are you just going to give them what they want?" He leaned forward to indicate his seriousness, as though to whisper a secret. "Because you know I'm not what they really want. Or at least, not all of it."

"I know, I know. They're aiming to realign the balance of power in the world."

Shahse straightened up in his seat and tried to sound mildly shocked. "And you're just going to let them do that?" Ruben's tie was really bothering him. And the green of the chairs wasn't doing anything for him either.

Ruben looked very troubled, and had difficulty getting his next sentence out. "Do you—do you really have a superweapon that can disintegrate millions around the world?"

Shahse laughed, long and loud, until his was snorting and chocking. He beat his free hand on the arms of the chair, and had to set his glass down to keep from spilling it. After a minute he managed to calm down. "So that's what this is about! That's what you want from me! You want me to do your dirty work for you!"

"And can you?" asked Ruben, not at all in a joking mood. He was not at all pleased by what he was asking. Indeed, it made him downright sick.

"Oh, no, no, heavens no!" said Shahse. "Look, all that stuff I said was just made up. There was a group of prominent people trying to take over the world, but they were just using the situation to angle their way into power. No such weapon exists, trust me."

"But I don't understand. Then what caused all those people to disintegrate?"

"The Rapture, of course!" exclaimed Shahse, delighted at being the bearer of bad news. "You know what the Rapture is, don't you?"

"Of course I do. But it couldn't possibly be the Rapture."

"And why not?"

"Because," he said, sulking, looking every bit like a child who's told that no, he can't have any ice cream before dinner, "I wouldn't still be here." He could see the twinkle of amusement in Shahse's eyes, and continued, insisting, "I'm saved. I surrendered my life to Christ and invited him into my heart when I was 23. I was in a terrible place, and he saved me from my sins and turned my life around."

"I thought you were in law school when you were 23," said Shahse, smiling in spite of himself.

"Spiritually, I mean. You know. Really, I have a strong, loving, personal relationship with Jesus."

"Oh, I understand completely," he said nodding his head vigorously. "That's exactly why I believe you are still here. God needs you here on earth to perform certain actions, that he can only trust to a believer who knows his Will to perform."

Ruben seemed interested, and leaned forward. "What kind of actions?"

"Actions necessary to fulfill divine prophecy. Early in the Book of Revelations, it describes the Four Horseman of the Apocalypse, who will bring famine, plague, and war, and destroy over a fourth of the earth."

"A fourth?" Ruben quickly calculated. "That's one and a half billion people! The population of China....Are you saying God is commanding me to launch a nuclear holocaust?" He looked very earnest as he said this.

"Well...," said Shahse, drawing it out, as he did not want to commit to anything so drastic. Any answer he gave at this point would probably make him look foolish, as he didn't know for certain whether Ruben was serious or not. Besides, he hadn't actually intended to push a war at all; his remarks were only meant as part of the setup for what was to come next.

"Of course," said Ruben, mostly to himself, and sounding very serious indeed, "I'd have to launch against the other nuclear powers too, to keep them from attacking us."

"What other powers?"

"Oh, all of them, I suppose. The ones that aren't our committed allies. Russia, Pakistan, Iran, North Korea. If I'm going to do it, I might as well take them all out."

"I thought a full-scale nuclear war wasn't winnable?" said Shahse, growing more and more alarmed by the second. He was going to have to get out of the city as fast as possible. Hopefully Ruben wouldn't ask him to stick around and watch.

"No, it can be. They might get a shot or two at us, but we can take 'em out. All in the name of God." He said this with sadness in his voice, the same sadness one might feel at having run over a deer. It had the clear ring of finality to it. He'd already made up his mind.

"Well, okay, if that's what you want," said Shahse, hoping to steer the conversation back to himself. "But if anyone gives you any trouble, maybe you should skip the 'name of God' stuff. You can always tell them I made you do it."

"You? Made me? If there's no superweapon, why should I play along? In fact, if I need to use nuclear missiles at all, doesn't that negate the very possibility of such a weapon existing? Since if did exist, you'd have just have used it, instead?"

Shahse paused a moment to parse that out and then watch it sink into oblivion, then said calmly, "The reason God left you on earth was so that you could give all of America's power to me."

Even in his grim mood, Ruben had to smile. "And why would I do that?"

"Because as a believer, you recognize the fulfillment of prophecy. Specifically, the prophecy of the Antichrist, the one who is to rule the world."

They stared at each other in silence for at least a full minute, maybe two. Finally, Ruben shifted slightly in his chair and said, "Go on."

Shahse stood, feeling energized. The time had come to play his trump card.

He stood over Ruben and spread his arms wide. "Sei Shest Shahse," he said, carefully annunciating the words of his name. "A bit of a transliteration, but 'sei' is 'six' in Italian, 'shest' is 'six' in Russian, and 'shahse' is 'six' in Romanian."

Ruben smiled, and Shahse felt overjoyed to the point of bursting that he understood it. "So," said Ruben, "*you're* the Antichrist."

"Exactly!"

"And I should just give my authority over to you? Why would I do that when you're the enemy?"

"Because you recognize the necessity of it. My rule is prophesied in holy writ. *It is the Will of God.* And he has granted you the special mission of ensuring it comes to fulfillment!"

"But," said Ruben, still smiling, getting it but not quite, "you're evil."

"It's in the Bible! All scripture must come to pass exactly as written. Christ will not come again otherwise. The destiny of the world lies in your hands, Mr. President. Destiny! You are needed to fulfill scripture. It is an act of *reverence.* It is your purpose." Shahse added, as an afterthought, "Unless of course, *you* wanted to be the Antichrist, since you're the one who's going to be doing all this killing."

Ruben kept looking up at him, half-smiling, a strange, confused look on his face. His hands dropped down to his lap, and he held them together. They were trembling slightly.

"Destiny," he said quietly.

CHAPTER 8

Captain Manly managed to hitchhike his way back to Virginia, but when he finally got home, discovered to his dismay, that his entire family had vanished and gone to heaven.

Worse, he quickly learned that all the airlines had shut down, which meant he was, at least temporarily, out of a job.

And if that wasn't enough, not a single person had broken into his house or stolen a single thing from it. Not even the hose in the garden. So what, his stuff wasn't good enough to rob? He lived in a very nicely decked out split-level, if he did say so himself. The nerve of people.

But was he put out by all this? Did it send him spiraling into a funk that could only end with him sitting locked in his bedroom, reading comic books and eating cheese puffs? Hell no! Not Captain Manly! He could see the bright side of things. Family gone? Well, who needed them, anyway? More freedom for him to fulfill his own needs and desires, which after all was the most important thing. No job? Who wanted a job when the world was going to end soon anyway? He had enough money saved up to last him the few years remaining to the earth. Of course, most of it had been tied up in airline stocks, but, hey, he didn't think he'd require too much anyway. Besides, he did have a job, in a sense. He had been given a mission.

He guessed he had nothing else to do now but to get started right away on that mission, to organize an armed resistance to the coming Antichrist, a massive Christian army that would seek to undermine his evil society with assassinations, improvised explosive devices, and martyrdom missions.

So he immediately began scourging the area for fellow believers to join him. He went around to the various churches, which were now full of people desperate for answers, delivering a spiel about the need for this Christian army, which he would lead, to stand firm against the onslaught of Satan, then asking people to volunteer. And volunteer they did. There were thousands of people, new to the Lord, who were burdened with the excessive zeal of all new converts and were eagerly willing to do anything everything they could. He recruited dozens of ministers, poor souls who had missed the Rapture due to their ignorance of the right Jesus, but who could now be counted on to know that The Time Was At Hand.

His name and his mission quickly spread throughout the area, as people everywhere were encouraged to choose sides now, to sign up with Jesus—and Captain Manly—or with the Antichrist. And if you didn't sign up with Captain Manly and Jesus, you were basically sided with the devil by default, and were going straight to hell. It was that simple.

CHAPTER 9

President Ruben ordered the nuclear attack against "everyone," as he kept putting it, and thus in a matter of an hour killed a billion people or so.

It was just that easy!

While waiting for an inevitable third strike, he and Shahse hid in an underground bunker at an undisclosed location. He went on television to announce what he'd done, telling the world that Shahse had made him do it, and that furthermore he was surrendering all his authority and would basically be second fiddle to the former ambassador from an OEEC (Obscure Eastern European Country). He told his audience all of these things in as grave and morose, on-the-verge-of-tears tone as he could muster, to impress upon the world the inevitability and hopelessness of his situation.

Shahse, meanwhile, was quite pleased, because now he was indeed ruler of the world, just as he'd always known he would be.

Ruben introduced him and then went off screen, leaving him at the podium to make his first speech as the new, albeit title-less, Guy In Charge.

"Ladies, gentlemen, and other people of the world," he began, "I'm not going to dance around the facts or try to blind you with fancy dazzling metaphorical lights. I'm going to give it to you straight, the short and sweet, as short and sweet as I can make it, though of course it's not really that sweet, though it is short, but not sweet, definitely not, unless you're masochistic or something, but then I can't help that, and in fact wouldn't want to help that at all. I would encourage that, actually.

Shahse continued, "In any case, it's like this. The end of the world is coming. Seriously, it's right on our doorstep. This is the time if the Tribulation, when all hell breaks loose, just before the Second Coming of Christ. But I'm sure you all guessed that already, didn't you? All those people disappeared in the Rapture. The Rapture! Of the Church! See, I believe in that sort of thing. In fact, I don't just believe in it, I know it's true, because all that nonsense I told everyone about having a superweapon that could instantly dissipate millions around the world is just that, total complete nonsense. Nonsensical as Santa Claus, or Hinduism. A complete fiction. Really, the truth is, it was an Act of God, his divine plan for bringing history to a state of completion.

"And so, you may be asking, which of course I'm sure you are, if I'm not the nefarious villain behind things, then why should I get all this power over the world? Well, I'll tell you. It's because I in fact am a nefarious villain, just of a different sort. You see, I'm the Antichrist, the Son of Satan, the Devil who walks the earth. I'm the one who is appointed by God to reign over the world during the last days. Yes! It's all true! I am the incarnation of evil, here specifically to bring about misery and suffering in the world. I am Sei Shest Shahse, 'six' in Italian, 'six' in Russian, 'six' in Romanian! None can oppose me, for my sovereignty is the fulfillment of scripture!"

He gleamed into the camera in triumph, then continued on a more subdued note. "For those of you out there in TV land who don't believe I could be the Antichrist because you don't believe in Christianity, good for you! You just keep on believing whatever silliness you believe now, and everything will be all fine and good.

Just remember that I'm here to bring peace on earth by killing everyone who doesn't go along with me. Oh, and when you find yourself burning in hell, don't say I didn't warn you.

"Thank you and good night!" He took a deep bow and walked off the stage, and the transmission ended, returning shocked viewers to even more shocked anchor people, who shook their heads in astonishment before saying, live on air, "What the fuck was that?"

Back at their underground bunker in a secret, undisclosed location, President Ruben was also perplexed. He grabbed Shahse by the arm.

"Why the hell did you tell the whole world that?"

"Because it was fun," he shrugged.

"Excuse me? I thought the Antichrist was a great deceiver who would ensnare the nations with promises of peace and security through diplomacy and pacifism and the unity of all humankind."

Shahse laughed. "Well, that would be a pretty stupid thing to promise, since I don't have the faintest idea how to deliver on it. Not that I could anyway. Honestly, you know that. There's going to be all sorts of horrible plagues and terrors rained down upon the world by God in the next few years."

"Yeah, okay, but to tell everyone…"

"I told them for the same reason I told you. Eventually people were going to figure out that I don't really have a superweapon. That wasn't a pretense I could keep for any length of time. It's better, in this case, to tell them the truth. Because, ironically, if people understand that I really am the devil they'll be less likely to try to overthrow me."

Ruben couldn't respond to this immediately and wouldn't let go of Shahse's coat because he was still trying to puzzle through it. He stammered a few times, trying to put together his next question, which was very unlike him, being that he was a smooth-talking professional politician, and not being able to talk on the spot was like not wearing any pants, if not far worse. Finally he said, "But don't you want to trick people to steal their souls, so they'll go to hell?"

"Oh, sure. But honestly now, how realistic do you think that is? People can see the signs. The portents! The stars in alignment! They're not idiots. At least, not all of them. They'll get it quickly enough no matter what I say. But don't worry, I'll get those souls one way or another. It is written, remember."

"I'm not worried," Ruben huffed. "You're the enemy, remember? I'm on God's side. I want to you fail. It's just that I don't get what's going on. Your methods are pretty confusing, you have to admit."

"Oh, I do!" he agreed expansively. "In the *Rapture* books, the Antichrist establishes a secular government and appeals to people in the name of nondiscrimination and nonjudgmental religious libertarianism, just like you suggested. How silly is that! That never works, and anyway I could never pull that off, because at the very least I don't believe in any of that stuff myself."

Dear God, Ruben thought to himself, *this man is completely insane.* He was beginning to have very subtle second thoughts about having killed a billion people and handed over his country to a complete psychotic and self-proclaimed devil. He was also having second thoughts about wearing his usual pale blue tie for his speech, instead of an appropriately somber black one. Did he even have a black tie? He hadn't noticed one in his closet, but he must have one somewhere. He couldn't believe that he, the president of the United States, could lack such a basic and essential fashion item.

"I'm sorry," Ruben suddenly said, frowning, "but I was going to say something, and now I've completely forgotten what it was."

"Happens to the best of us," said Shahse, patting him on the back.

CHAPTER 10

A few days later, Lucious D. Griffin, PsyD, Forensic Psychologist, sat in his living room, reading the Bible. As a professional forensic psychologist, he couldn't help trying to use what he was reading to get inside God's head, but frankly it was a daunting and ultimately futile task. Or rather, not that it was futile, but that is was so easy it disturbed him, and he had to assume he was looking at it wrong. Because it seemed to him that God was an obsessive-compulsive, nitpicking over the slightest detail of the one thing he was fixated on, while oblivious to everything else in the world as it screamed on around him. For instance, he was always after the Jews to stop worshiping idols and having sex, threatening to whack them if they didn't stop, while meanwhile everyone else on earth was busying themselves with as much idol-worshiping and fornicating as they could and nothing ever seemed to happen to them. Oh yes, obsessive and paranoid. Very paranoid. And then he was always telling people that "wicked ways" inevitably lead to ruination, while wisdom and virtue always brought blessing and bounty, and this simply wasn't true, because if it was, nobody would need so many innumerable reminders from on high. Really, the way he railed against his beloved "chosen people," and went out of his way to ruin them while proclaiming his eternal devotion to them was almost schizophrenic.

He suddenly shut the Bible and set it down on the end table, realizing that if he kept reading it he'd almost certainly end up in hell.

There was a knock on his front door. He pulled out his gun before going to open it, because these days you could never be too careful, not with the world in total chaos. He unlocked the door, and tugged at it, letting it swing open of its own accord.

Standing on his front steps were Detectives Tenney and Haversham.

"Hi!" said Tenney, grinning. "Remember us?"

He holstered his firearm and ushered them in. Their presence, if you're paying attention, which of course you are, since reading a book isn't like watching TV, where you can just zone out and let the story pass you by. It's an active medium requiring your participation, like a video game only without the flashy, violent graphics and sounds, and much more boring. There's no progression if you fall asleep, meaning that all the main characters are now in the same area, where they can begin to interact and their stories can intertwine, not that there hasn't been intertwining already, but real intertwining, to where they're in the same room, all intertwined together in some sort of literary game of Twister, only without the colored dots.

"What are you doing here?" he asked, confused. "How did you even get here? And how did you managed to survive the, um, total destruction of New York?"

"Oh, we weren't actually in the city when the bomb fell. We were out in the fringes, actually over in Yonkers, on a case," said Tenney.

"I see. And you came all the way here, instead of staying and rescuing people and helping the city recover and rebuild, because...?"

"Oh, what's the use? New York is gone, and it'll never be put back together before the world ends. And since our jobs and homes were gone, and everybody's dead, we figured we'd come down and see you."

Now Griffin was really alarmed. He hoped they weren't expecting him to let them stay here, in his home. Company, especially the uninvited type, was the last thing he wanted. He realized to his horror that their clothes were rumpled and dirty from having been slept in for several nights, at least. He might have to shoot them, after all.

Haversham, as though sensing his distress, smiled and said, "Don't worry, we brought you something that'll make up for our rudeness."

"What?"

"Something very interesting. Something significant. You'll like it, trust me."

With the mess the world was in, what could possibly be so valuable? "Okay, what?" he demanded, not giving an inch.

"Can't we at least sit down?"

"Do I need to wave my gun at you some more?" he said harshly.

"Boy, are you cranky," said Tenney. She reached into her purse, the only bag she had with her, and pulled out a manila envelope and handed it to him. He quickly opened it, only to find prints taken from the security tape of the car with diplomatic plates that had been captured leaving several Slasher crime scenes.

He looked up at them with a questioning, angry look. But before he could yell at them, Tenney quickly explained. "Before everything was destroyed in the bombing, things were starting to work again, and we managed to get the name of the owner."

"Who cares about that now?" said Griffin, growing more furious by the second. "He's probably dead along with everybody else. Who cares about a few miserable murders now, anyway?"

"He's not dead," said Haversham.

"Well?" said Griffin, after waiting a beat. God, it was like pulling teeth. They were doing this on purpose, to make it look like whatever they had to say actually mattered, just to get back at him for showing off.

Tenney, annunciating carefully through her grin, spoke the name, "Sei Shest Shahse."

Okay, that did matter!

CHAPTER 11

In the gymnasium next to the spa room, Shahse was fencing with his new instructor, his old fencing instructor having tragically died in one recent tragedy or another. His new instructor, Jean-Paul, was a top Olympic fencing contender, not that there would ever be another Olympics again, but if there were, he would definitely be in them, fencing.

They lunged and feinted and parried and dodged and ducked and et cetera and et cetera for an hour or so. They were using the basic fencing weapon, the lightweight foil. Shahse preferred the more difficult saber, but his saber, along with the rest of his beautiful sword collection, had been destroyed in the nuclear blast, and the foil was the only replacement he'd been able to acquire so far. No matter, though; it was more than adequate for his training needs.

Shahse was wonderfully lithe and graceful in his movements, and very aggressive in his attacks. Jean-Paul had thought, when he'd first been hired, before he learned who Shahse was, that he would just be teaching the basics to another rich snob, but this man was clearly an expert in his own right. He could reasonably expect to compete at an Olympic level himself, except, of course, that there were never to be another Olympics. Exhausted, Jean-Paul called it quits, and they removed their masks. As he grabbed a towel from his bag to wipe the perspiration from his face, Jean-Paul noticed with surprise that Shahse wasn't the least bit tired. He wasn't breathing hard; he hadn't even broken a sweat.

"Am I not challenging enough for you?" he quipped through his short breaths.

"Well, I've also been studying Tai Chi, which has helped me control my body's internal systems and retain stasis even through stress."

Jean-Paul, who knew Tai Chi masters, didn't believe it. He grinned. "Nonsense. How did you acquire such skill? You make a deal with the devil?" He instantly regretted the last line, because one did not want to make jokes, especially on that subject, with the self-professed Antichrist.

"Oh yes," said Shahse, returning the grin. "Would you like me to hook you up?"

"No, no," said the fencer, shaking his head quickly, fearing he might be serious.

"Well then, I guess I'll just see you next week. Toodles," said Shahse, who turned around and walked over to his private elevator. He turned to Jean-Paul and tipped his foil in a salute as the doors closed, and rode directly all the way up to the penthouse, which had become his new home.

He lived and worked, for the time being, in the fabulously appointed penthouse suite of an office tower in the highway- and mall-intensive landscape of Tysons Corner, Virginia, about a dozen or so miles from the White House. It was a nice enough area, filled with office towers, condominiums, upscale shopping centers/malls, and many dining establishments, yet dispersed and interspersed with wide, curving and heavily-trafficked roadways, making it somewhat pedestrian challenging. Shahse had a terrific view from every single window on his floor. He felt this vantage was safe enough should a nuke hit the Capital, while still close enough to maintain an immediate presence among the decision makers. Although, really, he had

wired the place with the most advanced, secured communications system on the planet. He could talk to anyone, anywhere on earth, at any time. He could conduct all his global business without ever leaving, if he chose. That, however, was not his style, and he already had a major trip scheduled to take place in the next few days.

Besides, he didn't want to live in DC. Practically, he couldn't throw Ruben out of the White House, because Ruben was too valuable, too useful. He felt he could ring some more out of the president before the man realized what an idiot he'd been, and did the noble thing by shooting himself (assuming he wasn't too much of an idiot to realize how much of an idiot he'd been). Even then he'd still have some president in charge. He was going to set up his evil one-world government as an overarching, international institution that would not replace national governments, but stand above them in a global federal system like the United Nations, if it ever had any power or did any good. (He was already miffed that things seemed to be backwards, that he was relying on America's missiles to control the rest of the world, instead of needing the UN's blue-helmeted peacekeepers to reign in an unruly US with their iron-fisted grip. Ah yes, a last lament for the noble UN peacekeepers, their powder-blue helmets striking fear into the hearts of rebels and warlords the world over.)

He would much rather have preferred to stay in New York City, and make that his new global capital, because he felt at home in New York, but alas, it was not to be. Checking his *Rapture* book, he found that LeVay had the Antichrist setting up shop in Rome, because Rome was supposedly the "Whore of Babylon which sits upon seven hills," as described in the Book of Revelations. Shahse wasn't one to quibble with the master's Biblical exegesis, but decided to depart from him on that one tiny detail, as he didn't want to live in Rome. He didn't like Rome. It was old and cramped and decrepit, like so much else in Europe, which he'd seen enough of to last a lifetime. He didn't want to live next door to the Catholic Church, even though they were supposed to be working for him. And despite his first name, he didn't even speak Italian. No, he wanted a better city, someplace gleaming and new, someplace filled with power and awe. New York, of course, was his first choice, but with that out of the picture, he was imagining maybe Tokyo or Hong Kong. Or had those been destroyed in Ruben's counterattack, too? He didn't even know. How absurd was that? Oh well, there was always San Francisco.

He stepped out of the elevator into the living room, whose walls were painted teal, but so far bare save for an unlit fireplace and four wall-mounted plasma-screen televisions mounted in a row, each turned to a different news station. He scanned them all briefly as lay his sword on the mantle of the fireplace, before picking up the remote from his crystal coffee table and shutting them all off. He replaced the remote, and dropped his wire mesh mask beside it. He picked up his sword and lay it down alongside the other items. Then he sat down on his white leather sofa, pulled off his gloves, and picked up his schedule that he'd left there earlier.

Before he could get comfortable, the phone on the oak end table next to the sofa buzzed. It only buzzed when it was his security guard at the front desk downstairs. He picked it up, mildly annoyed at the disturbance.

"Yes?"

"Sir, there are three FBI Agents here. There say they have a warrant for your arrest."

Shahse paused for a moment, confused. Of course, while his location was supposed to be classified, it was probably an open secret by now, so the fact that people had found him was expected. But FBI agents? With an arrest warrant? For what? He could not possibly believe, that after all he'd done so far, Ruben would suddenly decide to get rid of him and then do it in by having him *arrested.* Assassinated, perhaps, that he could understand. But arrested?

Most likely this was a small group acting on their own, without the consent of Ruben or any government agency, trying to be heroes and save the world by getting rid of the Antichrist. Poor fools. Still, he supposed he could admire them for their audacity in even coming here. Threatening the devil—did they even expect to walk out of here alive? And then there was whatever judge had actually signed such a warrant, who wasn't going to be a judge much longer. Unless it was Judge Judy; he liked her. So he was curious to meet them, and decided not to send them away by declaring immunity, or privilege, or whatever he had now, and instead invited them up.

Of course I don't need to tell you it was Griffin, Tenney, and Haversham, the latter two having fortunately gotten a shower and a change of clothes. And Griffin probably also showered and changed his clothes too, one would hope, given that this chapter is taking place at least a day or two after the last. In any case, they were all dressed pretty casually.

"Well, hello," said Shahse, folding his arms when the stepped out of the elevator and into his living room.

"Sei Shahse, we have a warrant for your arrest," said Griffin, leading, stepping right up to him, aggressively getting in his face. He was shorter and stockier than Shahse, who had the tall, elitist look of a liberal.

"Ah, yes, straight to business, hmm?" He casually, smoothly moved to the side, around Griffin, and approached Tenney. "No introductions, first?" he said, speaking directly to her.

She seemed a little flushed. When necessary, she could easily slip into the no-nonsense, tough-as-nails-and-that's-the-thick-kind-not-the-little-skinny-ones, policewoman role necessary to advance in a male-dominated field, but being flirted with by the most powerful man in the world made that somewhat more difficult.

"I'm Detective Tenney, with the NYPD, and this is my partner, Detective Haversham, and that's Agent Lucious Griffin, with the FBI," she said, somewhat nervous. NYPD?" said Shahse, in a higher pitch, sounding like he was trading gossip. "A little far from home, aren't you? I thought you were all FBI. And, pray tell me," here he touched his hand to her arm, "why is Agent Lucious Griffin the only one of you with a first name?"

"Because I'm the main character," said Griffin, testily.

"Oh, no," said Shahse, with a short laugh. He touched Tenney's shoulder before stepping away to face Griffin again. "Don't be silly. *I'm* the main character."

Griffin's eyes took on a luster as he stared intently into Shahse's face. "And so the man of sin is revealed, the beast from the sea with the name of blasphemy written upon his forehead, coming on cue to pluck the putrid, rotted fruit of this debauched age from the soddened branches of its warped history. And so in these last days sin has brought the world full circle, to stand in a garden of desolation before the Tree of Death."

Shahse said nothing for a moment, just sort of frowned, perplexed. In the silence, Haversham chuckled and said, "You're getting better at that. You should write this stuff down."

"What for? We're all going to die anyway."

"My, but you're crazy," said Shahse, smiling now. "I like that. So I understand you have some sort of warrant involving myself in some fashion?"

"An arrest warrant," said Griffin. "For six counts of murder."

"Murder! Goodness!" Then he frowned again. "What, only six? I mean, I suppose it fits with the whole weird 'number of the beast' thing, but I thought I had a little more notoriety than that."

Griffin pulled the warrant out of his pocket and waved it in Shahse's face. Shahse snatched it from his hand, unfolded it, and quickly read it through. It listed the names of the deceased, and of course he recognized them instantly. He began laughing again, very loudly, before folding the paper up and handing it back to Griffin.

"The Wall Street Slasher?" he said, giddily. "You think *I'm* the Wall Street Slasher?"

"There's no use denying it," said Griffin, maintaining his steely glare.

"All of New York City's been destroyed, the world is ending, and you're here about *this*? This trivial nothing?"

"A case remains open as long as the perpetrator remains alive. And I can't think of a better time than now."

Shahse still couldn't believe it. He looked past Griffin to the others. "Are you guys serious?" he asked, still grinning idiotically.

Tenney pulled from her purse the same manila envelope she had brought with her from New York, pulled out the photos, and held them up so Shahse could see them.

"These," she said after taking a moment to clear her throat, "were taken by security cameras at the three of the crime scenes. Your car appears at all three scenes, leaving just moments after the killings."

Shahse recognized the license plate number, and stopped smiling. "That car was left in New York and has consequently been destroyed, along with any other evidence you may have obtained."

"Doesn't matter," said Griffin, speaking in a clipped tone. "We still have the photos and the evidence of your ownership of this car. That's all we need."

"That car," he said, beginning to feel peeved, "along with duplicates of its keys, was left at the embassy compound. There were several employees who would act as my chauffer. Anyone could have gained access to the vehicle, and borrowed it for his own use."

"And unfortunately for you, anyone who could have testified to that is now dead."

Shahse shook his head. This whole thing was just too absurd. "Look, I know who these people are, and I have met with them, as they were all involved in investment in my homeland. But I didn't kill any of them! They were helping my country. What possible motive would I have had?"

"Obviously, it was an element in your grand scheme to weaken America and take power for yourself," said Griffin. "Just like everything else that's happened."

Shahse realized what was going on, and started laughing again, though not nearly as boisterously as before. "Oh, you're a crazy one, all right," he said, point his finger at Griffin. "But don't you see how perfect this is? Someone's obviously trying to frame me. I mean, clearly, I have a lot of enemies, and someone's trying to get rid of me."

"That's pathetic," Griffin spat at him. "These pictures were obtained immediately after the murders, well before anyone knew who you were."

But that wasn't true, thought Shahse. He could easily guess who would have framed him, had he indeed been framed.

"Of course! This has to be the work of the Zionist Committee!" he said, with the triumphant conviction of Sherlock Holmes declaiming to Dr. Watson.

"The who?"

"The Zionist Committee. It's a secret group of Jews who have been controlling the world for centuries."

Griffin slowly turned and looked knowingly from Tenney to Haversham, then turned back to Shahse. "A secret group of Jews, you say? Who control the world, you say?" he said in the slow, childish tone of one talking down at the mentally ill.

"No, it's true. They were the secret group I mentioned in my speech. I mean, they didn't really have anything to do with the Rapture, they were just using it to their advantage. But they did control the world. That is, they did, you know, past tense. They're not around anymore, understand, they were killed in the attack on New York."

"But if they control everything, how did they die in an attack which they caused?"

"Well, obviously they didn't have anything to do with that. They don't literally control everything, they just have a lot of influence."

"Uh-huh," said Griffin, nodding his head slowly. "That's fascinating."

"Come on, man, I'm telling you the truth. It was a real thing, and they must be the ones who had me framed, so that after I came to power and established their authority they could just get rid of me."

"And why would they do that, instead of just killing you?" said Griffin, sounding disgusted but at least no longer speaking in the tone of a woman to her poodle.

And wasn't that a good point indeed? Hadn't he just dismissed a similar concern about President Ruben? But there was a difference, a most significant difference. The Committee didn't know what Ruben did. "They didn't know I was the Antichrist."

"So?"

"If I was just an ordinary patsy I might be easy to remove, but nobody would dare touch me now, knowing I'm the Son of Satan."

Griffin reached out with his index finger and touched Shahse on the little red heart on his fencing suit.

"Ha-ha. You know what I mean," said Shahse, who then smiled. "But I admit that was pretty funny, so look, here's what I'll do. Not only will I not kill any of you, I'm going to offer you all top positions in the new global security apparatus I'm setting up."

"Excuse me? You're trying to bribe us?"

"No. It's not bribery. It's an offer of a position because I admire your courage in coming here and approaching me like this. Especially yours, Agent Griffin. And now that I think about it I do recall reading about you in connection with the Wall Street Slasher investigation. You're the forensic psychologist, right? The profiler. Your skills are highly valuable. But look, there's no bribery involved, because you simply can't arrest me. My authority supersedes all other authorities on earth. I'm absolutely immune, and you know it."

Griffin said nothing. Haversham leaned over and said into his ear, "Why are we even bothering with this? We're already here, why don't we just shoot him?"

"Because you can't possibly harm me," said Shahse. "Don't forget, I'm the Antichrist. My sovereign reign is prophesied in Holy Scripture! How many times to I have to explain this? Obviously you can oppose me, but to overthrow me would violate the Will of God. I'm predicted to have absolute dominion for a set period of years. Don't you know that? Nothing can interfere with that, under any circumstance. No bullet, and certainly no warrant, can stand in the way."

Griffin frowned and grumbled. To Tenney, he said, "He's right, you know. It is the Will of God."

"Then what the fuck did we come here for?" asked Haversham, annoyed.

"I don't get it," said Tenney. "God is protecting the Antichrist?"

"All things must take place as they are prophesied in the Bible," said Shahse, smiling again. "God ensures it. So in that sense, yes, he is protecting me. Pretty cool, huh?"

"Fuck this," said Haversham. "Let's just get out of here."

"All right," said Griffin. He pointed at Shahse. "But we're not through with you. We know you killed those people."

"I didn't, I assure you. But even if I did, what difference would it make? I'm the Man of Sin. What do you expect?"

"Then why deny it?"

"Because that's the truth."

"What do you care for truth?"

"I don't know." Suddenly Shahse drew himself up, and with great drama, said, "And Pilate said to him, 'What is Truth?'"

"Asshole," Griffin muttered. "Let's go," he said, and the three of them turned and walked back to the elevator.

"I was serious about that offer," Shahse called after them. "Come by again if you should change your mind. I'll tell the security people to let you in if you do."

As they were riding down, Haversham, still feeling very frustrated, asked, "So what exactly did we get out of all that?"

Griffin reached into his pocket and very carefully, using only his fingertips, pulled out the warrant. "We got his fingerprints," he said, and cracked a smile.

CHAPTER 12

On the sidewalk outside Shahse's building, the three continued their heated argument as they walked along. Or at least, Haversham, who was furious at this turn of events, argued the point with Griffin.

"What good are his fingerprints going to do us?"

"I'd like to find out some more about this man, and these will provide an excellent starting point."

"An excellent starting point? What the hell! Listen to yourself, man! And we already know everything we need to know about him." Haversham started counting on his fingers as he went through a check. "Rich son-of-a-bitch, ambassador from some godforsaken OEEC, terrorist mastermind, self-proclaimed Antichrist. What, is that not enough for you? What the fuck more do you want?"

"You don't think he really is the Antichrist?" asked Tenney, sounding distracted.

"I doubt it. You heard him, it's just some game he's playing to keep people from simply shooting him."

"But there is an Antichrist somewhere. We are in the last days. The Rapture has already happened, it's settled," Griffin reminded Haversham.

"Fine. You know what, I'm not going to argue with you. There is somebody. But it's somebody else. This guy's a few pegs short of a wallboard. At best there's somebody controlling him."

"Who else is there? President Ruben?"

"Maybe!"

"I thought you liked Ruben," said Tenney.

"That was back before he went all Dr. Strangelove on us."

Griffin turned around and held up his hand. They stopped walking. "Okay, look," he said. "I think we can all agree that Shahse is a dangerous person who will inevitably lead the world down a very dangerous path. We can agree that we can't just stand by and watch. We have to do something about this."

"Yeah, like shooting him when you're standing at point blank range!" cried Haversham. "We're not going to have that chance again."

"That would be murder," said Griffin.

"The man thinks he's the fucking Antichrist! What better justification could there possibly be? Wouldn't we be saving lives? Making the world a better place, all that? I mean, assassinating Hitler would have been good thing to do, right? What the fuck is the difference?" ranted Haversham.

"If it's not done in self-defense, it's still murder."

"Is that why you didn't shoot him?" shrieked Haversham, frantic now. "Because he wasn't pointing a gun at us?"

"Well...."

"Ha!" Haversham grinned and seemed to regain some control over himself again. "Well," he said, "I guess that's a good thing, isn't it? I was starting to worry you actually believed all that prophesy shit."

Griffin just shrugged. To be completely honest, he did think that Shahse fit the bill, and most likely was the devil incarnate, and as matter of fact had thought so since the very beginning, but he certainly wasn't going to remind everybody about that now.

Haversham ran his fingers through what hair he had left. "Look, this isn't going to work out. I can't play it your way, Dr. Griffin. I need to be doing something."

"What do you propose?"

"If we are in the last days, and if he is the Antichrist, he's going to try and wipe out all the world's Christians. They'll turn around and stage a global rebellion against him. I would rather join up with them and be planning things, serious, rational things that don't rely on your inscrutable hunches."

"Okay," said Griffin, non-committal and not actually caring. He'd be perfectly happy if Haversham, or both of them for that matter, went away, far away, and left him and his house alone.

"And we have to get started now, while we still have freedom of expression and freedom of association, before the suppression and tyranny begins."

"Okay, fine, then go."

"Fine, I will. How about you, Sam?"

He turned to face Tenney, who was startled. "Sam?" she asked.

"Yes, Samantha, what are you going to do?"

"Samantha," she repeated, letting it roll off her tongue, feeling elation. "I do have a first name!"

Haversham sighed. "Are you going to come with me, or are you going to stick with Dr. Griffin?"

She briefly considered her options. "Well, I was thinking the best course of action would be to take him up on his offer, and join his security service."

"Join him?" said Haversham, aghast.

"Yes. Then we can work to defeat him from the inside. Sabotage things, destroy data, plant bugs in his office and listen to all his conversations and diabolical schemes, those sorts of things."

"Why would you waste time planting bugs in his office?" asked Griffin, scratching his chin. "We already know what he's going to do. It's in the Bible."

"Take him down from the inside, is all I'm saying."

"You mean get close enough to shoot him?" asked Haversham.

"No, just undermine him, secretly."

"You can't undermine him any more than you can shoot him," said Griffin. "He must rule for the appointed time. I don't think there's anything we can do about it one way or the other."

"Fine, be a coward," said Haversham. "I guess this is where we part ways, then."

"I guess so," said Griffin, relieved. He stuck out his hand. "It's been nice working with you two."

He shook hands with Haversham, then with Tenney. Without another word he turned and strode off down the street. A moment later he realized he was being followed and spun around, only to see the two of them stop short right behind him.

"Oh, it's you," he said. "I thought we were parting ways."

"We are," said Haversham. "But we still need a ride back."

"You are not staying at my house any longer."

"Wouldn't dream of it. I would like to get my toothbrush, though, if that's okay with you."

CHAPTER 13

Pastor Mark Digby ushered Reverend Lars Trenton and his daughter Sarah into a secret chamber beneath the Christ Church in Herndon, Virginia, where Captain Manly had set up the headquarters of the Christian Army. It was a large room that until recently had been for storage, but had quickly been converted into an office bull-pen, with several desks and phones and computers. Here, the aspiring religious warriors waged their battle on the web, hacking into internet sites of the ACLU, Planned Parenthood, the Supreme Court, and other Satanist-run groups, to replace their content with truth-filled Christian propaganda designed to spread the wonderful Gospel message, that God so loves the world that he won't throw all its people into hell, just the vast majority.

"Reverend! Sarah!" said Manly, beaming. He was pleased the reverend could see how far he'd come in so short a time. He quickly got up from behind his desk and shook their hands, and kissed Sarah on the cheek. After introducing them to Digby, a stern, unsmiling, silver-haired gentleman who'd been a navy officer in a previous life, before going into the seminary, and who was Christ Church's pastor and Manly's second-in-command, he asked, "What are two you doing here?"

"I realized that you had been right, that I was needed out here. Once the Antichrist revealed himself, and it became clear that he was staying in this very area, I knew I had to come to his turf and do battle directly."

"Wow," nodded Manly, impressed. "You had a divine vision?"

"Not really," shrugged Trenton. "I just got bored. I knew you were out here doing exciting things and I was sure you needed me."

"Well, yes, of course," said Manly, who, if he had been asked, would have said that he needed no one, thank you very much. Except for Jesus, of course.

"So here I am, ready to provide all the spiritual guidance your fledging opposition group needs!"

"Um, yes, well," said Manly. He cleared his throat. "You know, we do have several ministers working with us already." He motioned around the room, where many of the desks were occupied be people with black collars, busy typing or chatting away. In fact, all the desks were occupied by ministers. With all the vanished people, the need for workers was so great that the unemployment level in America had dropped to zero. So while Manly had thousands of enlistees in his Army who could take action when duty called, during normal times the only people who had nothing else to do but staff his office were these ministers.

"But surely I can provide you with some service of value?"

Manly thought for a moment. He wanted to come up with something. He didn't want to send Trenton away, if only because of his lovely, petite, blue-eyed, golden-haired daughter Sarah. Now that he was single again....

They already had one major mission planned, but it was only the beginning. Next they were planning on searching for some opportunity to directly and publicly confront Shahse, which if they could pull it off would be a bold move, but also one that carried a very real risk of arrest and quite possibly death. Trenton would be perfect for that.

"Perhaps we can find you something," said Manly, grinning.

CHAPTER 14

The major trip Shahse had scheduled was a jaunt to Jerusalem with President Ruben, to meet with the Israeli and Palestinian leaders. It was to be a very important meeting, he told Ruben, essential to the fulfillment of Scripture. It was a meeting in which he would bring about a supposedly final and permanent peace agreement between Israel and Palestine, but it would be an agreement that would in fact start the clock ticking on the remaining few years until the Second Coming of Christ and the ultimate destruction of the world, because as we all know the last thing Christ wants is a permanent peace agreement between Israel and Palestine.

They flew over in Air Force One (AFO), which was being flown by none other than Captain Manly. Yes! This was the Christian Army's first major mission! But how, you may wonder, did he manage to snag such a plum position, when it looked like he was all but out of a job forever?

Well, despite the fact that all the commercial airlines had shut down, there were, of course, still some private and government planes flying around, such as AFO, and they all still needed pilots. But in spite of the airline shutdown, pilots were a scarce lot, being that airline pilots in general are such a decent, devout group that almost all of them were sucked up into heaven in the Rapture. So Captain Manly, as one of the few remaining pilots, was called to duty. Basically he was the only one they could find, but don't worry, they had given him a run down of the plane's unique controls during which he was able to surreptitiously learn how to fly. It was actually pretty easy; he wondered why he hadn't learned this before.

Of course, in his travels around the area recruiting people into the Christian Army he was developing to rebel against the cruel tyranny of the Antichrist, just as soon as said tyranny started, he had met numerous people, some of whom were influential deep inside the government. Their sway had ensured that Manly got the job, and, as an added bonus, had gotten Sarah Trenton a job as stewardess. He was going to be in tight, close to Shahse, a furry little mole burrowed right in the center of the devil's soybean farm, a spy able to discover and relay crucial information, such as when the cruel tyranny would begin, so that they could plan their rebellion accordingly.

To that end, they had taken actions that put them several steps ahead of Detective Tenney, planting bugs to eavesdrop on Shahse's evil scheming not only in his office, but anywhere he might go, such as his bedroom, his kitchen, his bathroom, his car, the Oval Office (doubly handy in case President Ruben was also planning any evil schemes), and aboard AFO (ditto). So with the touch of a button, Manly, even while remaining in the cockpit and pretending to fly the plane, would be able to listen in on all Shahse's secret conversations and learn what evil he was plotting.

After takeoff, which he carried out without a hitch, at least in the sense that the plane didn't explode, and after everyone got settled back down again, Manly set his course, popped in a pair of earphones, and flipped on the secret listening device.

Silence.

A cough. Then silence.

More silence.

"So," said Shahse, "have you ever been to Jerusalem?"

"No," said Ruben. "You?"

"No. Ever been to Disney World?"

"No."

"Me neither. Let's go there next."

"They've probably shut down."

"Why?"

"You know, cause of the whole end of world thing."

"Oh, right. That thing."

"Yeah."

Silence for about a minute or so.

"Hey," said Shahse. "How about we go to Hollywood?"

Exasperated, Manly turned off the listening device. But, having nothing to do, he got bored after a couple of minutes and decided to try it again.

President Rubin replied: "Well, you know, I always like those old Warner Brothers cartoons better than the Disney ones, but that's probably just from repeated exposure. They were on TV all the time when I was growing up."

"Tragically I never saw any of either growing up in my OEEC, under the communists. They would never have permitted such Western filth to corrupt their children."

"Did you have any cartoons at all?"

"No, no, no cartoons at all, I'm afraid. But there was this one show, which featured a group of puppets...."

Manly switched the device off, biding his time before switching it back on.

"So I said that's the last time I watch a movie based on a video game!"

"Ha! I hear you."

Ack! He waited another few minutes, then tried again.

"So the Prime Minister said, 'You shouldn't send your troops in without UN sanction,' and I'm like, 'Who the hell is running this whole coalition thing anyway?' Well, no I didn't actually say that, I just thought it, but I wanted to. I mean, who do these people think they are?"

"Well, you've certainly evened the score now."

"I mean, the way these people talk, you'd think they own the world, or something."

"And we certainly know better, don't we?"

Come on, come on! Manly was beginning to feel extremely agitated. When were they going to get to the secret evil plot to take over the world? No, wait, that already happened. Okay, well, whatever came next. What did come next, anyway, after the bad guy had taken over the world? No story ever progressed that far because that wasn't supposed to happen. But his wasn't some story; this was real! Surely they had an evil scheme for something or other. When were they going to get to it?

"So what evil scheme are you planning next?" said Ruben, when he tried again.

Ah-ha!

"Well, I already told you. I'm going to bring peace to the Middle East."

So that was it! The nerve of him, thought Manly.

"Yes, yes. I mean after that."

"Oh, I don't know. Consolidate my rule, I guess. I think the only major thing I have to do for the next year or so is to just respond to the plagues and judgments that God rains down on the wicked sinners of the earth. You know, pretend to care and whatnot. But I don't know. I'll have to check the book again."

"The Bible?"

"No, *Volume 2* of *Rapture*."

"The series by LeVay?"

"The one and only. Unfortunately, all my books were at home in New York, so *Volume 2* is the only one I have left. But it'll do for the time being, until I get some new copies."

"So you really make your plans based on some silly work of fiction?"

"It's not silly. He's the master. He's got all those end-of-the-world prophesies interpreted, precisely for me. All I have to do is follow along."

"But you can't be serious?"

"Sure I am! His books have greatly inspired me. They have given me focus and guidance, if you will. They have told me everything I need to know."

There was a brief pause, then Ruben said, "But wouldn't it make more sense to just read the actual prophesies in the Bible?"

"Why? I told you, he interprets them perfectly for me."

"He might be wrong."

"Don't be absurd. He's an expert. He has a doctorate in Biblical prophecy interpretation. Everything's worked out so far. Well, not exactly according to the book, but close enough to keep my trust. Besides, I need his explanations. I can't read the Bible myself."

"You can't?" asked Ruben, sounding awed. "You can't touch it? Because you're cursed by God?"

"No," said Shahse, laughing. "Because it's so boring. I mean, have you ever tried to read it? You're asleep in ten seconds. It just drones on and on. Why does anyone worship a God so hideously dull? Sure, there's a few exciting stories here and there, like the one where God kills everyone on earth in a giant flood because they're 'too violent,'—I love that story—but that's maybe one percent of the whole thing. The rest is just mind-numbing dreck."

"Oh, it's not that bad."

"It is too. Please. I've read accounting textbooks that were more lively. *Grocery lists* that had more pizzazz. Have you ever actually read the whole thing?"

"Well, no," Ruben said, clearly uncomfortable.

"No, of course not. I've never met anyone who has. Frankly, truth be told, I think the only reason why anybody remains Christian is because nobody actually reads the whole Bible. So they just assume it's a really great book and all's well and good, even if in their whole life they've never gotten past the first ten pages, never realizing that God's just like that monotonous loaf of a history professor you always hated."

Another short pause. "Um, is this relevant to anything?"

"I don't think so, no. I'm just kidding anyway; of course I read the Bible. Say, you got any alcohol on this plane?"

And that was how Shahse and Sarah Trenton met.

CHAPTER 15

Detective Haversham was nowhere near as clever or intuitive as Dr. Griffin, but he was a pretty decent detective. So it wasn't much of an effort to uncover the location of Manly's secret Christian Army headquarters. There were fliers posted up everywhere. And I don't mean just at churches receptive to the message, I mean at all churches, and temples, and corner stores, and utility poles. Manly was determined to accumulate as many followers as he could as fast as he could, no matter how much it compromised their security, because he wanted the largest force possible to stand against the army of darkness, to overthrow the kingdom of Satan and establish his very own kingdom. For Jesus, that is. Right, Jesus. Anyway.

The group of administrators working in the secret headquarters were spinning around, terrified that at any moment the secret police would come swooping down on them and take them out. Fortunately the secret police didn't exist yet, being that almost all the police in America, being such good, generous, devout people, had been raptured, and the ones who remained were too terrified about the end of the world and all that to be too much bothered about enforcing any sort laws, let alone doing so secretly. But surely it was only a matter of time before Shahse brought in some evil police from Europe to do the job. Surely! Of course, then he'd have to find police from somewhere else to oppress the denizens of Europe....

When Haversham arrived at the secret headquarters, waltzing in, he found Reverend Trenton, the only person there unoccupied, looking very bored. He immediately introduced himself to Haversham and struck up a conversation. When Manly left for his major espionage mission, he had explicitly put Trenton in charge as leader and spokesman—which riled Pastor Digby to no end—and consequently left him with nothing to do.

"I want to join your group," said Haversham.

"Excellent!"

"I'm a former New York City detective."

"Good. We can use all the help we can get, and I'm sure your work has given you many valuable skills."

"It has, yes," he said, thinking of his deductive reasoning abilities and knowledge of human behavior and depravity.

"You're familiar with military hardware? Machine guns, missiles, explosives, that sort of thing?"

"Um, I do have extensive assault rifle training."

"That'll do for starters. We need all sorts of firepower to blow stuff up."

Haversham became excited. "To kill Shahse?"

"No, just to blow stuff up. You know, to demonstrate the love of God."

"Okay." He scratched his chin momentarily. "How about this: I also have evidence that can prove that Shahse is a serial killer."

This information didn't elicit the least bit of astonishment from Trenton, as Haversham had expected. "Yes, well, of course he is" he said. "He's the devil, what do you expect?"

"Yes, but I have evidence admissible in a court of law."

Trenton shrugged. "All that matters is that everybody knows he's the Antichrist and comes to a saving faith in the Right Jesus."

Haversham shook his head. "Don't you want to take him down at all?"

"Oh, no, that would interfere with the prophecy. We'd much prefer to spend all our time and resources scoring small and completely insignificant victories against him as a means of futile protest while he inexorably slaughters millions of innocents, all according to Scripture."

"Okay," sighed Haversham, resigning himself to the inevitable. Griffin wouldn't do anything, now these guys were too self-absorbed to care either. Maybe there was something to this whole prophetic, protected-by-God business. "I can go with that, if I must."

"Splendid! But first, I must ask the most important question: Are you a believer? Do you have a saving relationship with the Right Jesus?"

"Um, yes, I certainly am a believer. I think. Which one is the right one?"

"I'm still not entirely sure myself. But I know he definitely hates gays. And baby-killers. You're not in favor of baby-killing, are you?"

"Um, no."

"Wonderful! Welcome aboard!"

CHAPTER 16

A FO touched down at Ben-Gurion Airport without incident; Shahse and President Rubin then immediately deplaned to the waiting limousine. Shahse stared out the window taking in the magic city of Jerusalem, it's ancient and cracked streets and buildings and walls contrasting with its bustling, modern *cityness*, and in the epicenter, rising above it all, the gleam of the enormous golden Dome of the Rock.

Shahse felt an odd sense of apathy as they passed through the city. He was excited about what was soon to transpire and all his future plans, but the city itself seemed to be just another city, albeit one far older than most. Despite the fact that it was God's holy city, and he was supposed to be the antithesis of all holiness, being here made him he neither elated nor enraged. He'd expected to feel some strong emotional surge, something uncontrollable, but it was just a business trip. He had far too much travel experience under his belt to care about yet another moldy antique city.

The meeting was held in a small, cloistered conference room in the Knesset building. A large table was set up in the center of the room for everyone to sit at together, and there were smaller tables around the room for each group to consult independently.

Ruben introduced Shahse to the Israeli Prime Minister, Mordachi Heifetz, a stout, red-faced man in a rumpled suit who kept his white hair in a comb-over. Heifetz, in turn, introduced him to the Palestinian President, Yasin al-Tineri, who in addition to being the president, was also the prime minister, the security chief, the foreign minister, the finance minister, the UN ambassador, the ambassador-at-large, and the chairman of his party, the peace-loving PTO (Palestinian Terrorist Organization).

"Let me introduce you to my aides," said al-Tineri, motioning to three men behind him. The three men, like al-Tineri himself, all had thick beards and tan suits that made them indistinguishable. Only the chairman, who was much older and gray-haired, was set apart.

"This is Mustafa Mohammed, head of ADP, my largest security service," said al-Tineri, point to the man on the right. Shahse shook his hand.

"This is Muhammad Saed, head of BPI, my second-largest security service," he said, indicating the middle man. Again, Shahse shook hands.

"And this," he said, waving at the man on the left, "is Muhammed M. Mohammed, head of PSL, my third-largest security service."

"A pleasure," said Shahse, briskly shaking his hand. "And if you'll apologize for my asking, just out of curiosity, mind you, what does the middle 'M' stand for?"

"Mohammed!" said Mohammed.

"Ah," nodded Shahse. "Of course."

There were a few other aides and recorders for both sides, but that was the bulk of the attendees. No one else, including press, had been invited, per Shahse's own instructions. He had a revolutionary proposal, and wanted the proceeding divested of appearances and politics.

They all took their seats around the main table, with Shahse sitting at the head, in an imposingly ornate high-backed chair, with President Ruben sitting at his right hand. Heifetz sat next to Ruben, and al-Tineri and the Mohammeds on the opposite side. Shahse saw that he had been provided with a gavel, so he picked it up and banged it a few times. Everyone turned to him, expectantly, while he banged it a few more times.

"Stop that," said Ruben, grabbing it out of his hand.

"My, touchy, aren't we," said Shahse, glancing at him. Then he spread his hands wide and said to the group, "Okay gentlemen, let's get right down to business. Gentleman, and gentlemen only, I should add," he said with a grin, "I have a revolutionary proposal to propose to solve this once intractable situation. It's very simple. You guys," he pointed to the Israelis, "will give the Palestinians everything they want. While you guys," he turned to the Palestinians, "will move that big Dome thing somewhere else so that the Jews can build their Third Temple. Then everybody will be happy." He sat back in his chair, smiling beatifically upon them, as their jaws fell to the floor.

"Good lord," said Ruben, coughing several times. "I bring you all the way here, and *that's* your idea?"

"What?" asked Shahse, concerned that nobody seemed to be getting it. "That's what it says happens in *Volume 2*. You know that, right? That's exactly the deal I'm supposed to make. The Jews get their Temple, the Arabs get whatever it was they wanted and go away, and I get to be the wonderful, beloved peacemaker everyone will worship while setting the world on the road to the apocalypse."

Ruben stared. "Do you have any idea how offensive that is to everybody? The Dome of the Rock is sacred and the Third Temple isn't supposed to be built until *after* the messiah comes!"

Shahse raised his eyebrows. "Since when did you know all that?"

"Everybody knows that!"

"I thought you said foreign cultures were worthless because only America was perfect?"

Ruben launched into another coughing spasm. When he got it under control, he turned to Heifetz and put his hand on his shoulder. "I'm sorry about that," he said. "I probably should have warned you about him beforehand. He's completely insane." He nodded to Shahse.

"Then why is he here?" demanded al-Tineri, pounding the table. "Why are you doing what he tells you, if he's insane?"

Ruben hesitated, and Shahse waved his hand. "Well, tell them. Don't be ashamed of your faith." He lowered his head to meet Rubens' eyes. "Don't deny your Lord Jesus. You know what happens to people who deny their Lord Jesus."

"Yes, yes," said Ruben, running his hand over his face. He proceeded to explain to the attendees how the world was ending and how Shahse was the Antichrist and everything he did was according to biblical prophesy, and how he was acting in faith to ensure the fulfillment of God's word.

When he finished there was a long moment of awkward silence. Then Heifetz cleared his throat and said, "Well, I can't honestly say I understand where you're coming from, Larry. It seems the definition of recklessness. And Mr. Shahse, don't think you're the only person who's read the Book of Revelations."

"I know I'm not. In fact, I'm counting on everybody having read it. I need you to understand these things are necessary. The end is approaching!"

"Mr. Shahse, I'm only too aware that these prophesies predict that the so-called Antichrist will betray the Jewish people and instigate another holocaust. I hope you don't really expect us go along with that."

Shahse leaned back in his chair and wondered absently if Heifetz knew about the Zionist Committee. He must have, right?

"Secondly, you should know that, as President Ruben has already mentioned, it is well understood by Talmudic scholars that Solomon's Temple, the Third Temple you speak of, shall be built by Messiah himself, after he has returned. Not that I necessarily subscribe to Talmudic prophecies, but neither do I subscribe to yours."

Shahse glanced over to Ruben. "Larry..." he said.

Ruben sighed and, with hesitance appropriate to violating a well-established diplomatic barrier, said to Heifetz, "You have to know that Jesus is the messiah."

"That'll be quite enough."

"The Rapture really did happen! It's really all true! You must see that Jesus is the fulfillment of all the Old Testament Jewish messianic prophecy. You have to believe!"

Heifetz stood up suddenly. "I think we're done here," he said. "Coming, Yasin?"

Al-Tineri stood up as well. "We do not believe in your absurd prophecies, either," he said to Shahse. "This 'Rapture,' as you call it, is a judgment of Allah upon the infidels."

"What is with you?" replied Shahse. "You're supposed to be on my side."

"Your side?"

"Yeah, my side. I'm the Antichrist. I'm here to destroy the Jews and the Christians. You guys want to destroy the Jews and the Christians too, right? So you should be on my side. Enemy of my enemy, and all that."

"You should know," he said glaring with fire in his eyes, "that the *Haram al-Sharif* is holy ground to all Muslims. Every Muslim would sacrifice his life defending it before allowing it to be defiled by a dog like you!"

He turned away, and the two leaders made for the exit, united in their disgust, their aides quickly rising to follow.

"I can't let you do that," said Ruben forcefully from his seat. They both paused and turned back to him. "It has to happen or I will make it happen."

Heifetz stepped back to the table and stood above Ruben. "With more missiles, I suppose?"

"If need be."

"There shall be war without end and without limit if you dare commit such sacrilege!" bellowed al-Tineri from across the room. He folded his arms but remained where he stood.

"What happened to you, Larry?" said Heifetz. "You used to be such a friend to Israel. Now you will kill us all."

"I'm sorry, Mordi, but my God comes first. I have to do what's necessary to fulfill the prophecies. It's my destiny. And please, don't say it like that. The Jewish people are God's chosen, and he loves them and will protect them, if only they'll abandon Judaism and convert to Christianity."

"And if they don't?"

"I don't know. I guess they'll go to hell like all the other sinners."

Heifetz sighed deeply and briefly raised his hands, putting his palms on his temples. It was inevitable, he supposed. One fringe group or another had been trying to blow up the Dome for decades. They'd all been Jewish groups; he'd thought Christians would have more sense, but apparently he'd misjudged. In the past, the American fundamentalists had provided much needed support for Israel, and it had been accepted gladly enough. But they'd never really cared, had they? It had all been for this, even if Ruben didn't realize it. It had never been about protecting the Jews. The Jews were always just a means to an end for their own religious conquest.

On the plus side, he finally decided, at least the blood wouldn't be on his hands, and who knows, maybe something would come along to prevent it from happening and disprove their nonsensical prophecies, or maybe the Temple would be rebuilt and Messiah really would come. Who knew?

CHAPTER 17

Meanwhile, Captain Manly and Sarah Trenton were seated in the president's office aboard AFO. He had taken her around the plane, showing her the places where the bugs had been planted, bragging about his secret surveillance as though it had been his idea and his strategy from the first, and he who had planted them all, all by himself, finally ending up here in the main room. It was large for a room on a plane, but small for an office, and thus had only minimal furnishing, mainly the president's desk and chair, a smaller chair across from it, a phone, a computer port with it's laptop computer missing, as it was being carried about by an aide; a pen-rack stocked with roller-ball pens emblazoned with the presidential seal, a bowl of individually wrapped mints, the packing likewise festooned; a wall-mounted plasma TV directly behind the desk, and some framed photos of Ruben's wife Marisa and son Lawrence H. Ruben, Jr., currently at Yale, though of course who knew where he actually was at that moment. Manly, naturally enough, sat behind the big desk, and indeed had his feet up on it as he leaned back in the plush, ergonomically fitted chair, a chair much more comfortable than his chair in the cabin, and yet who was the one with the most responsibility for the plane?

"Yes, tragically, my wife and children were all taken up to heaven," he said to her. "Which makes me once again very single," he added with a wink.

Sarah, sitting up straight in the small chair across the room, which like all the other furnishings, including the carpet, was covered in a dark navy blue fabric, unsmilingly blinked her pretty blue eyes at him.

"I'm sure you and I will get along great, since I'm such good friends with your father. Heck, I'm practically his boss now." When Sarah continued to blink silently, he continued. "I mean, don't get me wrong. I'm not suggesting anything inappropriate here. I'm a changed man now, you know. Jesus has given me a new life, made me a better person. You can trust me. I'm just saying I think you're beautiful."

Lacking a response, he shifted his position, taking his feet off the desk, pulling the chair in, and leaning forward, considering her. "You shy? You can talk to me. How about your story? You missed the Rapture too, didn't you? But I know you're a good little girl. You don't have any secrets, do you?"

"We didn't believe in the Right Jesus," she said quietly.

"Well, yes, of course. Because otherwise you're a perfect little angel, aren't you? Of course you are." He stood up and walked out from behind the desk. He wanted to have her very badly. Her simple, honest purity excited him, and the improbability of his success with her only made her more enticing. "Hey, you want to go see what's in Shahse's luggage?" he asked with a grin, holding his hand out to her.

Looking at him gravely, she rose, took his hand, and let him lead her downstairs to the luggage hold. She felt entirely uncomfortable with him, and would have preferred being almost anywhere else, especially because she knew her agreement, silent though it was, would only encourage him, but she really did want to see what was in Shahse's luggage. It turned out he had brought nothing but a single change of clothes, some basic toiletries, and two books. One, of course, was a tattered copy of *Rapture, Volume 2*, and the second was a newer book entitled *Demented Depths: America's Leading Forensic Psychologist Probes the Mind's of America's Worst Killers*, by Former FBI Agent Lucious D. Griffin, PsyD.

CHAPTER 18

Reverend Trenton, with ex-detective Haversham in tow, wandered around the National Mall, haranguing the occasional passer-by about their need for redemption.

The Mall was in shambles. Where do I begin? One, it was a vast tract of vacant, uninhabited land. Everywhere in America, rioting in the aftermath of the Rapture, violence resulting for a lack of law enforcement, and the widespread fear of more retaliatory nuclear strikes, had all conspired to depopulate the nation's cities. People had poured out of them screaming in terror like Tokyoites fleeing Godzilla, leaving them barren wastelands of such desolation it was poetic.

Two, what was left was uncared for, both because of a lack of people to mind it and because of a lack of concern. I mean, even for a sacred place like the Mall, it's hard to care about keeping the grass trimmed and litter-free when total annihilation is peeking straight at you from over the horizon. The Smithsonian Museums lining the Mall were kept locked and shuttered, protecting their invaluable treasures inside, but anything outside was uprooted, scarred, or graffitied. Even the Lincoln Memorial had garishly colored gang signs painted all over the building, and even the statue itself. You don't want to know what was painted in the spot above his crotch.

Three, I hardly need mention the roaming bands of thugs and punks who were basically the only people remaining. At least, they were in a majority over the frightened gerbil government workers who still held on to their jobs, either out of patriotism or stupidity, I don't know which.

"Yes, very post-apocalyptic," said Haversham as they wandered around. Even though he was a decorated police officer, he was extremely nervous, and only kept his gun holstered because Trenton insisted. They were on a mercy mission, he explained, trying to save souls by winning them to Jesus. Waving a gun at them would not help, even if the objects of their mercy were waving guns of their own.

"No, it's not. The Apocalypse has not occurred yet! Not for some time!" he said, exclaiming loudly so that anyone nearby might hear, if there were anyone nearby. They hadn't encountered any passers-by for several blocks. "But it is coming! Make no mistake! Repent and be saved!"

Suddenly he spied someone, a scrawny young office worker scurrying about, hiding behind trees, benches, sculpture, et cetera, as he made his way through the city, probably trying to get home. Trenton chased after him, shouting "Repent and be saved! Believe in the Lord Jesus! Believe, believe!" The poor guy squeaked fearfully and raced away as fast as he could, Trenton tracking until he ran out of energy and collapsed, huffing desperately.

"You okay?" called Haversham, who hadn't moved from his spot.

Trenton raised his hand, indicating he was still alive. Haversham waited patiently for him to get up and trudge back.

"You know, if something happens you'll just die. There's nobody out here to help you."

"I would gladly sacrifice my life for the cause of Christ!"

"Yeah, okay. All I'm saying is why don't we forget this and head back to the suburbs? There's nobody out here anyway. It'd be pretty stupid to die here when cause seems to be lacking."

Reluctantly, Trenton gave in, and they began walking the four blocks back to where they parked their car. Hopefully it was still there. They passed by a string of deserted government buildings, imposing in their solitude, and abandoned, boarded up restaurants, their facades already grimy, some already broken into and ransacked. When they reached the car, an old Buick Trenton owned and had driven all the way from Iowa, they saw someone, a red-haired woman, leaning against it, back to them. Haversham had an inkling as to who it was, but pulled out his piece as they approached, just in case. "Hey!" he shouted. The person turned around and grinned.

"Jeeze! Samantha! What are you doing here?"

"Oh, I heard there were some crazy people wandering about, and I came to investigate," his old partner said, sauntering up to them without concern for her surroundings.

"Investigate, huh? What, are you DC's lone cop now?"

"Not exactly." She came up and hugged him. "I came here looking for you."

"That's nice of you. Do you mean, just for old times' sake, or did you change your mind about saving the world?"

"Actually, thanks for bringing that up so quickly and sticking it to me, but yes, I do want to join your Army."

"Uh-huh. Finally came around to seeing things my way, huh? What happened to your plan to undermine things from the inside?"

She grinned. "On schedule. I got a job with the Department of Homeland Security."

"DHS? You're kidding. In two days? Well, whatever, these days… I'd congratulate you, but I thought you were seeking something more direct. Doesn't Shahse have his own global security network?"

"Nope, nada. I did some research. This guy doesn't have *anything*. I mean, except for that office we already visited. Everything else belongs to the same American government it always has. He just tells President Ruben what he wants, and Ruben does it for him, no questions asked."

"But why?"

"Beats me."

"Sounds like we're going to have to assassinate him, too."

"We can't do that!" cried Trenton.

"Shoot Ruben? Why not? He works for the Antichrist!"

"So? He's still the President. And a *conservative*, I might add."

Haversham then proceeded to introduce Tenney and Trenton to each other. Trenton, of course, wanted to know right up front if she had received Jesus and been saved. When she didn't respond instantly, he began his eclectic lecture about the coming Apocalypse, and her need for salvation from her sins, and how Jesus was the fulfillment of Old Testament Jewish prophecy. "His divinity is proven by the fulfillment of prophecy! Every prophecy—dozens of messianic prophecies—every one in the Old Testament was fulfilled in the person of Jesus Christ! What are the odds of that happening!"

Tenney decided not to even bother to calculate the odds of one part of a book being in agreement with another part of the same book, especially when the former was written with the express intention of being considered a continuation of the latter. Nor did she comment on the oddity of arguing over such a thing while standing in the middle of a crumbling, deserted city. So instead she used the momentary pause in his speech to quickly and empathetically promise him she, in fact, was a believer and had been saved. And yes, to answer his next question, she was also against baby-killing. She then reiterated her desire to join their group.

"Sure, that'd be great," said Haversham. "You can work for us and for him at the same time, by doing a little espionage for us. We actually already have some spies, but we need all the help we can get."

She sighed. "Yeah, about that. I was actually ordered by them to come and join your Army. They sent me to spy on you guys."

"And you're just going to admit to that?" he said, shocked.

"I want to be honest with you. I want you to know I'm on your side. And I sort of figured I could act just as you said, as a double agent."

"Ah, yes, the old double agent."

"And I'm not really going to spy on you. I mean, I'd still have to tell them some stuff about what's going on, but it's not like they don't already know everything anyway. I mean, this Manly character isn't exactly subtle. He might as well be buying air time on national TV."

"Really?" interrupted Trenton. "Is he in danger?" he asked, quickly explaining about his mission aboard AFO.

"Oh, yeah," she said, shaking her head. In fact, she already knew about the mission. She hadn't known about the bugs, but considering she herself had previously thought of the same idea, it wasn't too much of a stretch to guess that Shahse had thought of it too, and was already taking precautions. He could easily have his office swept, though he might not bother until he learned who was planting them, otherwise once removed they'd just end up being replaced, and removed again, and replaced, and removed, and so on. "You bet. It's too bad; now I'll never get to meet him. Oh well, his loss."

"What about my daughter Sarah?" he demanded frantically. "She went with him as a stewardess!"

Tenney shot a worrisome glance towards Haversham. She didn't quite know what to say, how to deliver the bad news. But what she had to admit, and couldn't bear to say in front this poor man, was that sending such an innocent, youthful girl to pour coffee for Satan was a monumentally stupid idea. I mean, what if she spilled it on him, or something? His suits must cost a fortune to clean!

CHAPTER 19

After their success in Jerusalem, Shahse and Ruben decided to stop in Rome before retuning to Washington. To Manly's distress, they said nothing about what they planned to do there, or what they hoped to accomplish. The only significant moment was when Sarah, bringing them their coffee, gushed to them how pleased she was to be there, to meet them, such important people, how wonderful they were, et cetera. Ruben, used to such things, curtly acknowledged her praise and then proceeded to pointedly ignore her, while Shahse, less accustomed, mumbled something that Manly couldn't hear. When Sarah left, Ruben laughed at his apparent embarrassment.

It turned out they wanted to see the pope.

His Holiness, Pope Perfect I (Pi to his friends), was initially disinclined to see them, but after being told about what happened in Jerusalem, condescended to grant them an audience. They were brought into the Sistine Chapel, where the wizened pope, decked out in full ostentatious papal regalia, including his fancy tall hat, sat in a chair that had been placed before the alter, above which loomed Michelangelo's fresco, *The Last Judgement*.

Shahse was awed to be standing in front of the actual masterpiece itself, but apart from that he thought it was nothing but an amusing broadside. Personally, he never much cared for the painting because Michelangelo downplays hell, depicting it in a single scowling demon, a cave entrance, and a few anguished looking individuals, which seemed terribly dismissive. He much preferred Last Judgment depictions that really emphasized the point, in which the souls were neatly divided between clusters of joyful robed saints on one side and of despairing naked sinners on the other, in which heaven and hell were given equal space, or better, in which hell was the foremost feature. He felt it deserved serious respect, and in any case, it was more fun to look at. Pictures of heaven, even good ones, not those silly caricatures of people with harps and halos, just showed people standing around, maybe lit by bright lights, idiotically staring off into space. They always failed to convey any essential aspect of the place. Hell depictions, on the contrary, were always vastly superior, even in their most primitive forms, because it was so easy to empathize with the misery and suffering, to create a palpable sense of the intensity of emotions involved. Shahse was always moved by such drawings, with the crowds of people and big wide O's of dismay on their faces. He had tried drawing some of his own, but unfortunately, like Hitler, he was a terrible artist.

Ruben, however, looked up, disconcerted, into the downward gaze of Christ, and found himself fixed to the spot, his mouth working silently as his emotions became unglued. Shahse had to give him a gentle push from behind to get him walking again.

They stepped up to where the pope sat, and Ruben immediately fell to the ground, knelling at the pope's feet. He started to weep openly. Everybody looked on in surprise, except Shahse, who stared down in disgust. Of course he'd been expecting something of the sort eventually, but this was just too much.

Ruben was clearly no longer going to be of any help to him. Oh well. Shahse brushed it off in his mind, as ultimately of little concern, since he'd already accomplished all his main goals, and no longer needed the president.

Perfect leaned down and stroked his head, quietly repeating some chant as Ruben continued to blubber.

"Oh, this is just pathetic," said Shahse. "Hey, anybody taking pictures?" he shouted to the small assembly, made up almost entirely of red-robed cardinals.

It was some time before Ruben managed to calm down. He refused to get up off the floor though, and lay down in a fetal position. Perfect muttered something—in Italian, of course, which as we've already established, Shahse dose not speak—and his translator whispered to Shahse, "You should go now."

"Excuse me? I came all this way; I have some things to discuss, and I'm not leaving until I do."

Perfect muttered some more, and the translator said, "His Holiness is not interested in anything you have to say."

The nerve of these people!

"Look," said Shahse patiently, "As the world's most revered religious figure, I need the pope to help me create a one-world religion that will encompass and thereby replace all other religions, so that I can begin to divvy up the globe and eventually force people to worship me as a god."

When Perfect's aide translated this, the pope turned livid. He jumped up out of his chair, literally hopping over the prostrate Ruben, and started screaming at Shahse, who, again, didn't understand a word, but nevertheless managed to get the general drift of things.

"He says 'no,'" the aide said sardonically, when Perfect stopped because he'd run out of breath.

"Hey, I don't need this," said Shahse. "It's prophesy. It's in *your* Bible, plain as day. People are going to worship me. The will revere me as a deity. It will happen. It is *written*. It's the will of God."

Perfect calmed down upon hearing this, and seemed to consider it.

Seeing the effect his words were having, Shahse plowed on. "Helping to make this come to pass is fulfilling the will of God. God *wants* you to do this. God *needs* you to help me. Think about it. You missed the Rapture—God left you here on earth—for a reason. Was it because you're a sinner? Hardly! Was it is because you weren't devout enough? Patently not! Was it because you're Catholic, and Catholics aren't real Christians? Well, we won't go there. No my friend, He left you here because only someone as understanding of his word as you could be trusted to do what's necessary to see to its fulfillment. You Holiness, this is your destiny!"

"Don't listen to him!" cried Ruben plaintively from his position on the floor. "He's evil!"

Shahse sighed dramatically. "Well of course I'm evil. I'm the Antichrist! What do you expect? Look, Larry, you may be having some regrets just now for killing all those hundreds of millions of people, but you needn't be. You did the right thing. You did exactly what God wanted you to do. You should be proud! You're part of God's plan. And Your Holiness, you can be part of God's plan, too, or you can refuse, and make your Father in Heaven very unhappy, and you don't want to do that, do you?"

Prefect was nodding his head. He stepped right up to Shahse, and placed his hand on his back, and said in halting English, "Come, my son," and led him out of the room, with the bishops trailing, leaving the President of the United States of America lying on the cold stone floor, curled up and sniffling like a toddler.

CHAPTER 20

Captain Manly simply couldn't contain himself. During their layover in Rome, he went to a jeweler and spent a ridiculous amount of money, far, far more then he could afford, by the way; but of course with the world ending it's not like he needed to worry about paying off his debts or anything, and purchased a ten-carat diamond ring. And yes, I know, the world is ending and there are still jewelers selling expensive diamond rings. Go figure.

After completing his purchase, Manly rushed back to the airport and, after asking around, found Sarah eating dinner in a little café nearby. He walked right up to her, fell to his knees, gave her the ring, and proposed.

"Will you marry me?" he asked breathlessly.

She stared at him in wide-eyed horror, with her mind instantly going into overdrive: Marriage? With him? Dear Lord, how old was he? He must be at least in his forties, and she was only eighteen. It was perverse, it was ghastly and repulsive. But by asking her here, so importunately, in this restaurant, where the other patrons and the staff stopped all their own activity, and were now all turned to her, staring, awaiting her answer, silently pressuring her into agreeing. Maybe she could get out of it by telling him she needed to consult with her father before making such a tremendous commitment. Yet what would that get her? He probably had his cell phone handy, so she could call without leaving the table. And what would her father say? He liked Manly, thought he was a great leader, a hero meant for important things. He'd go out of his way to encourage her to say yes. Heck, for all she knew, it had been his idea. After all, he was the one who wanted her to go along with Manly on this trip as a stewardess, ostensibly as a backup spy, in case anything important was said between Shahse and Ruben during the few minutes when Manly was doing actual piloting and couldn't listen in on them.

No, she knew in the end she'd be pressured into this, if Manly was insistent, which it looked like he would be. She really had no choice in the matter, yet she simply didn't want to. *Seriously* didn't want to. The fact was, she loved someone else, but unfortunately that wasn't something she could ever discuss with either Manly or her father. They wouldn't understand.

So, feeling immensely embarrassed, she forced herself to put on a smile, and as disingenuously as possible, said "This is really very sudden. I have to think it over. I have to talk to my father first. You know how it is." She handed the ring back to him.

"Sure," he said smoothly, standing and putting the ring in his pocket. "I get it. You just take your sweet time." He patted her on the shoulder and walked out of the café.

The other people returned to their meals, whispering about her no doubt, and she finished eating as quickly as she could, then dropped some money on the table and ran out.

He had sounded angry at her response. She was going to be pressured into marriage, all right. She felt so trapped. It was almost a physical sensation, like a weight on her chest, restricting her breathing. Oh, what was she going to do?

CHAPTER 21

Shahse stood in front of the television in the Executive Suite of a swanky hotel in downtown Rome. Ruben had absolutely refused to leave the grounds of the Vatican. When Shahse left, the president had been shouting about how he was "safe" inside the walls of the Sistine Chapel, although what gave him that idea, or what it was he needed protection from, Shahse couldn't fathom. So he and the members of the president's staff had left him there and taken rooms for the night. Hopefully things would be better in the morning.

The meeting with the pope had gone splendidly. Perfect had agreed to everything Shahse had proposed and was now, for all practical purposes, on his side. Of course, having the pope on his side was, while far more satisfying, was not nearly as significant as having the president, because the president had lots of weapons and could push other nations around; the most the pope could do was give nice speeches praising him and holding a pan-religion conference to "work through all those issues which needlessly divide the peoples of earth seeking the life of the spiritual," or something like that. The exact words still had to be ironed out, but the conference was already in the works. Soon all religions would be melded into one amorphous, blob-like gelatinous mass which would ask only one thing of people: that they worship Shahse as a divine incarnation and surrender their souls to burn in hell forever. You know, simple stuff like that. It's not like he was going to ask anyone for their money.

In fact, right now he was watching the pope on TV, making the first of what promised to be many, many nice speeches praising him. Of course, again, Perfect spoke in Italian, and this being Italy there were no subtitles with the translation, so Shahse had no idea what he was actually saying, but the pope was smiling as he said whatever he said, so it certainly seemed nice.

Shahse was in the process of undressing before bed. At the moment someone tapped gently on the door, he was barefoot, his jacket and tie were hung up, and his shirt was partially unbuttoned.

When he opened the door, he found Sarah Trenton standing outside, still dressed in the blouse of her uniform, sans the hat and jacket. She stood there primly, holding her hands clasped together in front.

Surprised, he fumbled a moment for her name. "Miss, um, Trenton, right?"

"Yes," she nodded. "But call me Sarah."

"And what is it you're doing here, Sarah?" He peeked out to see if anyone else was around, but the hall was empty. The floor he were on, the top floor, had three suites, all executives like his, and the other two were empty. Still, he thought there might be a security guard, or something, but no. Which was fine, since he hardly needed any security, but still. Well, they were probably all downstairs, keeping out protesters and unruly reporters.

"May I please come in?"

He looked down at her, into her eyes. "You understand, if anyone sees you here, well, you know what they'll think."

"No one will know. Please?"

He could sense some eagerness in her voice which she struggled to hide. But he got the impression that it was more than just the standard enthusiasm of being in the presence of a celebrity, so he stood aside and let her enter.

Shutting the door behind her, he asked, "Well?"

"I thought you should know that there are listening devices planted all over your plane."

Interesting, thought Shahse, mildly surprised. He had suspected all along, of course, but had only gotten confirmation within the last hour from his spy in the Christian Army. And now this unexpected second confirmation. Plus she'd said 'your plane,' not 'the President's plane,' which was flattering. He grinned, patted her arm, and played it cool. "Oh, that. Don't worry. I know all about the bugs on AFO, as well as the ones in the Oval Office and in my penthouse suite in Virginia."

"You do?" she asked, startled. Manly hadn't said anything to her about bugs anywhere else.

"Oh yes. And I know all about your friend, Captain Hiram Manly, and his so-called Christian Army."

"You do?" she repeated, now very shocked.

"Yes, of course," he said, laughing. "I have spies of my own. You needn't worry about me."

"Do you know about my father?"

"The Reverend Lars Trenton, formerly of Corny, Iowa? Of course."

She was so overwhelmed she staggered over to the sofa in front of the television and sat down. Shahse clicked it off and sat down next to her.

"Well, I don't see why that surprises you. America may be in shambles, but you don't seriously think the Secret Service is going to let someone on Air Force One without conducting at least a cursory background check, do you?"

"I guess not."

"Of course not! The only thing I don't know is why you came to give me this warning. Why are you betraying your friends?"

"I was hoping," she said, now sounding glum, "that when you found out what Hiram was doing you'd kill him."

"Kill him?" Shahse laughed again. "I'm not going to kill him, don't be silly."

"Aren't you even going to arrest him?"

"No. There's no need. The man's a buffoon. He's not a threat to me. If anything, I find him amusing. But why on earth did you want to get him killed?"

She looked dejectedly at the floor. "Because he wants to marry me."

Shahse waited for the next sentence, and when it failed to materialize, stood up and said, "Ok, this may surprise you, but I can't actually read minds. Okay? So, if you want to tell me, then tell me."

She looked up at him. "I don't want to marry him. I hate him."

"Okay...so tell him 'no.'"

"He's going to make me. And my dad will make me. He practically idolizes him. I don't have a choice; I'm so trapped."

"That is unfortunate," he said, still not quite grasping it.

She stood up and embraced him. "Please, please get rid of him for me. I'll do anything you want."

He pushed her away. "Um, I don't think so."

"Please, I mean it. You can have your way with me."

"Excuse me?" he said, gagging suddenly.

"Anything. You can hurt me, if you want. I bet you like to hurt people. A real sadist, right? You're into pain."

Shahse choked. He could not believe he was having this conversation, especially not with such an innocent-looking girl. Granted, being the Antichrist did put a little weirdness into his life now and again, okay maybe more than a little, but this seemed just a bit on the extreme side. Still, he thought as he gained control of himself, if that's the way she wanted to play....

He smiled. "I'm sorry, Sarah, but you know better than that. You want a favor from the devil, it's going to cost you a little more than a night in bed."

Her eyes lit up, like she'd been waiting for this all along, even hoping for it. "You want my soul."

He dropped his smile and stared at her. "Come, on, don't play games. That might have been funny once, but not anymore."

"I'm not joking! I'll give you my soul. Just tell me where to sign."

Shahse briefly debated with himself how far he wanted to take this. It didn't feel right, making light in this manner. After all, he certainly wasn't kidding when he told everyone he was the Antichrist. He really was. He knew it. Still, while this was not remotely typical behavior for a celebrity admirer, the odds were she wasn't being serious. Long before all this Rapture business, when he was nothing more than a youthful and fabulously wealthy telcom executive, he'd hit the underground bars in the various global cities he traveled to, looking for genuine Satanists. He'd wanted to find others who shared his beliefs, but never did. He found punks with dyed hair and pierced tongues and army boots, and Goths all in black who wore pentacle necklaces and listened to heavy metal, but to a one, they were only doing it to mock society and be rebellious and nihilistic, to excuse their often crude sex and violence. They would say interesting things, but when he pressed, nobody actually believed in the devil. He'd found Wiccans and other occultists who sought magic powers and worshiped pagan gods which most preachers would call demons. But the occultists themselves denied it. For them, it was about nature, or the old religions of Europe, or space aliens, or something along those lines. They didn't believe in the devil, either.

Even the most depraved people he found, the would-be vampires, who literally drank human blood, usually each other's when no willing donors could be found, disappointed him, too. Their favorite word was "darkness" but they were just playing, as far as he was concerned. They didn't really care about theology, and didn't expect to wind up in hell. Most didn't believe in any afterlife, when they took the time to think about it at all. It was about nothing more than extremely debauched and wanton sex.

And yes, there were a few self-proclaimed Satanists that he found, but they were no better. More sex and drugs, no concern for the large picture, no understanding of the true nature of evil. As far as Shahse was concerned, they were just atheists who chose to mock God and the Church, instead of ignoring them to focus on science. It seemed almost everything he'd ever heard about Satanists was all just the invented fantasies of fear-mongering religious believers. Only the devout believed, and they of course trembled, but apparently without cause. It had been so unsatisfactory.

He hadn't played any of their stupid games. He hadn't participated in the Wiccan's silly spellcasting rituals, or drunk any blood with the vampires, or engaged in any of the violent, domination-themed sex orgies. He didn't even like the heavy metal. It all disgusted him. These people didn't know *anything*. He was a sun god living among naked mole rats.

Only once before had he made a deal to buy another person's soul, and that had been done as a joke, too. He had met an atheist in a bar in London who gave him her soul in exchange for a martini (an apple martini, naturally), simply to prove how strong her convictions in the non-existence of God were. She laughed about it with her friends afterwards. Where was she now, he wondered. Hopefully in hell, but, he thought sadly, she'd probably long since repented.

He put his hands on Sarah's shoulders and looked intently into her eyes. "Sarah, please understand what you're getting yourself into. It's really all true. The Rapture did happen, that proves it. There really is a God. And I assure you hell is a very real place. If you do this, you will burn for all eternity."

She compressed her lips and met his eyes with a steely gaze of a far deeper intensity than his own. "Good. I hope so."

He let go and stepped away from her again. "Okay," he said quietly. His heart was beating heavily with amazement.

Her smile and voice softened. "Why even tell me that? Are you trying to frighten me? Don't you want people to go to hell?"

"Oh yes," he said quickly. "It's my job, you know. My *real* job, I mean. I want to get as many people damned as possible. Stuff the place full. But most of the people headed that way are only going to end up there out of ignorance, ignorance about the true nature of God. Pure, foolish ignorance! It saddens me, when I think about it. But you…well, I've never met anyone who knew and was willing. You're…interesting."

"Thank you. So where do I sign?"

He sighed softly. They were really going to do this, weren't they? Unfortunately, there were practical considerations to factor in as well.

"Look, I'm not going to kill him. I don't know if I have that authority, legally."

"But you rule the world!"

"Well, sort of. But listen, first I need him to fly us back to Washington. After that I can have him arrested, and even if I can't kill him, I promise you you'll never see him again."

She didn't hesitate. "Good enough. Are you going to write it down? Do I have to sign it in my own blood?"

"No. This isn't 'The Devil and Daniel Webster.' I don't need a contract. A simple handshake is enough."

"Okay," Sarah held out her hand.

Shahse still felt uncomfortable doing this, for some reason. Was her forthrightness intimidating? Or just that he didn't like the idea of someone as young and as pretty as she was facing eternal damnation? The thought didn't excite him the way it usually did.

He took her hand in his and gave it a vigorous shake.

When he let go, she returned to the sofa and sat down, looking at her hand, as though to see if there was anything different. There wasn't. After a moment, she looked back up at him. "So that's it," she said, sounding awed. "I'm really damned."

"Oh, yeah," he said, folding his arms. "Though to be honest you were already damned before. You know, Original Sin, all that? Everyone's on the path to hell as soon as they're born. They have to beg God to let them into heaven."

"Yeah, but this is different. Now it's permanent. It can't be undone. It feels different."

He smiled at her again, experiencing a bit of gentle paternalism. They had a special connection now. "Scared?"

Sarah shook her head and returned his smile. "No. Not at all. I feel kind of excited."

Shahse nodded slightly. Strange as it was, he knew exactly what she meant. He had, of course, made his own deal with the devil, and had felt pretty excited about it afterwards, too. That had been a little over a decade and a half ago, when he was just a bit younger than she was now. And yes, he's a normal person, in case you were wondering. He's not a demon ascended from the underworld and now in human form, or any silly nonsense like that.

Perhaps that was what was bothering him. He was beginning to think he'd finally found someone who *understood*. More than that, she reminded him of himself. But if what she was doing was extremely freaky, and he had to admit it was, what did that say about him and what he'd done? He'd been going along with all these ideas in his head for years, but to be sitting here quietly talking about it with a perfectly innocent-looking girl exposed the perverseness of it. Of course, it wasn't exactly the same. He was getting more out of it, namely fame and fortune and control of the whole world, while she was just getting rid of some guy. Plus, he'd made his deal before the Rapture proved that God really did exist, so even though he had been far more sincere than the punks, there was still the possibility it might not be true. Now that thin sliver of deniability no longer existed, so she had no excuse. Not that he did either anymore, but still.

"Well, Sarah, I wish I could tell you that things were going to be great for you from now on, but I can't. I mean, things worked out splendidly for me, but I'm the Antichrist and God needs me to do certain things. He doesn't need you, and this is after all the time of His Judgment and Wrath upon the earth, so even though Lucifer looks out for his own, some bad things might still happen to you."

"I'm not worried."

"You're not, huh? Well, that's good. Since you don't seem the type to get all wracked with guilty you'll probably be able to appreciate your new position, at least on an emotional level."

"My new position," Sarah repeated, grinning. "I like the sound of that."

"I'm glad. It's just that I can't promise that you'll get any fringe benefits from worshiping Lucifer, much as I'd like to."

"I have to worship Satan now?" she asked, mildly amused.

He shook his head. "No, of course not. I was just saying. You don't have to do anything, Sarah. You're completely free. There are no more rules for you."

"I'd much rather worship you, Mr. Shahse."

Shashe laughed, but it was strained, embarrassed. "Oh, you don't want to do that, trust me. Don't forget, I'm the Antichrist, the infamous 'Beast,' and the Bible says anyone who worships me will wind up in the Lake of Fire."

With that, she slid off the sofa onto the carpet, where she got on her hands and knees before Shahse. She crouched close to the ground and bent her head down. She kissed him on his bare feet, first the right, then the left. His heart was thundering with shock, but remained motionless, fighting an urge to jump back.

She sat up on her calves and looked up at him. "You are my god," she said. "My messiah, my lord. I devote myself to you with my whole being. I will praise your name and obey your every command."

He stepped away and collapsed onto the sofa, astounded. She remained on the floor but turned around and shifted her position so that she was no longer kneeling but sitting cross-legged.

Shahse couldn't believe what she'd just done. Dear lord, was she incredible, the flat out most amazing person he'd ever met. He felt extremely stimulated, and for a brief moment wanted to pull down his pants and have sex with her, right there on the carpet. But really, as he let the moment pass while he considered her, sitting on the floor looking up at him, he remembered she was only to be the first. He knew from *Rapture* that millions upon millions of people would come to see him as a divine being and worship him, so he should get used to it. Of course, all those people weren't going to be knowingly damming themselves as she had done, rather they would worship him because they would actually think he was some sort of god. He had no idea how that was supposed to happen, now that he'd brazenly declared to the whole world that he was the Antichrist—surely millions upon millions wouldn't go completely insane, although, he had to admit, it would be pretty cool if they did—but it would. It was prophecy. God would see to it. With God, all things were possible.

After a moment, he said weakly, "I was going to say, 'You must really hate this guy,' but I think it's safe to say this goes way beyond Captain Manly."

"Oh, well," she blushed. "Yes, there is more. You see.…" She paused, and looked down at the carpet and smoothed out her skirt.

"Tell me, Sarah. Please."

She faced him again. "It's just that the person I really hate is God."

Shahse smiled, he hoped kindly. "Ah, I see. Is this some kind of rebellion against your father?"

"No," she said, frowning for the first time. "It's not about him. I mean, I can't stand all his rules, and his insufferable preaching, and all that. But it's not about him. It's about God. I hate God. I really, really hate God. I hate him so much it hurts, sometimes. I want to go to hell just to let him know how much I hate him, so that he knows I'd rather burn for eternity than worship him. That's how much I despise him."

"Wow," said Shahse, genuinely amazed. "That's pretty powerful. But what did God ever do to you?"

"He killed my mommy," she said quietly.

"Oh."

"She died when I was fourteen. She had cancer. It was in her bones. They cut off her leg and she still died. It spread everywhere in her body, and she was in pain all the time. All the time! She would lie in bed all day moaning, and at night she'd cry in her sleep. And that was when she was on her morphine, all doped up and barely there. When she wasn't, when she tried to be herself, her face would be all tight and she would grimace in pain. All the time. It went on for months and months, that she lay in bed in agony, and all this time I had to take care of her. Daddy was always off busy with his church and his sermons. He just didn't want to see. And then he'd say it's the will of God, it's all his perfect plan." She had tears in her eyes by the time she finished. Even Shashe was moved with pity. He moved to the edge of the sofa, leaned forward, and put his hand on her forehead. He stroked her hair, trying to comfort her.

"But Sarah, dear, don't you want to go to heaven and see her again?"

"No!" she shrieked, and the suddenness of it gave him a start. The tears started flowing down her face freely now, and she sobbed quietly.

"But why not?"

"Daddy didn't go to heaven in the Rapture. They believed the same things, so why should I think she did? She went through all that pain and suffering just to wind up in hell."

"But you don't know that."

"How could I stand it if I went to heaven and found she wasn't there? How could that be heaven? What would God do? Just make me forget her? Forget she ever existed? Does that sound like heaven to you?"

Shahse pitied her, and felt awful about having doubted her sanity earlier. He still didn't quite agree with her decision—there were, after all, centuries worth of theological studies dealing with these questions—but he now realized the tremendous depth of her sincerity.

"I'm sorry," he said. He patted the seat next to him on the sofa, and she climbed back up. She sat next to him, rested her head on his shoulder. He put his arm around her.

She had stopped crying by now, and wiped her tears. "You understand, don't you?" she asked, looking up into his eyes. "You hate God too, right?"

He sighed. "No. I'm sorry to tell you this, and I know it's going to surprise you, but I actually don't."

Puzzled, she sat up straight, pulling away so that he let go of her. "How could you not hate God? You're the Antichrist!"

"Yes, well. How can I explain this to you?" he asked rhetorically, as he rubbed his chin in absentminded thought. "Have you ever read *Paradise Lost*?"

She shook her head.

"A shame." He thought for a moment, then said, "Essentially, it's destiny for me, being the Antichrist. I didn't decide to do this because I wanted to conquer the world, or re-imagine society in my image. I didn't set out to destroy anything or anyone. This was a path that opened itself up to me, and I believe God chose me. You see, he's written this story, an ultimate tale of good versus evil, which he wants now played out in the world for his own inscrutable reasons. But to have such a story, you need a villain, and that's me. He picked me, and I accepted. Had I truly hated God, I might have refused to help him bring his story to life. But I didn't, Sarah. I don't hate God at all. I've actually always been very devout, it's just that I knew I didn't belong. I'm not a bad person, despite being what I am. I follow the commandments to the best of my ability. I've never killed anyone, really and truly. I've never had sex, either, believe it or not." Sarah tilted her head questioningly at this, and he said, "It's true. I'm still a virgin. I play by the rules. I don't even like lying. I've told some in my time, I admit, but I try to avoid it as much as possible. That's why I'm so open about who I am, and what's happening in the world. I'm not going to fabricate some alternate reality. I'm going hold fast to the Will of God. Please understand, I honestly love God. He chose me, and I accepted his command. I will be his villain, and when it's all over with, I'm going to go to hell, forever. I will happily sacrifice my immortal soul to follow the Will of God."

She grew amazed as she listened to his speech, and when he had finished, she hugged him.

"You're better than Jesus," she said with quiet joy as she held him. "He only gave his life, and not even for very long, since he got it back anyway, and everybody thinks that's such a big deal and all, but here you are giving your eternal soul. That is so much greater, so much more meaningful. That just proves how horrible God is, that he would ask you to do such a thing when you love him so much. You're far better than he is."

"Well...."

"I'm going to be good, too, just to spite him."

"You do that." He lifted up her head and kissed her on the cheek. "You should be going now. You need to get some sleep."

She looked into his eyes, completely enamored with him. She was disappointed they weren't going to have sex, but she found his commitment enormously inspiring. She wanted to devote herself to him, to become just like him.

"Thank you so much for everything," she said.

"A pleasure." He stood up, and led her back to his door. Before they parted, he added, "Goodnight Sarah. And welcome to the Kingdom of Darkness."

CHAPTER 22

Sarah skipped back to her room, humming and walking on clouds, then giggling at the inappropriateness of such a metaphor, given her "new position," as Shahse had put it. She felt so much better now, so much more at ease. She'd kept her hatred for God buried deep for a long time, so that it had indeed become painful, physically so at times, and finally being able to share it, to express it fully, had given her a tremendous sense of release.

She hoped fervently that she would meet with Shahse again in the near future, and, while she thought his purity in spite of his dark nature was very awesome, she also hoped that he might reconsider making love to her. Certainly someone as powerful as he would never marry her, but at least they might have sex, if only so that she could express to him how much she loved him. And it wasn't just because of her pledge; what she felt was a genuine, intensely emotional love. She had loved him from the first, from the moment he lit up her television screen. How much had she wanted to tell him! But if she had, he would have just dismissed it as just some infatuation. Worse, he might have been offended, assuming the offer of her soul was just some cheap trick to get into bed with him, which it most certainly was not. Would he have made such a deal, she wondered absently. Instead of her soul in exchange for disposing of Manly, would he have taken it in exchange for making love to her?

She doubted it, given how sincere he was about his devotion to God, which she didn't want to upset. She didn't want to change anything about him, such was her love.

When she arrived back at her room, she kicked off her heels and though about taking a nice hot bath before going to bed. But no sooner had she taken her stockings and blouse off than there was an insistent knocking at her door.

"Sarah, open up, please open up," said a voice which was unmistakably that of Captain Manly. She peeked through the peephole, and yes, there he was. The nerve of him, showing up unannounced at this hour. But now, knowing what was in store for him, she was unconcerned. Perhaps, she thought, if he asked for an answer to his proposal, she would say yes, just so it would be that much more painful for him when he was sitting in solitary confinement.

"Hey, what are you doing here?" she asked cheerfully, as she let him in after putting on her bathrobe.

He pushed the door shut behind him. "Get dressed," he said hastily. "We have to get out of here, right now."

"What?" she said, shocked. "Why?"

He gripped her shoulders. "They know. They know everything." He then quickly proceeded to give her the disastrous news he'd received when he called her father back in Washington. The reverend had told him about their newest member, Detective Samantha Tenney, now an employee of the DHS, and now also a secret double agent, and how according to her, the DHS and Shahse himself knew all about the mission and the bugs and the spying and the Christian Army in general, so they were literally standing on the brink, possibly only moments away from being arrested and taken to a CIA-run prison facility where they'd be waterboarded into revealing all their secrets, or died, or knowing the CIA, most likely both.

Sarah began to freak out. Of course, she knew perfectly well that nothing of the sort was going to happen, and in any case Shahse had made it clear he wouldn't arrest Manly until after he'd flown them back to Washington. But now he wanted them to run off, together, and become fugitives, roaming Europe, together, melding seamlessly into the anonymous great masses, together, where the would hide out for years if necessary, slowly making their way back to America, or maybe Israel, where something important and prophecy-related was bound to happen. Together. Just when she thought she was rid of him, just when she thought she was free, now they were going to be stuck with each other for a very long time.

Manly noticed her starting to cry, and thought naturally it was related to their impending arrest and imprisonment. "Don't worry, we'll make it. Here, look." He pulled out from his jacket not one but two pistols, and offered one to her. "Take it," he said.

"What—where did you get these?"

"I brought them with me, of course. Just take it. It's a semi-automatic. No safety, no need to cock it, just point and shoot. Now please hurry up and get dressed."

Trembling, she took the gun in her hands, while he held up his, Bond-like, muzzle skyward, and peeked out the edges of the drapes. The metal was weighty, menacing, with an oily smell to it.

She looked at his back, hating him, her guts boiling with her inflamed emotions, all feeding into each other. He was going to ruin everything. Everything! He was going to take away the freedom that for the first time in her whole life was close enough to taste, and he was going to keep her away from any possibility of every seeing Shahse again. But the absolute worst part of it was the realization that she had sold her soul and was now going to be cheated out of the one tiny, itty-bitty thing she'd asked for. All she'd wanted was to be rid of him, and now was going to be denied even that. Fate was against her. No, God was against her. This was all his doing. God must have it in for her, she decided. God had ignored all her prayers and sacrifices and pleas, but now that she'd done something bad, now he was going to start paying attention to her. He'd just been biding his time, waiting for her to give up waiting for him, before pouncing. Wham!

"Sarah, hurry!" said Manly without moving from the window, as he could still hear her whimpering where she stood.

"No," she choked.

"What?" he said, turning toward her. She pulled the trigger and blasted him right through the middle. The world exploded, and he was slammed back against the wall right next to the window, spraying the drapes and wallpaper with gobs of blood, along with almost all the rest of the furniture in the room, and Sarah herself, her bathrobe and her face.

She shrieked as loudly as she could, dropped the gun, and ran out the room and down the hall as fast as she could, screaming all the way, collapsing at the far end of the corridor.

CHAPTER 23

A few hours later, she was sitting in the hotel's deserted restaurant, in a fresh bathrobe, talking to an Italian inspector with a mustache who spoke decent English, named Gulipe, and a bald, black Secret Service agent named Alexander. Over a cup of hot tea, she told them how she had shot Manly because he had tried to rape her. Gulipe took a few notes on a pad of paper, yawning throughout. He asked only one question, about the guns, and all she could say was that Manly had brought them, and she'd managed to wrestle one away from him. Gulipe was entirely uninterested. She got the clear impression he could have cared less about her and would have preferred being anywhere else. She hoped it was just him, and not some general police-wide apathy resulting from the enormous levels of recent apocalypse-related violence, although it probably was. Before leaving, he said that they had taken her passport and that she should plan to stick around for the next couple of days, while they investigated, which would screw up her trip back home, but tough.

Afterwards, she was alone with Alexander, who gave her a key to a new room in the hotel.

"How...how is he?" she asked.

He shrugged. "They took him to some hospital. Touch and go, is all I heard."

"Oh."

"Well, goodnight, Miss Trenton."

She slept fitfully, twisting about anxiously, filled with fear about what she'd done and about would happen to her. But she was able to comfort herself with the thought that it was ultimately his word against hers, and he was a middle-aged pilot and she was an innocent young woman. Plus, there was the fact that he was spying on the president of the United States, which she was sure would eventually come out. And besides, even if the worst happened, what was she afraid of? Going to jail? It seemed ridiculous to be afraid of going to jail when she'd been eagerly planning on going to hell. Was she afraid of her father, and how upset he'd be when he found out? She had to admit the thought of it made her uneasy, yet that seemed pretty stupid too, if she seriously expected she could stand before the Almighty on Judgment Day, and curse him to his face.

Still, a thick sense of fear, and yes, guilt, pervaded her. And she couldn't get over the fact that she'd shot him in cold blood. It was a monstrous thing to do, so unlike her.

After lying awake for what seemed like hours, she got out of bed and down on her knees. She started to pray, "Lord God, I...I...."

Beyond that she couldn't think of anything to say. Prayer had been increasingly difficult for her in the last few years, since her mother had died. She persevered nevertheless, praising God and asking for his blessing, but she never felt him respond, and her prayers became formulaic and forced. Now she couldn't even do that much.

So she prayed to Satan instead, asking for comfort and strength to face the future. And when she finished, she could indeed feel a soothing presence surround her. It was as Shahse had said, Satan looked out for his own. Feeling much better, she climbed back into bed, and easily drifted off to sleep.

In the morning she was awaked by Agent Alexander, knocking at her door. When she opened it, he handed her passport back to her. "Get dressed, ma'am," he said. "We're leaving in two hours."

"I thought I was staying here."

"They changed their minds. There's no case."

"But...."

Alexander put his hand on her shoulder. "I'm sorry, ma'am. He didn't make it."

She put her hand on her mouth, went back into the room, and sat on her bed. Her shock turned to tears. Alexander quietly shut the door, leaving her sitting there alone, sobbing. She sat there like that for at least ten minutes before she was able to get up and turn on the shower. Everything that happened after that, dressing, packing, going to the airport, getting on the plane, all went by in a blur as she wrestled with her emotions, trying to contain her grief. A grief not for Manly, whom she could have cared less about, but for herself. She was no longer a good person. Now she was a murderer.

When Shahse had told her about how dutiful he was to God, she had immediately and completely empathized, because for so long she had felt exactly the same. She felt persecuted by God, and for nothing. She had never done anything wrong. She always obeyed her parents, she was a virgin, she was a hardworking student, she was honest, and she was a faithful, sincere believer, going to church, reading her Bible, earnestly praying, singing in the choir. She had never smoked or drank, let alone taken any harder drugs. She was just about perfect in every way, even her father had said so. So the way God treated her was simply unjust. She did have to admit she had a sense of self-righteousness about being so victimized, but now, of course, all that was out the window. Now she'd become genuinely evil, truly guilty, deserving of whatever mistreatment she experienced. In essence, God had ultimately won out.

She tried to regain control by convincing herself that it didn't matter. If Shahse had agreed to kill Manly as she had requested, she'd have still been a murderer, at least in a legal sense. But then at least she wouldn't have done it herself, wouldn't have felt the kick of the gun in her hand, wouldn't have seen all the blood, and wouldn't have seen the look on his face, the look of shock, of hurt at her betrayal. And at dying, which had probably been pretty painful, too.

Aboard the plane, for which they'd apparently found another pilot, she was sequestered in a small conference room in the back, away from everyone else, especially the reporters. Now she flew as a passenger, her stewardess position rescinded. She sat there alone, at a small table, wishing she could speak to Shahse again. He'd help her out. He probably already had, probably pulled some strings to squelch the investigation. Who else could she turn to? He was her lord now, after all.

She got up and carefully wandered throughout the plane, slinking around to avoid other people, until she found Agent Alexander, guarding a door. She went up to him and offered her thanks for his help last night.

"No need, ma'am. Just doing my job."

She smiled awkwardly, and said, "If it's at all possible, I'd like to speak to Mr. Shahse, and thank him too."

Alexander regarded her curiously, with a raised eyebrow. "For what, ma'am?"

"Well, I'm sure he must have done something. I mean, everything was cleared up pretty quickly, so he must have said something to someone."

"Ma'am," said Alexander, hesitating, "they dropped their case because there was no evidence against you. Ambassador Shahse had no influence on their decision that I know of."

Which didn't mean that he hadn't, of course. "Well, I'm sure something must have happened. Maybe you could ask him for me?"

"What happened, ma'am, was that Mr. Manly died on the operating table."

"Could you ask him, please?"

"Ma'am—Miss Trenton—I have to caution you against any interaction with the Ambassador. He's a very dangerous individual."

She laughed at this. "But you're protecting him!"

"The Secret Service protects all foreign dignitaries, no matter how insane they may be."

"Listen to yourself! You shouldn't be talking like that. And besides, you're wrong, he's a sweet, gentle man. I already met him, the other day on the trip over here. I poured him some drinks, and he didn't bite my head off or…steal my soul, or whatever you're so worried about. So could you please just ask him?"

Alexander said nothing for a moment, but finally nodded his head, slowly. "Very well," he said, his tone having dropped several degrees. "Stay here." He opened the door and went inside, closing it behind him.

Fifteen minutes passed before he returned. "Ma'am," he said, "The Ambassador denies any involvement with the Italian authorities regarding your case. But he did ask me to give you this." He handed her a sealed envelope with her name scrawled across it.

She thanked Alexander, kissing his cheek, then raced back to the conference room and tore open the envelope. Inside was a typed letter and an index card with a phone number.

Dear Sarah,

I want to express my sympathy for what occurred last night. But as they say, "The Lord works in mysterious ways." I just hope you've finally begun to realize the seriousness of what you've done. I fear this may only be a harbinger of worse ills to come. God is not your friend. On the contrary, he can be quite vengeful, and I'm sure you've not seen the end of this. All I can offer you is my support, and my friendship. On the enclosed card you will find my personal cell phone number. Due to the fact that your Christian Army friends, and possibly others, will likely continuously have my office bugged and my phones tapped, calling this number will expose you, so use it only in an extreme emergency. But if you need me, I will provide you with all the assistance I can.

With Love and Sincerest Regards,
SSS

She read the letter twice, and though she wanted to weep, not a tear was shed. Everything he'd written was true, but she'd so overtaxed her capacities for fear and guilt that she seemed to have lost them. Her heart had become hard and cold and cruel, and she thought that, having crossed the line and killed one person, she could easily kill more. Others should suffer as she had suffered.

The only redeeming part of her situation was the clear evidence that Shahse really did care for her, as she'd hoped. True, things were bleak indeed if even the devil pitied her, but she was warmed by his empathy; it seemed he was the only one who had any compassion for her. He'd given her his phone number, and he'd even teased her. Here she was, her hands stained with blood, her future promising nothing but misery, and he was making jokes—"The Lord works in mysterious ways," indeed.

CHAPTER 24

Shahse sat in a small, private section of the plane, a sort of lounge area with two sofas and a coffee table. Ruben, of course, had locked himself in his little office and refused to see anyone, least of all Shahse. But that was okay; the solitude gave Shahse time to finish reading Griffin's book, *Demented Depths*. It was a weird book, all right. Shahse had been expecting a collection of police procedural stories documenting the cases Griffin had solved. And while there was some of that, along with some of Griffin's personal story, including his time at the FBI, the tragic death of his partner, and the resulting Incident that sent him into the private sector, much of the book was devoted to his psychological analysis of various killers, each more twisted than the last. Griffin had talked to all of them, often interviewing them in prison, but many of these interviews took place long after the convictions.

Griffin wrote quite luridly of the atrocities they committed, as well as the murders' own, often pathetic, explanations. You know, how they were abused as children, left home alone without anyone to read them bedtime stories and tell them they were special, and that's why they grew up to stab elderly couples and rape little girls and eat the livers of their next door neighbors.

Most of these stories disgusted Shahse, some to the point of actual physical nausea. He had no taste for the macabre. Shahse, a man who amused himself with the thought of people burning in hell, was not a sadist. The infinite misery of hell was too abstract for him to get upset about (though his encounter with Sarah had left him strangely uneasy), plus that was something *God* was doing, so that made it okay. But real-world cruelties disturbed him with their unfair and arbitrary destruction. For instance, he had so far been very successful in avoiding all news reports of the lives of the people in Asia who had survived Ruben's nuclear strike, if the suffering and depravations they endured could be called life. All Shahse knew about it was what the Bible said, that the Four Horseman of the Apocalypse brought war, pestilence, famine, and death. How that played out in the real world, he remained blessedly ignorant of.

Shahse endured *Demented Depths*, though, because he expected to cross paths with Agent Griffin again. Not that he was concerned about it. Griffin couldn't do anything to him, and besides, he was pleased to note that according to the eminent shrink's symptomological descriptions—particularly regarding the triumvirate of childhood factors that supposedly predicted murderous aggression in adulthood: bedwetting, arson, and animal cruelty—he did *not* fit the profile of a serial killer, which was certainly good to know. He had never been cruel to animals.

CHAPTER 25

A week later, Shahse was at the White House, knocking on the door to the Presidential Bedroom, standing beside a Secret Service agent.

"Larry, please," he called.

"Go away!" a muffled shout came.

"Come on, Larry, don't do this. People are getting very worried."

"Go away!"

"Larry, they attacked your country, you were entirely justified in responding. Do you hear me? You didn't do anything wrong!"

"Go to hell!"

Shahse sighed and shook his head at the Secret Service agent. "Look, Larry, saying that to me isn't an insult."

"Get out!" Ruben screamed, and this time he must have been standing right at the door, given the volume.

Shahse jerked back, recovered himself, then said to the agent, "Well, at least he got out of bed."

Shahse wandered around the White House for a little while, dispirited, taking no notice of the guards and officials staring at him from around corners, meandering over to the West Wing, where in the Oval Office he found the vice president seated imperiously behind the president's desk.

"Oh, hello," he said.

Vice President Prescott Baines looked up at him forbiddingly. He was known to be an intellectual, far too intellectual and serious minded to have ever been elected president but handsome enough in a stark, John Wayne sort of way to wrangle the second slot. Actually, his appearance seemed to have digressed since the election. Probably all the stress of the apocalypse and whatnot, but he'd grown gaunt and pale, his eyes hollow. Not eating very well, it seemed. Plus he'd stopped shaving and now had this short beard. Upon reflection, Shashe thought the degradation of natural attractiveness gave him a terribly sinister look. In fact, Shashe thought the vice president looked more satanic than he himself ever would. It was so unfair.

"Well, if it isn't Mr. 6-6-6," said Baines in a deep, glowering tone that Shahse was envious of.

"You have no idea how much I was teased for that when I was little."

"I'm sure."

Shahse took a deep breath. "Um, so Larry's still, um, recuperating, I take it?"

"Recuperating? I don't know what you did to him, but it seems he has suffered an irreparable emotional breakdown. It is only a matter of time before he's declared unfit to perform his duties and removed from office."

"I didn't do anything to him."

"Didn't you?" He rose from his seat and stared menacingly at Shahse. "I can assure you, when I am president, there will no longer be such condescending to your whims. You status here will undergo a significant revision."

"Oh, come on," Shahse sighed. He was getting real tired of having to explain to every single person he met how the Rapture had happened and he was the Antichrist and Biblical prophecy was being fulfilled in accordance with the will of God and so on, et cetera, et cetera . "Come on, you already know this. I'm the Antichrist, et cetera."

"Do not patronize me, Mr. Shahse."

"You know what, fine. You just get in the way, and see what happens. I don't really care anymore." He turned and walked out.

He was driven back to his office tower in a funk. Things were not going well. Actually, no, things were going fine, prophecy-wise, it's just that he'd lost his enthusiasm for it.

First, there was Ruben. The president had been thrown out of the Vatican when he demanded absolution but then refused to convert to Catholicism, due to the pope being in league with the devil, or something. He scurried aboard AFO, avoiding not merely the press and the local dignitaries there to see him off, but also, mainly and especially, Shahse. He locked himself in his little office and refused to see Shahse, a state which he maintained from then on. According to White House staff, Ruben had locked himself in his bedroom, refusing to come out for any reason, fanatically washing his hands, sitting half-naked on the floor amidst tissue boxes and bottles of milk, opening the door only to admit a tray of food, which at least thank goodness he was still eating, but otherwise avoiding all other people, including his wife. Shahse couldn't really fault the guy for his turnabout; he had, after all, killed a billion people. But if this sort of behavior continued, he'd not only be stripped of his office, he'd be carried off to a mental hospital in a straight jacket, and wouldn't that be entirely undignified.

Shahse had been counting on Ruben's continued support for his own power, so naturally this split was very troubling. Still, for reasons already delineated, he was hopeful that the loss of support would prove not a disaster but the impetus to propel him into acquiring power on his own accord.

Second, there was the al-Tineri situation. After Shahse's triumph in Jerusalem, the former terrorist denounced him publicly as the greatest threat ever to the Muslim world, far worse than those Crusade things that happened in the Middle Ages, thus riling up said Muslim world, then renounced his position as the president/prime minister/et cetera of Palestine to resume his terrorist career, swearing to destroy numerous yet unspecified infidels, of which Shahse was presumably one. A bare week had gone by, and the construction, or rather de-construction, of their ridiculous Dome had barely begun, and already there had been several massive bombings in Israel, resulting in dozens of deaths. Shahse wasn't particularly concerned with this, since, as the Antichrist, according to LeVay, he himself was supposed to be a Jew-hater plotting a second Holocaust, so really, the more Jews al-Tineri killed, the fewer there would be for him to worry about. And of course he wasn't the least bit concerned about his own security. It's just that this wasn't supposed to be happening. It made Shahse look bad, to be upstaged so, not to mention the fact that the Muslims were supposed to be on his side. They were supposed to fall in place and help him oppress the Christians, not muddy up the beautifully pure good versus evil symmetry he had going.

So there were the Christians in North America, South America, and Europe, all hating him for being the Antichrist, and the Muslims in the Middle East and Africa hating him for the same reason, and the nations in Asia who had survived Ruben's rather broad nuclear strike hating him big-time for all the massive fallout-related pollution that was quickly making their countries uninhabitable, which wasn't exactly his fault, but who'd listen to him? That was his third problem, his lack of supporters. Where was his coalition of the willing, he wondered. How exactly was he supposed to rule the world when everyone hated him?

Fourth, and strangely enough this bore on his mind the greatest, even though it was the least important, there was Sarah Trenton. He hadn't heard from her all week, which was probably a good thing, but he realized he was aching to talk to her again. He wished he'd given her a different number. Obviously, he had alternative means of contact that were protected from taping and bugging, but they were indirect. His spy in the Christian Army, for instance, could get reports to him that avoided those problems, but they had to be written and delivered by courier, which could take a day or two. He had given his direct number to Sarah because he believed she would be in immediate danger when she returned, but apparently no one had found out, or else they had found out and then locked her up in some sort of telephone-deprived location, both equally realistic possibilities. He couldn't wait until he received the spy's next field report to find out what had happened. Of course, the spy didn't know about Sarah and the commitment she had made, but as the only other member on the ill-fated AFO mission there would surely be some focus on her from the group, at least for a while.

Until then he was in despair with uncertainty as to her fate. Had she been discovered? Did any further disasters befall her? He had horrible thoughts about all the awful things that might happen to her, the dreadful curses God might inflict upon her. He imagined her in misery, unable to stand in direct sunlight, forced to hide in the darkness and drink the blood of the living when night fell, in order to survive. Well, no, that was an unlikely curse, but he had to admit it would be pretty freaking cool if it did happen.

He felt dreadful about all that had transpired, and worse, he actually felt guilty for causing her ruin. Did that make him one pathetic Antichrist, or what? He was supposed to hate humanity, to be eager to sweep souls into perdition, and now that he'd actually gotten one, one that hadn't even been tricked but fully and happily acquiesced, here he was racked with regret, wishing he hadn't gone along with it, wishing he'd stopped her before it was too late. This couldn't be healthy. How was he supposed to deceive the innocent multitudes when he was so upset over one rather demented little chick?

Shahse was in a general state of despondency. Even that day's fencing lesson with Jean-Paul failed to cheer him up. He easily defeated Jean-Paul, time and again, without breaking a sweat, but it just wasn't fun anymore. He went up to his apartment, showered, had lunch brought up to him, and tried to read from *Rapture, Volume 2* while he ate, but that, too, failed to sustain his interest.

He went to his office and looked through his paperwork, but that only made him more depressed, so he gave it up. It was entirely unimportant drivel! The way things had developed, he had indeed become the ruler of the world, but found it was in name only. His was a figurehead position, like the UN Secretary General, only with less bureaucracy, hence fewer scurrying underlings to prop up his sense of importance. It was just him in his office. Without any machinery, and without Ruben's threats, he had only that power he derived from the willingness of people to go along with the whole antichrist/prophecy-of-God thing.

Wandering back into his living room, Shahse turned on the television, where there was breaking news regarding a catastrophic explosion. Great, just what he needed, another bombing from al-Tineri and his posse. But this time it happened in Italy. So they were expanding, he thought. More bad news.

He switched it off and sat thinking about Sarah. He could easily find her number and call her, but of course doing so would expose her. But did that really matter so much? Why not just take her away from them? She could live here, with him. Wasn't that what he wanted? But no, he thought, that couldn't happen, the antichrist was supposed to be unattached, just like Jesus had been. LeVay had made that pretty clear. See what he was giving up in the name of prophecy?

Such was his dejection that when the guard from downstairs buzzed him to say that the crazy guy from the FBI was back, he could have danced for joy. Finally, some real excitement!

Agent Lucious D. Griffin, PsyD, had been spending his time rather inconsequentially, sitting at home reading, and doing heavy loads of behavioral profiles for the FBI, mainly regarding terrorists, of which there seemed to be a lot of these days, and that was even before the al-Tineri situation had got started. This end of the world stuff was getting to people.

He'd sent those prints he'd gotten off the arrest warrant to the FBI's forensics lab, and, given the naturally lengthy time periods processing took even under good conditions, plus the general messed-up current conditions, it had taken quite a while to get the results back. But now he had them, and boy was Shahse screwed this time.

Shahse, standing in his living room, clapped for him when he got off the elevator. "Agent Griffin, I'm so glad you came back! I was beginning to wonder about you. You seemed so hot and bothered last time you were here, and then you just disappeared on me! Your friends both ran off to join that Christian Army thing to fight the good fight, yet you just went back to your boring old life?"

"Not quite," said Griffin, dressed in his usual casual corduroys, stepping into the living room but remaining several paces away from Shahse. He held up a thin manila folder he was carrying.

"Oh, is that another criminal case?" Shahse asked in mock disappointment. "Too bad. I was hoping you came to take me up on my offer. You know, I read your book. All those twisted psychos you've put away—I was quite impressed. I'm not like those people, though; I could never do things like that. I could barely stand to read about it. Some of those crimes made me nauseous just thinking about them."

"I'm glad you were so entertained," said Griffin.

"No, no! I wasn't entertained, I was horrified! The world is a terrible place, isn't it? It almost makes you glad it's coming to an end."

"Yeah, I'm real happy about that," he deadpanned.

Shahse sighed and decided to move on. Poor man, he thought, he's endured so much he can't even take a compliment. "So, what's this case you have? Can I assume it's a new angle on the Wall Street Slasher case? Or something else, perhaps? Who am I this time? The Zodiac Killer? The Southwith Strangler? The Anthrax-letter mailer?"

"How about Jack Wilson Snell?" said Griffin, opening the folder to show Shahse a picture clipped to the inside, of an intense young man in a uniform who bore an uncanny resemblance to Shahse.

Shashe launched into a fit of coughing, doubling over and grabbing his stomach. His face turned red as he coughed loudly and repeatedly, hacking uncontrollably, like he was choking on something.

Griffin watched with pleasure, a hint of a smile creeping onto his lips. He'd interrogated numerous criminals in his career, and always loved this part, the part where you played your trump card, that piece of evidence that unequivocally fingered the suspect and destroyed whatever pathetic excuses and alibis he was shelling out. Only the professional criminals who had been around this particular bend before could remain steady. The rest of them were always entertaining. Sometime they went bug-eyed. Sometimes they just collapsed in on themselves. Sometimes they started talking a mile a minute, vainly trying to explain away the unexplainable. Shashe, well, he must be great fun at poker games.

"Well now," said Shahse, holding up his finger while still holding his guts with left hand, slightly bent over, "that fellow does bear an slight resemblance—"

"Your fingerprints are a twelve-point match," said Griffin, and Shahse started coughing again, though not quite as ghastly as before, finally collapsing on the sofa. Griffin decided it was just an act and rolled his eyes; no one who spent years living under an assumed identity could have such little self-control.

He turned the file around and began reading it. "Jack Snell, from Blue Gulf, California—a bit away from Eastern Europe, I notice—joined the Army on your eighteenth birthday, then after basic training you were stationed in Germany where you spent almost a year before coming under suspicion during an arson investigation. Why am I not surprised? Shortly before they charged you, you went AWOL, never to be seen again. They've still got an active warrant for both charges, you know."

"Is that why you're here?" Shahse said weakly, holding his head in his hands. To try to arrest me again? Didn't I tell you that was impossible?"

"That was when you were the Antichrist. Now you're just some Army dropout. Named *Snell*, for God's sakes. I don't think the president's going to be quite as awed as he was before."

"Oh, come on, so I changed my name, so what? You don't really think anyone's going to be so stupid as to name their kid '6-6-6,' do you?"

"Well, actually—"

"You want to arrest me, you go right ahead, I don't even care anymore."

"I'm not here to arrest you, Jack. I accept that you're the Antichrist."

Shahse dropped his hands and looked up plaintively. "Then what do you want from me?"

Griffin pulled up a chair up against the crystal coffee table, right across from where Shahse was, and sat down. They two were face to face now. "Let me tell you something. I've spent my entire professional life studying psychotics: serial killers, kidnappers, rapists, terrorists, even cannibals. Everything. You said you read my book, so you know all about it. The vilest monsters you can imagine. I've read about them. I've written about them. I've talked to them. But in the end, no matter how much I learn, no matter how deep I go, I can't help but feeling that I always miss something, some subtle yet fundamental aspect that separates them from everyone else, which lets them commit the atrocities the commit." He pointed at Shahse. "But you, you're the Antichrist. You're the ultimate evil, the absolute extreme. If I can get to the heart of what makes you tick, I can finally discover the key to the essence of evil."

"Okay." Shahse recovered himself, and smirked at Griffin. "Good lord, why on earth would you want to find such a thing? Do you think it'll help anything? Because it won't. You can't save the world; the end is inevitable. And after that, nobody's going to care about evil anymore. You think they talk about serial killers in heaven? Unless, that is, you were planning on joining all us cool people in hell?"

"No."

"No, didn't think so. Too bad, you'd probably enjoy it. So anyway, what good's it going to do you? Two, you're playing a dangerous game, going around, looking for the heart of evil. I feel compelled to throw that in. A very dangerous game, et cetera, et cetera. However, not with me. That's three. I'm actually not a very evil person at all, at least not in the way you expect. I mean, what you've just found out about my past is probably the worst thing I've ever done. And I just mean going AWOL. I had nothing to do with the arson."

"I doubt that."

"I didn't kill those people, either."

Griffin shrugged, playing indifferent to the crimes he's so puzzled over. "Even if."

Shahse sighed. "Look, I've met all those types of people you seem to find so fascinating. Brutish thugs and degenerate fetishistic sex fiends. I've met people who claimed to be witches and vampires, I've met Satanists, and I have to tell you, it was all so disappointing. None of them *believed*. For them it was all just a way to excuse their perversions and cruelty. I'm so far above all that it isn't even funny. For me, it's purely philosophical."

"How are you above it?"

"Because I'm sincere. I believe, in all of it. And I really do worship the devil. Well, maybe *worship* is too strong a word. I pray to Lucifer—sometimes—but I don't do any of those stupid rituals. You know, all that black magic nonsense."

"No, I don't know."

"Besides, my evil is so much more refined."

"What's more evil than murder?"

"See," said Shahse, grinning, "that's what I mean. Murder is just another form of rude violence. It's so pedestrian. Do you know Dante's *Inferno*?"

"Of course."

"Right. It used to be my favorite story, before I discovered the *Rapture* series. I must have read it a dozen times, though come to think of it, I never did get around to reading the rest of the story."

"The *Paradisio*?"

"Yeah, the one about heaven. Who needs that, right? Anyway, he describes a journey through hell, how it's multi-tiered, and how different sins are on different levels, or circles, going from least to most offensive. He puts murder on the seventh circle, out of nine. Not too good, but hardly the worst of sins. See, murder and other forms of violence are bestial in nature, the province of animals. They're criminal, of course, and beneath the dignity of humans, but they don't warrant the lowest position, because they're just things animals do. The sins on the eighth and ninth circles are sins like fraud and treachery, which Dante considered worse than even murder, because they abused that which was uniquely human, the God-given power of reason. Abusing the gift of reason was far more sinful than simply brutality."

"And you believe this?"

"No, of course not. The twentieth century provided the world with a whole new look at just how deep cruelty can go. There's no way I would say that fraud is worse than killing. But the point is that there are worse things."

"Such as?"

"It goes to the heart of what it means to be the Antichrist. I've asked myself this often. Napoleon and Hitler, in their days, were both considered potential antichrists, and afterwards they were seen as prototypes. But what were they, except thugs? Simple killers, albeit very effective killers? I'm unique. I'm not another despot in a long line of despots, nor am I some cheesy supervillain with a giant laser; I'm the opponent of God Almighty. Killing is simply beneath me."

"All right, I get that," said Griffin, becoming frustrated, "but what's worse than murder?"

"No, I don't think you do get it," said Shahse, his voice rising, sounding angry for the first time. "I am the Antichrist, the very antithesis of Jesus Christ. Do you hear me? I'm the evil Jesus. I am as far above these petty killers, as Christ is from the prophets. Isn't there a parable in the Bible, where Jesus compares the prophets to mere servants of the master, while he is the son? It's the same way with me. I am the son of Lucifer. I am a Prince of Darkness. These vile monsters you obsess over are nothing but servants in my father's house, going around performing menial chores. I would no more stoop to their level than would the Prince of Wales scrub his own toilets. Do you understand?"

Griffin swallowed and nodded. His heart rate became momentarily elevated, which was as close as he came to fear. Never in his life had he been truly afraid; the emotion had long ago been tamed and driven out by his steely self-will. But he began to think he had underestimated Shahse.

"Okay, Sha—Jack," he said, and flashed a tight smile, both to let Shahse know he wasn't intimidated and to restore his own confidence. "You've made your point. Now will you please tell me what, specifically, you're talking about?"

Shahse sighed and shrugged his shoulders, no longer upset. "A world that thinks only in terms of death and sex will be turned on its head by what I represent. It's not a one-word thing. I think the closest approximation would be 'sacrilege,' but that's not quite what I'm going for."

"Sacrilege? How is sacrilege worse than murder?"

"If you don't already know—and you really should, a man in your position, with your expertise—I'm not going to explain it now. Maybe some other time."

Griffin's first impulse was to demand an answer, but he didn't because he decided Shahse's mention of "some other time" was an offer to give him what he wanted, namely an in-depth psycho-evaluation. He calmly steepled his hands together. "So you agree to let me psychoanalyze you?"

Shahse smiled and nodded. "Sure, why not? Come back in a day or two and we'll talk some more. I'll try to explain things in a clearer manner then. And I think I could actually use it, too. I've been feeling a little depressed lately; maybe you could help me with that."

"You? Feeling depressed? What for?"

"Oh, well, a number of things," he mumbled. "There's this girl ..."

"A girl?" said Griffin, allowing himself a chuckle. After all his bragging, this was what was on his mind? "The Antichrist has relationship problems?"

"No," Shahse huffed. "It's not a relationship problem. I'm not in a relationship. It's just, I'm sort of concerned about her."

"Who?"

"Hey, you know, I've got an idea," Shahse said, lighting up. "Would you do something for me? Would you go and join the Christian Army?"

"Excuse me? I'm not going to spy for you."

"No, that's fine. I don't want you to be a spy. I just want you to talk to her."

"This is about the girl? She's one of their members?"

"Yeah, maybe you can tell me what's going on, maybe help her out if she needs it, I don't know."

Now *this*, Griffin thought as he considered the implications, is very interesting indeed. Not only was Shahse fraternizing with the enemy, he was letting his image of careless control and malicious perfection slip, by revealing his worry for another person, and thereby giving Griffin a whole new angle to work with. It was definitely worth pursuing; relationships were so essential to life, this girl could prove to be the key to understanding everything that was going on. Plus it sounded like there was someone in trouble, and he was absolutely not against helping someone in trouble.

"All right, I'll join them. But I have to know who this girl is before I can help her."

Shahse was anxious not to compromise Sarah and make things even worse for her, so he demurred. "Just get established first. I'll tell you next time I see you."

"Jack, I'm a professional. I can promise you confidentiality. No one else will know."

"Next time," he said, thinking of the bugs.

CHAPTER 26

Right at that very moment, Sarah Trenton was sitting in the front office of Christ Church, at the receptionist's desk, slowly reading through a copy of *Paradise Lost* she'd borrowed from Pastor Digby—there wasn't one in the church's small library. The office was tiny and cluttered, with one wall taken up with mailboxes for the different church officials and programs, and the wall across covered with pre-Rapture posters about the imperative outreach work the church was doing in the community and through missions around the globe. Below the posters was a table filled with various cards and pamphlets on the church's work and values, and beneath the table were open boxes where there was donated food they had been collecting for the needy which they were now keeping for themselves. The wall directly in front of Sarah had a large window through which she could see the church's main entrance, as well as the doors to the sanctuary. The office door beside the window opened and a woman walked in. Sarah looked up and saw it was Agent Tenney, and internally sneered. *The double agent*, she thought. *The traitor.*

"Hi, Sarah," said Tenney.

She put on a smile and said, "Hi, Miss Tenney. What can I do for you?"

"Can I talk to you for a minute?"

"Sure," she said politely, closing the book.

A week after returning from the AFO mission, Sarah wasn't exactly delighted with her current situation, but was contented enough. Certainly, Shahe's doom and gloom predictions had been way off the mark, at least for the time being.

The group had, of course, been extremely upset by the death of Capitan Manly, but grateful for her own survival. She came up with a story, which she related amidst a stream of tears in an Oscar©-worthy performance, about mysterious European police working for Shahse bursting in on the two of them, in her hotel room (in which she and Manly were having a private Bible study, naturally). Manly pulled out the gun he was carrying, and they immediately started firing. She saw him collapse, then she fainted, to awaken downstairs in the hotel restaurant, where she was interrogated extensively by police shining bright lights into her eyes and shouting at her. She told the police some half-truths, but denied any connection with Manly, and that seemed to satisfy them. They took her to the plane and left her in the conference room, where she was told only that Manly was dead, and that she had lost her job, but could leave upon their return to the States.

Everyone was so concerned about her and her well-being, profusely blessing her and praising God for her safety. They accepted her story without question, and held a big funeral in which her father had told the audience in a stirring crescendo how Manly was a noble saint who had been martyred for the cause of Christ, and that they might all be called upon to take a similar stand for God. She had to pretend-cry some more to keep from laughing.

The only downside was that her father became extremely paranoid, and, convinced she was still in danger, he prohibited her from leaving the church, for her own safety. So now she slept in the underground bunker, alone among the computers and the canned food and the stockpiled explosives, and spent her days working as the receptionist (the church's previous receptionist having been raptured, and a replacement proving impossible to find, given that receptionists were now a scarce commodity, since receptionists in general were such a good, hardworking, devout lot). She was a bit exposed in the front office, even though she could see anyone who came into the building, so her father had given her a gun to carry, one of the 9mm Berettas the group was stockpiling. All day she answered phones, read mail, talked to visitors, and listened delightedly to the frequent shouting matches down the hall between her father and Pastor Digby. Manly had left Reverend Lars Trenton in charge, when he left for his trip, overstepping his previous second, Digby. He'd only done it to score points with the reverend in advance of his planned marriage proposal, but now that he was dead, Trenton, despite being the newcomer, was trying to claim the position permanently, which naturally infuriated Digby. Sarah could hear them screaming at each other at least once every hour.

When she wasn't busy in the office she sat in with one or another Bible study group that met in the library or the centrum or the fellowship hall, all of which were naturally focused on the Book of Revelations. Nobody said so, but she understood it was expected of her, and she readily complied. She didn't mind. It was kind of fun.

No, she didn't try to manipulate the groups into incorrect theology, thus preventing them from knowing the Right Jesus, thus damming them eternally, as nice as that might have been. She didn't think she could get away with it, what with so many ministers around, and anyway she was beginning to get a morbid kick out of all the talk about death and destruction and hell, just like Shahse did. In her own participation, she always maintained the strictest, most extremely fundamentalist interpretation, which pleased her father when he learned of it.

On Sunday she also sang solo during each of the services. She'd sung in the choir before, but now her story had made her a star, and she easily took to the limelight. She was a good singer, too, and her heartfelt rendition of *Amazing Grace* moved the audience to tears. Her own tears were tears of laughter, driven by the irony of it.

Doing these religious things tickled her, because it was all blasphemy for her. Good, right, holy things were now all blasphemous. She took part in the sacred rite of communion, too, which was a sin in and of itself. That had frightened her a little; she had been scared the Host would burn her, like it did to the possessed and to demons and vampires and all other unholy creatures in the movies. The potential pain of it hadn't worried her as much as the fact that it would expose her, right in front of everyone. But fortunately, nothing happened, and the Host proved to be just a tasteless cracker. Probably a deep metaphor in that, but we won't go there.

So things weren't too bad. Then this morning, things had gotten even better when she'd had a real triumph. It started when one of the parishioners, a young man, had sought her out for confidential counseling. This had actually happened several times already. People would come up to her to talk about their fears in private and ask her to pray with them. It seemed she was more approachable than any of the dozen-plus ministers who worked there, but there was also something special about her, as the people would tell her. Her survival of the AFO mission seemed to them indicative of divine protection, the hand of God rescuing her from the clutches of Satan. She now had an aura of saintliness about her, which was the most entertaining thing of all.

Unfortunately, the problem this young man was having was not something she could fix with comforting words. Quietly, and with great embarrassment, he told her he was gay. He had a boyfriend and everything, but now that he'd missed the Rapture he realized how wrong and sinful it was to be gay, and was frightened, and wanted to know what to do.

Well, obviously, she said, he had to repent and turn to Christ and stop being gay.

But he couldn't, he protested. His feelings were so strong and so real; he was so very deeply in love with his boyfriend.

Sarah had a really wicked idea at that point. Perhaps, she suggested calmly, he should just stop worrying about it. Perhaps, if God had it in for him, he should stop wasting his time trying to change the unchangeable, just accept the fact he was going to hell, and enjoy his life.

Needless to say he was a bit startled to hear such advice from a veritable saint, but as they argued about it he realized she was right, and decided to just accept fate.

And since God has basically spit in your face, she continued mischievously, you might consider spitting right back by worshiping the Antichrist instead. You know, just something to think about.

He realized then she wasn't quite the holy woman she was made out to be, and she gave in and told him her story, about her mother, and about how she had met Shahse and how he was actually a wonderful, pure-hearted man who completely sympathized. She got the nice young man to sympathize, too, so she didn't spoil it by mentioning such minor, insignificant details as selling her soul and killing Manly, or that worshiping Shahse would irrevocably condemn the nice young man to eternity in the Lake of Fire.

So she jokingly led him in the Happy Sinners Prayer, which she made up on the spot, in which he confessed he was a sinner and completely happy about it, and did not want any forgiveness, thank you very much. And yes, she got him to renounce God and accept Shahse as his Personal Lord and Savior (or was it Non-savior? Un-savior? De-savior?)

They promised to keep each other's secrets safe, and he went away smiling, and Sarah felt ecstatic. Her first convert! She'd won a soul! (Or lost it? Damn these opposites!) It was such a shame she couldn't tell Shahse about it; he would be so proud of her.

So when Tenney showed up to talk a few hours later, she at first thought the nice young man had gone and ratted her out. Not that there was anything for her to be concerned with, even if. Who here would take some pervert's word over hers?

Tenney pulled up a chair to the side of the desk and sat down, leaning in close to Sarah, so they were eye-to-eye. "You know how I work for DHS, so I have a lot of law enforcement connections?"

"Yeah."

"So your father asked me to see if I could uncover any information about Shahse's plans, and especially anything about Hiram Manly's death."

"Okay," said Sarah cautiously, already guessing where this was going and cursing herself for not having planned better. It looked like she was going be in some trouble, after all.

"I read the official report from the Secret Service. Do you know what it said?"

Just how did she want to play this? Obviously a shooting involving a member of the president's staff, even if just his pilot, was bound to generate a lot of investigatory-related paperwork, some of which Tenney had apparently gotten a hold of. It was surprising enough that there hadn't anything more than a brief mention of the incident in the media, but Shahse might have done something to prevent that, and in any case the media, like everything else these days, was no longer the clockwork-like model of perfection it had once been.

It would be disastrous if she got caught in a lie. But if she denied everything and stuck to her story, clamming any discrepancy was cover-up, she might convince her father and a few others, but Tenney,

Haversham, and anyone else with a government background would instantly be suspicious, and hound her unrelentingly until they learned the truth. Government people, especially police, hate conspiracy stories.

With no time to think things through, she decided to go with the story she had told the investigators in Rome and talk to Tenney woman-to-woman, and try appealing to her feminine side. "It said I shot him after he tried to rape me."

Tenney's eyes widened, clearly surprised at her candor. "And is that what actually happened?"

"It is," she said, nodding, already concentrating hard on getting those tears flowing again.

"Then…why did you lie to everyone?"

Sarah reached over and took her hands. "Oh, Miss Tenney," she pleaded, beginning to whimper, "he tried to force himself on me. He'd bought a diamond ring and proposed to me, and when I told him no he got very angry and came after me. I didn't have a choice. Please, Miss Tenney, please understand. I didn't have a choice."

"Okay, okay, it's all right," said Tenney softly, leaning in closer and touching her shoulder. "But then why did you lie about it?"

"Oh, Miss Tenney, who would believe me? You heard my father's eulogy. Everybody here thinks he was some kind of holy man, a martyr for Christ and all that. They don't want to hear he was just another creepy pervert, lusting after someone young enough to be his daughter. That he was a braggart, a liar, a hot-head. I got to know the real Captain Manly while we were alone over there, and no one here would ever believe me."

"Not even your own father?"

"Especially not my father. Daddy idolized him. He would defend Hiram over me anytime, I know he would."

"I have to admit, I find that hard to believe," Tenney said, sounding apologetic. Sarah thought the tone indicated she was winning and only had to press a bit further.

"Please don't tell anyone, Miss Tenney, please! I'm terribly sorry about everything and wouldn't have done it if it hadn't been absolutely necessary. Please, if you tell anyone all you'll do is get me in trouble, and you'll ruin everyone's faith in their precious hero. Why upset everybody? Let them remember him like they want."

Tenney withdrew her hands, moved them to her lap, and leaned back in her chair, giving Sarah a sharp look, as if contemplating her critically. "I won't tell anyone," she said at last, and Sarah gave a small sigh of relief. "But you shot someone. That's not something to take lightly. As a police officer, I know how traumatic that can be, even when it is necessary."

"Did you ever shoot anyone?"

"No, I never had to, thank God, not once in my entire career. But I've know people who had, and how greatly it affected them, even the macho guys who claimed nothing fazed them. They'd become very introspective, at least for a while. It can take some time to process."

"I'm fine, really," Sarah said, cautiously.

"Of course, those were the decent ones, who got introspective. The other guys, the sociopaths, the ones who became cops so they could beat people legally, they just shrugged it off."

Sarah clenched her teeth; this was a trick, after all. "Okay, I'm not fine. It's really eating me up inside only I can't say anything to anybody because it'll just make things worse, but I'd be so grateful for your help Miss Tenney."

Tenney smiled wanly. "Just Sam, please. And if you want my help, Sarah, stop lying to me."

"I'm not lying to you," she said, a chill unavoidable touching her voice.

"You know I'm supposed to be here in the capacity of a spy for the DHS, don't you?"

"Yes, except you're a double agent."

"No," she said, shaking her head, "I'm not. I just tell everyone that so they'll trust me. But I really am a spy for the government, for Mr. Shahse. My reports go directly to him."

Another trick, thought Sarah, this one rather pathetic. "I don't believe that."

"He trusts me, Sarah."

"Why would he trust you? I thought you tried to arrest him."

Tenney leaned in closer again and spoke sweetly. "I spoke to him yesterday, in fact. He wouldn't tell me exactly what had happened, but he said he met with you in Rome, and that there was a special bond between you two. He told me he's very worried about you."

Sarah was taken aback, and felt a lump form in her throat, and swallowing hard, had to stop herself from spurting out any response. All of a sudden, she felt a rush of dependence on Tenney commingled with a desperate yearning to reconnect to Shahse. She so much wanted it to be true, but how could she trust Tenney? But how else would Tenney have known about the meeting if Shahse hadn't told her? The hotel had been chosen at a moment's notice; no one could have bugged their rooms. And how could she have known about Shahse's concern for her? If it was true, Tenney could become a conduit between them, and they'd be able to communicate. If only it was true. It was difficult, but finally all Sarah allowed herself to say was, "I don't know what you're talking about."

"Sure you do. Don't worry, it'll be just between the two of us. You can tell me what happened. You're in love with him, aren't you? Did you have sex with him? Did you shoot Hiram because he told you to?"

Sarah smirked; she'd been right to be cautious. It looked like Tenney couldn't be trusted after all. "See, that just proves you don't know Sei in the least. He's such a good, kind man, he would never, ever do anything like that."

"You call him 'Sei?'"

"He's completely pure and would never try to take advantage of anyone. He didn't want sex from me at all."

Tenney arched her eyebrow. "Perhaps because he's gay?"

"What?" she cried sharply.

"Sarah, how would you know anything about him? Unless I'm right, and you did talk to him. Just admit it, Sarah."

"Of course I talked to him. On the plane, when I brought him his drinks."

"Okay, fine, be that way," said Tenney, pushing the chair back and standing up to leave.

"He's not gay," she pouted, mostly to herself. Although, given how evil homosexuality is, it would make sense that the Antichrist would be gay. She shivered; it made *perfect* sense. She had to fight an urge to grab the phone and call his private number just to ask him.

Agent Tenney, meanwhile, left the office and wandered down the hallway, pondering her next course of action. Should she go directly Pastor Digby to tell him, or wait a few days and try to wring some more out of Sarah? She was leaning towards an immediate exposure. If Sarah really had shot Manly in cold blood, she was far too dangerous to leave alone. Unfortunately, Reverend Trenton would be extremely resistant, even if he accepted her accusation, because there was very little they could do about it. It wasn't like they could just lock Sarah up anywhere. Any confrontation with her would invariably result in her leaving and heading straight into the arms of their enemy. And that was if they were lucky. With one phone call, she could bring him to their doorstep.

And even if they did manage to confine her somehow, what then? With the authorities in Rome having already cleared her, they couldn't simply have her arrested and taken to jail. Even if they did, Shahse would simply intervene and order her released. Besides, Trenton would want to keep her nearby so they could attempt to save her soul. But that too, was bound to fail, if Sarah really was in love with Shahse. Tenney wondered how long it would be before they resorted to medieval torture to get her to repent.

Another idea suddenly occurred to her. Since she did work for Shahse, she could always go over to his office and speak with him directly. He'd admit her. Then perhaps she would have the conversation she'd pretended to have a minute ago. She could play the same trick on him she'd tried to play on Sarah, and claim that she could be trusted because Sarah confided in her. But no, on second thought, that would be a waste of time, if not outright suicidal. No matter what Shahse said, he'd demand an assurance that Sarah would be protected, and then when she wasn't, he'd know exactly who to blame.

She reached into her pocket and took out a piece of paper, unfolded it, and reread the letter Shahse had given to Sarah. Agent Alexander had opened it and made a photocopy before sealing it in a new envelope and handing it to Sarah. He sent the copy on to Tenney when she called to do research on behalf of Reverend Trenton. Alexander was another member of the group in government service working for them undercover; it had been he who had placed the bugs aboard AFO, as well as in the Oval Office and Shahse's penthouse suite.

She reread the letter, frowning. Sarah was clearly in love with Shahse, that much was obvious, but just what was it that had happened between them? What had she done? It was maddening.

Her cell phone rang then, and it was Agent Griffin, which surprised her; she hadn't expected to hear from him again. "To what do I owe the pleasure?" she asked, returning the letter to her pocket.

"I need you to get me in with this group."

"The Christian Army? Sure, I can do that, no problem. There're pretty lax about their admission standards, for a bunch of people who think they're fighting to determine the fate of the world. But I thought you weren't interested? What made you change your mind?"

"I went back and spoke to Shahse again."

"Really?" she asked, amused. "Did he want you to spy, too?"

"No. What do you mean, 'too?'"

"That's what he wanted me to do, when I went and talked to him. He got me a job at DHS, but then I had to come over here to spy. Of course, I'm actually a double agent. I'm willing to do anything I can to undermine Shahse. The thing is, though, I don't have all that much actual spying to do; we have his place bugged, and he seems to know everything about these guys already."

"Wait, back up. Why would he want *you* to spy? You're obviously against him."

"God only knows. The man's deluded, thinks he's invulnerable. Maybe it's some kind of test, I don't know. So what does he want from you?"

"He wants me to protect his girlfriend."

Tenney paused a moment. "So he has a girlfriend," she said carefully, stating it more to herself.

"Yeah, and she's part of your group, but that's all I got out of him. I don't suppose you have any ideas?"

"Doc, I know exactly who it is."

"You do?"

"I was just talking to her. She all but confessed."

"Well, who is it? Don't keep me in suspense."

Tenney allowed herself a smile. "I should, you know. It's exactly what you would do to me if our positions were reversed, isn't it?" Someone moved behind her, and she turned to find herself staring down the barrel of a gun. Behind the gun was Sarah's gloomy face. She stared with a crestfallen, hopeless look.

"Look, Sam," said Griffin, his voice floating from a very long distance away. He continued speaking, but Tenney could no longer hear him.

"I gotta go, Doc. Call you later." She snapped her phone shut, and slowly raised her hands. In all her years as a cop, she'd never once had a gun directly in her face, and while her training allowed her to remain steady and think clearly, her heart was jackhammering. She was convinced Sarah had killed Manly in cold blood at Shahse's behest, and if that was the case, knew she wouldn't hesitate to fire.

Sarah reached over and pulled Tenney's own gun from its holster, and slipped it into her pocket without ever breaking her gaze

"Please, it's not what you think," said Tenney in clear, natural sounding tones that disguised her terror.

"Of course it is. On your knees!"

Tenney sank to her knees, struck by the horrible realization that in a moment she would die. Sarah meant to kill her, that was clear. She was a sociopath. The pretty little girl that everyone adored and respected was a heartless killer without the slightest hint of a conscious.

"Please," pleaded Tenney. "You won't get away with it."

"Sure I will," Sarah said, sadly. "Everybody here is so fucking paranoid, they'll just assume some intruder did it. I'm the last person they'll suspect."

And even if they did, thought Tenney, what difference would it make? No one could do anything to her, not when she had an intimate connection to Shahse, the man who ruled the world. She could murder a federal agent without any consequence; one phone call would get her out of any prison.

"Look," Sarah continued, "I was really hoping I could trust you, that we were on the same side. It would be nice to share with someone, to really honestly say what I'm feeling. I get kind of lonely here, you know."

"I am on your side, Sarah,"

Sarah shook her head, then smiled wanly. "I know you'll never forgive me for what I'm about to do—"

"Please don't kill me."

"I'm going to give you one chance to prove that you're not a traitor."

"Anything, just tell me," said Tenney, her mental grip degenerating and desperation becoming apparent. She tried to maintain her focus by reminding herself that she would soon be in the presence of her Lord, kneeling at the feet of Jesus, but the thought didn't bring her any comfort.

"It's easy. All you have to do is say one little sentence. You just have to pledge your loyalty to Sei. That's it. Just say that you reject God and embrace Sei Shahse as your Lord and Master." Her smile broadened a bit, but she still seemed anxious.

"That's it? How will you know I'm not lying?"

"It doesn't matter, I promise."

"But...." Tenney was terrified, and very confused to boot. There was something extremely wrong with this whole situation; it didn't take any special detective skills to see that. "This is some kind of trick, isn't it?"

"It is, yes. But is it worth your life? If you don't say it by the count of three, I'll have no choice but to shoot you. One. Two...."

"Okay," said Tenney, holding up a hand. She believed Sarah's threat absolutely, and the only trick she could imagine being involved was that Sarah had a tape recorder and somehow thought she could use it to discredit her, or for blackmail, which at the moment seemed entirely insignificant. "I'll say it. I reject God and pledge myself to my Lord and Master, Sei Shahse."

Sarah sighed, relieved. She lowered her gun, then reached into her pocket and withdrew Tenney's weapon, and offered it back.

Tenney snatched it out of her hand, jumped up and took several steps backwards. She raised the gun at Sarah, but Sarah only pocketed her own without showing the least bit of concern.

"Don't worry. Now we're on the same side. Now I can trust you."

"What did I just do?" Tenney demanded, her heart racing as her body, now out of danger, finally allowed her to feel the effects of the stress she'd been under.

"You gave your soul to the devil."

"Okay," she said, not understanding.

Sarah shook her head. "You don't get it. You can't repent for this. It's the unforgivable sin. You're eternally damned now."

Tenney looked at her wildly. She was still new to all this religious stuff, and wasn't sure what was going on. She got that there wasn't a tape recorder involved, but beyond that she was at a loss. "I'm sorry?"

"It says in the Book of Revelation, 'All who worshipped the beast were cast into the Lake of Fire.' That's all. No exceptions. Look it up yourself. Anyone who worships the beast—that's the Antichrist, Sei—will be thrown into the Lake of Fire. You worshipped him, so that includes you."

Tenney's head was spinning and she had to put her hand on the wall to keep from falling down. "But I didn't mean it."

"That doesn't matter."

"You had a gun to my head!"

"That really doesn't matter," Sarah said with a slight chuckle. "If you love God you're supposed to die as a martyr. Weren't you listening to the eulogy?"

"But…you can't be serious."

"It's in the Bible. Look it up. Or ask anyone, don't just take my word for it."

Tenney lowered her gun and put her back against the wall. Her whole body was trembling. Everything here was crazy in a fun-house mirror sort of way. How seriously could she take Sarah? Obviously Sarah only wanted her to keep her mouth shut about what she'd discovered, and driving her insane was probably a very intelligent way of going about it. Could it possibly be true? Why would God do such a thing?

"Why are you so sure you can trust me now?" she asked. "If I really thought you'd stolen my soul, why shouldn't I expose you? Or just shoot you myself?"

"Why would you? When you realize I'm right you're going to be extremely upset, and you're going to want to make others miserable, too. But killing me won't fix anything, and besides, I'm going to hell, too. You can't make things any worse for me then they already are. What you *can* do is hurt other people. You can steal their souls. You can work for Sei and help him rule the world. I mean, you're going to do the time, so you might as well do the crime, right?"

Tenney looked Sarah over carefully and saw that beneath her friendly smile, she was anxious, too. She thought she understood, and began to feel some sympathy for her. "Is this what Shahse did to you in Rome? Did he steal your soul?"

"No, silly. Sei would never do anything like that. He's much too nice."

"So, what, you're a worse person than the Antichrist?" she asked, amused in spite of herself.

Sarah frowned briefly, confused. "I hadn't thought of it that way, but I guess so. I think that's why he's the Antichrist. He's supposed to do all these evil things but he doesn't."

"That makes no sense," she said, with a desperate shake of her head.

"He's exposing God as a hypocrite, which is what God hates the most."

"That still doesn't make any sense. Please, Sarah, just tell me what happened between you and Shahse."

"Sure," said Sarah with a shrug of her shoulders. "I'll tell you everything. But we'd better get back to the office first. If that phone is ringing and I'm not there to answer it, I could get into real trouble."

CHAPTER 27

The next morning, Griffin stepped out of the elevator onto the second floor of Shahse's office tower, where the spa room and fitness center were located. There was also another room, a basketball court, into which a medium sized trampoline had been brought. Griffin watched through the front window as Shahse, wearing gray boxers and nothing else, jumped up and down on the trampoline, swinging a sword as he did so. It was a double-edged broadsword, clearly very sharp, with the light glinting off its edges, but Shahse handled it like a toy. He swung it around, tossed it up in the air, and flipped it back and forth between his hands, doing the types of acrobatic twirling with it that a cheerleader does with a baton, all without slicing off any limbs. Griffin thought it was extremely reckless, a stupid adolescent-kind of spectacle, but obviously Shahse was very skilled at it.

His interest in swordsmanship was clearly significant. It was very peculiar, after all, for a man who claimed to abhor violence to be so adept in handling weaponry, and that was even besides his having been in the military. But while the swords related to his ideas about the use of the knives in the Wall Street Slasher attacks, as Griffin watched he considered Shahse a less likely suspect than he had before. By the way he handled the sword, Shahse was evidently right-handed, and Griffin had previously determined the killer was left-handed. Which was odd in itself—you'd expect the Antichrist to be left-handed, wouldn't you?

Griffin entered the gym, and Shahse did a backflip off the trampoline, landing just a few feet in front of him. "Agent Griffin, what a surprise! I wasn't expecting you until later this afternoon, if not tomorrow." He swung the sword back and forth a few more time before laying it on top of the trampoline.

"Who's your girlfriend, Jack?" Griffin gave Shahse a quick once-over, and noticed two things. One, he must not have been jumping for very long, because he wasn't sweating, or even breathing hard. His face was not flushed, nor was his hair mused. He might have been merely standing there all along, given his calm demeanor.

Two, whatever his exercise methods, Shahse obviously took care of his body. His muscles were well defined and solid. And it wasn't just his muscles. His skin was unblemished, and not just in that he had no tattoos, or that he lacked any cuts or bruises one might expect from his reckless handling of the sword. He lacked even natural blemishes. No birth marks, no moles or rashes or even pimples. There was only one tiny thing that marred the statuesque perfection of his flesh, and that was a small, circular, brownish-white mark on his inside left forearm, just below the crook of the elbow. After a moment, Griffin realized what it was, and it gave him pause. It was definitely also something of significance; he made a mental note to ask about it later, assuming there was a later.

"She's not my girlfriend, okay?" said Shahse. "But look, now that you mention it, I guess it's best that you're down here. I'm pretty sure there aren't any bugs in this room, so I can tell you. But afterwards, when we go back upstairs, remember not to call her by name, just an initial. We'll just call her T, okay? I was going to get the bugs cleaned out of my office, but since I still don't know who put them there, I can't trust anyone to take them out. I'm sure the Secret Service is in on it. I'm sure Vice President Baines ordered them to do it, at least, if not Larry himself. Everybody's after me, you know. It's far more involved than just the Christian Army."

"If she's not your girlfriend, why all the secrecy?"

"Well," he smiled, looking embarrassed. "We sort of made a deal, she and I, and technically she ended up with exactly what she wanted, so she really has nothing to complain about, but the thing is I didn't do anything to make it happen. Now, that doesn't particularly surprise me; coincidental stuff like that happens to me all the time. I always get everything I want without my having to lift a finger. I'm blessed, you know. But all the same, I feel I owe her *something*, so the least I can do is keep her secret safe and offer her my help if she ever needs it."

Griffin remained silent, and the two of them stared each other down for a moment. Finally, Griffin said, "Sarah Trenton, right?"

Shahse was genuinely surprised. "How did you know? Is that your amazing deductive reasoning at work, or has she been outed?"

Griffin glanced up at the ceiling, indicating his exasperation and also creating a dramatic pause, before he continued. "I spent all last night over at Sam Tenney's apartment, talking her out of a total mental breakdown. She was in hysterics. She had a rather disastrous encounter with your girlfriend earlier in the day." He proceeded to explain what had transpired between the two, how Tenney had confronted Sarah, and Sarah in turn had stolen her soul. Shahse listened in wide-eyed wonderment.

"My little Sarah did that?" he said, in complete amazement. "Wow. That's incredible, just incredible."

"You little shit," Griffin sneered at him. They stared at each other for another moment, then Griffin suddenly ran at him, grabbing Shahse the neck and slamming him against the nearest wall. Shahse was momentarily surprised, but then calmly reached up, took Griffin's arm, and pulled his hand from his neck. He was quite strong; Griffin's grip melted like ice.

In a single, fluid motion, Shahse hefted his right leg up, placed his bare foot against Griffin's chest, and simultaneously let go of his arm and gave a hard shove. Griffin flew several feet back, hitting the floor hard and sliding back almost all the way to the opposite wall. He lay on the ground a moment, calmly waiting, while Shahse stood motionless. They watched each other from their respective positions, waiting for someone to draw a weapon, before they mutually decided that the tension was over. Griffin stood up and brushed himself off brusquely, glaring at Shahse as he did.

"Sorry," said Shahse with a semi-apologetic shrug. He turned his head back and forth slowly to relax his neck muscles, "But hey, think about this: You wanted to know what was worse than murder, and now you do."

"Jesus Christ. That's what you were talking about yesterday? All that 'sacrilege' stuff?"

"Sure. What's more sacrilegious than worshiping the devil? I'm surprised you didn't figure that out already. I mean, that is supposed to be my job, the whole reason I'm here. Christ saves, and Antichrist damns. Pretty simple, really. I thought I made it clear to you yesterday. Did you think I was kidding? Do you think this is some kind of game?"

For a moment, Griffin was dumbstruck. Such moments of astonishment were rarities in his life, and he wasn't used to not being in control. His heart rate sped up a bit as he tottered dangerously close to the brink of being afraid. "What about Sam?" he asked finally.

"I'm sorry about her, really I am. I didn't even realize it worked like that. Did she ask any of those ministers about it? What'd they say?"

"She said she talked to eight different ministers, which I know doesn't encompasses all the ones over there, but that's all she could stand. Agent Tenney asked each of them about it in a very general-ized, Bible-study sort of question, and they all agreed with Sarah's interpretation."

"Then I guess it's true; I'm certainly no expert in theology, so if they all agreed, that settles it." He frowned, and said "wow" again, with a small shake of his head, still finding it hard to believe. And he was honestly sorry about Tenney, though it didn't quite bother him as much as it did regarding Sarah. Tenney's circumstances were much more unfortunate, of course, as she had been tricked into it, which he detested on principle, but on the other hand that was cer-tainly more rational and expected than Sarah's behavior. Plus he felt responsible for Sarah, having initiated her himself, while Tenney's loss wasn't one bit his fault.

On another level, he could begin to see plans being laid out for the future. The ease with which Tenney had lost her soul presented all sorts of enticing possibilities, clearly relevant to the looming question of how he would fulfill his purpose of deceiving millions, and bringing them to their eternal ruin. Maybe it wouldn't be so hard, after all. Which, when he reflected upon it, was not necessarily a good thing.

"So what is she supposed to do?"

"Nothing," Shahse shrugged. "There's nothing she can do. I'm sorry."

"Jesus." Griffin rubbed his temples. Had he been dealing with anyone else he would have pulled his gun already.

"Do you want me to talk to her?"

Griffin chuckled in a strained way. "No Jack, I think that would be a very bad idea."

Shahse waited another minute, as they both stood there in uncomfortable uncertainty, before finally picking his sword up off the trampoline. "Well then, I guess I'm going to go upstairs and take a shower. I don't know if you still wanted to analyze me...."

"Oh, more now than ever," said Griffin, fiercely.

"All right then," said Shahse, a bit surprised. "Come back in an hour or so." He headed for the door, then stopped and asked in an offhanded way, "I suppose you want to hear my whole life story?"

"We'll see. But we can start with that cigarette burn on your arm."

Shahse glanced down at the burn, as if he needed to confirm to himself it was really there. "Oh, that," he said, trying to sound nonchalant.

"Did you do that to yourself, Jack? Or did that happen when you were a child?"

Shahse laughed a little, and gave the sword a circular swing. "No, I wasn't abused, if that's what you mean. I, for one, will not fall back on *that* tired old excuse. And no, I didn't do it to myself. It's sort of a long story, but sure, I'll tell you about it."

And so, Griffin returned later that afternoon and was invited into the living room; Shahse sat on the sofa, while Griffin sat in a chair across from him impassively anticipating what was to come. The story which began that afternoon continued over the next several days.

CHAPTER 28

"First of all, there was nothing special about my birth. I know the Nativity is such an important story in Christianity, so it's natural to assume some spectacle of the same kind attended my own birth, but there was nothing that I ever heard of. If there was anything unusual, my parents kept it from me. Maybe that's as it should be; Christ's birth was a spectacular affair with a whole parade of colorful characters, so mine should be the exact opposite: entirely uneventful and unnoticed.

"Nothing of notice occurred in my childhood, either. I had a perfectly routine, normal childhood. Blue Gulf is a small town in northern California, about ten thousand people, and while it's not on the Pacific, it is within driving distance, and after a number of summers on the beach I became a decent surfer, though it was never a particularly favorite activity of mine.

"My parents were perfectly normal people, too. While I was an only child, I never heard any claims that my mother was a virgin when she conceived me, and I doubt it anyway, since my parents had been married almost two years before I was born. Nor was my mother the expected opposite, a, um…you know, a whore. She was a working mother, which I think is an opposite, of sorts. She was a secretary for a local construction company, my dad was a self-employed accountant, and between the two of them we were solidly middle class. They brought me up well, indulging me too much, I suppose, like every parent does.

"There's really nothing more to say about my childhood, or my adolescence. I was never popular, but I wasn't a loner, either. I had a number of friends growing up, and in my teens I dated several different girls. I never had sex with any of them, but that wasn't intentional; I certainly *tried*, it just never worked out for one reason or another. My strict morals weren't something I developed until later on.

"As you were so nice to point out, I enlisted with the army on my eighteenth birthday, and left for basic training shortly after graduation. My parents were not only okay with this decision, it had been their idea. Strictly speaking, as they were both college educated they would have preferred I follow them into higher learning, but it wasn't like there was much of a choice. I hadn't even applied to any colleges, and I doubt I would have gotten in anyway. My grades were dismal; I had barely graduated high school. So they decided the army was better than whatever pathetic unskilled job I could have gotten.

"I know what you're going to say, but no, I don't have a learning disability. Trust me on this; I had all the tests when I was a kid.

"My problem was that I had neglected most of my schoolwork because I was very depressed during my junior and senior years. There wasn't any cause; I was just another angst-filled, despairing teen. I often thought about killing myself, which is how I first got interested in hell and Satanism.

"We weren't religious, but occasionally we attended a nearby non-denominational church. I'd been baptized and gone to Sunday school when I was little, so I knew just enough religion to be unhappy. I knew that if I killed myself I would go to hell. This, in turn, inspired a research jaunt. I wanted to know what it would be like, before I went, so I read things about hell, bits of theology, stories of near-death experiences, even some classics. Well, that is, I read brief summaries of the *Inferno* and *Paradise Lost* and things like that. I even went searching through books on medieval art for pictures. Those pictures were fun. Everyone in them was invariably naked. Crowds of naked people being tortured, hot and sweaty, all pressed together. A bit titillating, actually. Of course, what I was doing was stalling, pushing back the time I would kill myself, further and further until hopefully I'd no long want to. And also, I was trying to scare myself out of it. That's the point of hell, right? To scare us would-be sinners straight.

"But you know something? At first it was frightening, but the more I thought about it, the more…interested…I became. The fear morphed from genuine dread into a sort of pleasurable chill, that tingly feeling you get from a horror movie or a roller coaster. And I could empathize with the lost souls in hell. You know the saying, right? 'Misery loves company.' It was so easy for me to imagine the sorrow of these people. I could never imagine the happiness of the people in heaven, or even the happiness of people here on earth. Feelings of joy and love were simply beyond me. I couldn't see myself as ever being in heaven, but I could certainly see myself in hell. I began to feel that I belonged there. That, even if I didn't kill myself, I would still wind up there, that it was… well, a good word here is 'predestination.' I read about that, too. No free will. God is all powerful and knows the future in advance, so how can there be free will? God determines where people go before they're even born. Some are predestined to be saved, some aren't. And I wasn't.

"Maybe you think it's too much of a ridiculous presumption to take seriously, but it's a real theological argument, with some significant weight behind it. I was convinced. In fact, I got so wrapped up in it, I became not merely stoic about my inevitable damnation, but actively willing for it to happen. That's when I first started thinking about Satanism.

"Most Satanists become so in order to rebel against authority, usually their parents. But not me. I wasn't rebelling against anything or anyone. I never made a big deal about it, and certainly never even told my parents. But I did take it seriously, not just as a pose or a means to an end. I was going to hell, and this was just, not formally acknowledging it, but embracing it.

"I didn't sell my soul to become the Antichrist, or to take over the world, or even to gain any sort of power at all. I didn't ask for a single thing. A few months before my eighteenth birthday, I wrote out a little pledge, disavowing my baptism and dedicating my soul to Lucifer. Really, that was it. I did sign it with a few drops of my own blood, which is what you're supposed to do, as I understood it, mostly from fictional accounts I had read, and then I burned it.

"It's funny, but afterwards I felt much more assured of myself. For once, I felt I knew with certainty who I was. And my depression went away. I guess maybe it's like those people who know they're going to die soon, and want to savor the life they have left. I was in sort of a similar situation, so I was able to enjoy life again. Everything became clearer, more vibrant. Whereas before, I had barely been able to drag myself out of bed, afterwards I got up feeling excited about whatever the day had in store for me. My grades actually went up markedly, though too late to save me, but of course by then I was already looking forward to the Army.

"You know, when I filled out all the paperwork, on the question about religion, I selected 'Wicca.' That was the first time I ever openly acknowledged my new beliefs, though as I'm sure you know Wicca is totally different from Satanism. But of course, 'Satanism' wasn't one of the options they gave me, and I don't know if at that point I could have been quite open enough to have chosen it even if it had been. But it was just a box to check off, some little note in your file, so they can put the right little symbol on your grave if you die.

"But I quickly gained confidence, and I did tell people what I was. At Ramstein Air Base, where I was stationed in Germany, I was the company Satanist. I never made a big deal out if, and I never did anything that might draw any attention to it. I never performed any odd rituals, I attended chapel when it was required, and I never complained about prayers or the proselytizing or anything else that was a violation of my First Amendment Rights. It was just that I was honest if anyone asked about my spiritual life. But otherwise, I was like everyone else.

"In fact, since I lacked the gloomy attitude people might associate with Satanists, and never took myself too seriously, nobody felt threatened by it. Most people seemed to find it amusing, and all I ever really got was some friendly teasing, to which I responded with the appropriate self-depreciation. I developed a few good jokes. 'Yes, I do want to go to hell—I'm a masochist, that's why I joined the Army.'

"When I say there was proselytizing, I didn't mean it was directed at me. Mostly it was directed toward the poor Jews. I guess they figured I was too far gone to save. Only two people ever seriously tried to argue with me, and one of them claimed he himself had been a Satanist during his wayward adolescence before maturing and seeing the error of his ways, and wanted to help me come to my senses. I politely told him I was sure that someday I, too, would become as enlightened as he, but for the time being I was happy enough with my benighted state, so thanks but no thanks, and by the way did you know it's against regulations to proselytize a subordinate. He was a lieutenant. The other guy, a sergeant, was actually afraid of me—the only one, I should add. He thought I was possessed or something, warned me to repent before the devil completely took over and destroyed my life. Once or twice he waved a cross pendant he wore in front of me to ward me off, like I was a vampire or something. He got mocked for that; even the chaplains thought he was being ridiculous. They certainly didn't waste time worrying about me.

"So like I said, nobody took it seriously. I made plenty of friends to pal around with. I'd go with a whole group of guys into Nuremburg when we had leave, or sometimes up into Berlin, and we'd go to bars and look for chicks. I never hooked up with anyone myself, although, again, this wasn't for lack of trying. Actually, most nights I was too busy translating for my friends. Because at first I'd been worried about being ostracized, I'd taken the trouble even before arriving to learn some German, which nobody else ever did, and while I didn't become fluent until years later, I'd learned enough within my first month to prove quite useful to my fellow soldiers, especially when they were horny and drunk and could barely make themselves understood in English.

"There was also a group of three gay soldiers who invited me along on their weekend trips, ostensibly also for my linguistic talents, but more for my sympathy. They assumed that because I was a Satanist, I was against traditional morality and would understand them, which I did. Everyone knew they were gay, you know, and they got razzed all the time, and they lived in fear of being discharged at any moment, but as long as they didn't admit to it, or *do* anything— you know, don't ask, don't tell—they were safe. Still, they wanted my support, as it were, and I gave it to them, though with a caveat. I told them I was not a silly mocking Church-of-Satan type but a genuine devil worshipper, meaning I believed fully in Christianity, but chose to be on the other side. We were all playing for the other team, in one way or another. I let them know that I believed, like all good Christians do, that homosexuality was vile and sinful and they were going to hell for it, but of course I wanted them to go to hell, so I strongly encouraged their wicked ways. They were all pretty amused, so we had fun hanging out together.

"On three separate occasions we all went to a gay bar in Berlin to meet people. I got hit on a number of times, and every time I had to say the same 'thanks but no thanks' brush-off. But this wasn't nearly as often as I'd expected. I was just as fine-looking back then as I am now, if not more so, but I guess I didn't give off the right vibes.

"The third time we went out only one person tried to pick me up, but that was the one that changed everything. He was a middle-aged guy, a bit overweight, married with kids, a businessman who made a lot of trips, during which he led a secret life. You know the type.

"I was sitting at the bar alone at one point in the evening, drinking a beer, and he slides up to me, said hello, and offered to buy me a drink. His words were difficult to understand, but the message was plain enough. I gave him the usual dismissal, but he noticed my accent and asked me, in English, 'You are American?' When he said this I realized he was French, and I knew that's why I had trouble comprehending his words—he'd been speaking German with a French accent.

"I'd taken French in high school, and I could still speak it partially, though again, it would be a while before I became fluent. So we switched back and forth between the three languages, but mostly we spoke in English, because his English was better than my French or German.

"I told him I was an American, and then slowly explained, in English, and without mentioning that my friends and I were soldiers, that I wasn't gay, that I was just there to translate for my friends, because I was the only who knew any German. He clearly didn't believe me, if only because I wasn't with any friends at the moment. They were otherwise engaged, and not in activities that required much translation. One I could see sitting in a booth across the room making out with some blond stud. So he said he understood, but maybe we could talk a little anyway, since he hadn't had any luck otherwise and could use the opportunity to practice his English, which as I said was pretty decent already.

"He told me he name was Emile, and I told him mine was Sei. I'd made up this name early on, back in Blue Gulf. I looked up the word 'six' in a bunch of different languages, then put together three that sounded like they might actually be a real name. It was just a joke. Totally and completely a joke. At most, I thought someday I might write horror novels about demons and stuff, and it would make a good *nom de plume*, more reminiscent of Aleister Crowley than, you know, the Antichrist. But when I went out to bars, it became my alias. Some of my friends heard it, but I never explained what it meant, and I didn't need to. It just sounded European.

"But this guy, Emile, he traveled all over Europe and had a passing acquaintance with most of the languages, not just the big three. By that I mean he probably knew no more than he needed to get a taxi, but it was enough for him to realize 'Sei' wasn't a real name.

"He gave me a sideways glance and asked me what my last name was. I understood he knew my name was fictitious, so I just told him. After I did, he smiled crookedly and asked me if I had a middle name. I told him that, too.

"He considered it for a moment, then laughed. 'Ah, so you are the devil, yes?'

"I was both surprised and impressed that he'd gotten it. I nodded and we started taking together earnestly. I told him a little bit about myself, and how I was a Satanist and wanted to go to hell. He got quiet and furtively asked if I liked pain. I said I did. Understand though, that up to that point I've never really *done* anything to myself, no cutting or anything. Nor have I ever had anyone do anything to me. I wasn't *that* far gone. What fantasies I had remained pure fantasies. The closest I came to any real pain was the exhausting workouts I did in basic training. Ten mile runs, five hundred push-ups, that sort of thing.

"When I told him I liked pain, his eyes widened, and he leaned in real close and asked if I'd ever been burned. When I said no, he asked if I wanted to be. You have no idea of the thrill I felt, what kind of tingling energy ran through me when he said that. It was so freaky to have that kind of possibility before me, the desire for it battling with the insanity of it. This complete stranger was offering to burn me, just like that.

"Now, after all the years I knew Emile, I believe what he later told me, that he wasn't 'that kind of person.' He's not the sick bastard he sounds like. He's a gentle soul who had never done anything else remotely like that before or since, and he spent sleepless nights worrying where such a debased urge had come from, that sudden, sadistic yang that awoke within him to match my masochistic ying. Of course, he'd never encountered someone like me, before or since. I think he fell in love with me the moment he saw me, and may have created a sadistic yang, at least subconsciously, because he thought it was what I wanted. For years I would catch the embers of lust in his eyes when he looked at me, but he always restrained himself from asking what he so clearly wanted because he was afraid of me, too. Whether it was some talismanic fear of me as the devil, or fear of the secret depravity crawling through the basement of his mind, I don't know.

"I let myself be tempted by his offer for a second or two before saying no. So as to not hurt his feelings, I allowed that I might be interested in other, softer forms of pain, but I didn't want to be burned because that would leave a permanent disfigurement, which I certainly didn't want. I have a pretty high appreciation of my body. I mean, I don't ogle myself in the mirror, or anything, but still.

"He responded by offering to pay me 100 marks. I was shocked. And I know how it sounds, how perverted he must have been to be so desperate as to pay me, but as I said, this was a one-time thing. A brief passion, however, that sized him completely, becoming a compulsion, a necessity. He had to burn me. When I rejected the money, he doubled the offer, then doubled it again. When he offered me five hundred marks, I realized I was going to say yes, but was just waiting to see how high he'd go first. It wasn't that I decided to say yes, it was just something I discovered. It was a decision that had been made while I was too busy listening to his increasingly desperate pleas.

"Finally I said I'd do it for a thousand marks. His face lit up then, a glowing, joyful shine. He said he didn't have that much cash with him, but he could write a check, though it would be drawn from a bank account in France, so it would be in francs. I had no idea what the exchange rate was at the time, but I agreed. A thousand francs.

"Only later did I find out how rich he was, how insignificant the amounts we were discussing really were to him. All this bargaining made it sound like he was mad with this desire, but wasn't all that bad. He could have offered me ten times that amount without missing it. Emile Jouve was one of the casual rich, the kind who wasn't into crass consumption, buying obscenely expensive stuff just because he could, but who was still able to drop large sums without giving it much thought.

"I went to seek out my friends, and met one who was on his way to the bar to get some more drinks for him and his date, and told him I was going off with someone and would see them tomorrow. He was pretty astonished, needless to say. I quickly explained it wasn't about sex, but since I couldn't tell him what it *was* about—the only other option I could think of on the spot was drugs, but that wouldn't have worked because they knew I wasn't into that either—he eyed me and gave me a wicked smile. 'You little bastard,' he said, with a grin. 'After all this time!'

"So my reputation was ruined, and I had no idea how I was going to fix it, but for the moment I just huffed out. Emile drove me to his hotel, and took me upstairs to his suite, one of the executive suites, with its own living room and kitchen. The living room had lush oriental carpets, with a fireplace on one wall and an Impressionist painting of people at a picnic above it; a 40-inch TV was in the corner on the other side. There was an upholstered sofa and two recliners in front of the TV, and I sat in one of the recliners.

"He'd bought a pack of cigarettes at the concierge before we came up, and now unwrapped them and pulled one out. I don't remember what brand they were. I know I should, but whenever I think about it, I always see them as Marlboros. I'm sure this is just a memory trick and that they were some German brand I'd never heard of, but I can only see Marlboros in my mind. They're an American brand, and I know they were available on the base, but I can't imagine he was able to buy them in a hotel in Berlin, but then again, what do I know. He might have bought American cigarettes for me, because I was an American. He didn't smoke, and I didn't either, but he gave the rest of them to me afterward, and I took them thinking I would hand them out to my friends who did.

"He asked me to take off my shirt. I wanted him to burn me on the back of my leg, so no one would ever notice, but he wanted to do it on my arm, so he could look into my face as he did and watch me grimace in pain.

"So I took off my shirt while he wrote out the check he'd promised me. I glanced at it before slipping it into my pocket. It wasn't a personal check, it was a corporate check, from some company called Q-Com, which I hadn't heard of then. That was a weird realization, that he was spending company money on this. What was he going to say to the accounting department, or to his boss?

"He lit the cigarette with a lighter. Then he took a few puffs to stoke it, and put his right hand around my left wrist, and pulled my left arm straight. I was pretty scared, trembling slightly with anticipatory fear. He was eager. He held the cigarette above my forearm, just below the inside of my elbow, very close to the skin. I could feel the heat, felt it singeing my skin slightly. He looked up into my face, like he wanted, while I kept looking at my arm, which I know now you're not supposed to do. You're supposed to look away and try not to focus on it or think about it, to lessen the pain. But that wasn't the point here.

"Then he plunged it down, pushing it hard against my skin, and I tried to jerk my arm away, but he held it tight. It felt…well, I don't know. It was burning, that's all. A pricking, tearing, searing pain. My whole world was reduced to that little spot, and the pain kept getting worse and worse every moment. I gnashed my teeth together, while making groaning sounds, sort of humming. Tears filled my eyes and ran down my face.

"He held it there for several seconds, maybe five, longer than he should have, before he decided he'd gotten what he wanted, before taking it away. I grabbed the spot with my other hand and sat there, sobbing a little, and he watched while he put the cigarette out in an ashtray.

"Well, I'm not going to say it felt good, or that I wish I could do it again, or anything like that, but I wasn't mad at him, and I never regretted the experience. I did feel embarrassed on occasion when someone saw the burn and asked me about it, and I had nothing to say, but that was the worst of it. It didn't scare me into giving up Satanism, either, because I…because they're not connected. Hell is supposed to be worse than anything else, and it lasts forever, so you can't make comparisons. It's too abstract. I think about it in terms of the fact that I'll be there with billions of others, and however awful it is, we'll all be experiencing it, together.

"Anyway, that was it. He took me back to the club, and I saw the car was gone, so my friends had left, so then he took me back to the motel where I was staying that night, and let me off, clearly never expecting to see me again. But I had his check, with his company's address on it, and his signature, plus he'd had some paperwork laying on a table in his room, and I'd surreptitiously seen his name spelled out, along with his title: President.

"Not that I had planned on doing anything, understand. I was just curious to know who this weirdo was, which is why I didn't cash the check immediately. I kept it, instead, which turned out to be a pretty good idea.

"My three friends teased me a bit the next day, but they all knew I wasn't gay and this didn't change their minds, although I refused to tell them what I'd done. Otherwise, things were normal, for about a week.

"What happened a week later was that a building on the base, near our barracks, burned down. It was only a small office building, with just one or two rooms, and no one was in it, but it turned out to be arson. Someone had splashed gasoline all over it, and broken a window and poured it inside, too. The building was completely ruined.

"And on a base with tens of thousands of people, guess who singled out right away? That's right, me, the Satanist. One person, the sergeant I mentioned who was afraid of me, claimed to have seen me fleeing the scene, which was the main piece of evidence against me. Personally, I always thought he'd set the fire himself, quite possibly just so he could blame me for it, and get rid of me once and for all. But I don't know. However, somebody was framing me. The MPs searched our barracks and found an empty gasoline can under my bed. But that wasn't all. They found an open pack of cigarettes and a lighter, which Emile had given me, among my belongings, even though I never smoked. People had noticed the fresh burn on my arm, just as I'd feared, and that certainly didn't help my case. Neither did my alibi. Nobody had seen me that night, and when I told them what I was doing, they must have assumed I was mocking them, all but admitting my guilt. Believe it or not, I'd been in the chapel, reading the Bible. I know, I know. I'd gone in there because there was some game on television, and everyone was watching that, making a big racket, so I'd gone to the chapel for some peace and quiet, and, I don't know, there was a Bible there. I was bored; it was just something to read. But I might as well have told them I'd been saying a black mass.

"When it became obvious they were going to arrest me and court-martial me, that's when I decided to leave. I packed a few things, climbed over a fence, and that was the end of my army career. Which was really a shame; I'd actually enjoyed running through obstacle courses.

"I traveled west across the country by hitching rides and doing a lot of walking, spending nights sleeping out in the open, buying food with what little cash I had. In a week I got to the border and managed to sneak across into France. Then it was another week to Paris and the address of Q-Com's headquarters.

"They had a nice gleaming, glass-walled office tower. I put on my dress uniform, which I'd kept with me and brought the whole way just to this moment, then went into the building. Moving with a group of people, I slipped onto the elevator and rode it up to the top floor, where the president's office was. I marched across the expansive front office and told the receptionist that my name was Sei Shahse and I was there to see Emile Jouve. Fortunately the uniform did the trick, because the secretary didn't even bother to check whether or not I had an appointment. She just buzzed Emile, told him my name, then hung up directed me inside.

"Emile's private office wasn't anywhere as big as I'd expected, especially not after seeing the reception area, but as I said he wasn't the ostentatious type. It was just a room, though he didn't have any file cabinets or stacks of papers or anything like that. Just a desk with a computer and a telephone. The main perk was that the back wall was entirely glass, with a stunning view of the city. You could see the Eiffel Tower in the distance.

"He was sitting at the desk in a leather chair, and seemed neither happy nor surprised to see me. I'd expected the former but not the latter. Literally, the first thing he said to me was, 'I suppose you are here to blackmail me, yes?'

"'No sir,' I said, approaching him. I kept the check in my pocket. 'I only need your help in sneaking back into America.'

"He guffawed a bit before realizing what exactly I'd said. 'Sneaking?' he asked.

"I told him how I'd left the base illegally, because I was being framed for an arson of which I was innocent, but he clearly didn't believe me. Or, at least, he didn't believe I was innocent of the arson. He sighed, and wrote something on a piece of paper and told me he'd find me a place to stay for a few days, and to wait in the cafeteria on the first floor. I thought he was going to call the police, but I dutifully went down and sat in the cafeteria for the remainder of the day. When at one point a security guard asked me if I needed help, I showed him the note Emile had written, and he read it, gave it back, and apologized. After that nobody approached me again until Emile appeared at six o'clock to fetch me, after everyone else had left for the day. I'd spent the whole day in dread, because Q-Com, whatever it did, was obviously a huge corporation, and as president, Emile was obviously a much more important and powerful man than I'd anticipated. I was worried I had gotten in over my head and would wind up in prison just for imposing on him.

"Fortunately that wasn't the case, but I was also concerned about a second possibility. He offered to let me stay at an apartment he owned in the city, someplace close to the office he could escape to during the day, which, I assume, he meant for illicit affairs, for a few days while he sorted out my problems. I thought he was only being nice to me because he wanted sex from me, that this was a set-up to becoming his kept boy, but I was desperate at that point, and I decided that if he really did help me get back home I'd be willing to give him what he wanted.

"So we got into his car, a silver Porsche, and he drove me to a dingy walk-up, and left after letting me in. I found myself alone, which was appreciated. There were some instant meals in the cupboard, for a quick dinner before going to sleep.

"I was left alone for the next several days, and didn't leave the apartment except once, to walk to a nearby grocer to spend the last of my money on some more cheap meals, when I had finished all the ones that had been there. The rest of the time I spent watching television, talking back to it to brush up on my French. I was nervous the whole time, waiting for Emile to return, worried about my fate, about what he would want from me.

"But he surprised me when he finally did show up. Believe it or not, he somehow obtained some fake documents for me: a birth certificate, passport, and an identity card, all in the name of Sei Shest Shahse. This had become my real name, and I was now an immigrant from some Eastern European country I'd never heard of. I had no idea where he'd gotten these documents from, but I guess that someone both wealthy and well-connected would have resources for every need. I didn't ask why because he assumed I knew, because he considered my demand blackmail. To that end, he gave me a thousand francs, cash, in exchange for the check I'd kept, which eliminated the only real evidence I had to prove my story.

"It didn't end there, though. Emile made me another offer. If I took the documents and money he'd given me, I should have no problem getting a flight back to the States and passing through customs. But there was a second option. I could choose to stay in France. He had a seat on the board of directors at Sorbonne University, and his company gave scholarships to a few students every year. He could easily get me in, and award me one of the scholarships for that year, while pretending I was some bright foreign student, and then when I graduated he could get me a job at Q-Com.

"Now the immediate question that arises is why on earth would he do all that for me, when he didn't know me, and my continued presence posed a threat to him? The obvious answer is, as I mentioned earlier, that he had fallen in love with me and so wanted to keep me around on the hope that we'd eventually develop an intimate relationship. An honest relationship, I mean, not just that I would have sex with him because he would pay me. He didn't want a whore, he wasn't that type. He wanted any relationship to be genuine, between two willing partners, with full acquiesce, whether with me, or his wife, or with any of the men he picked up in bars on his business trips. He wanted, in other words, for the other person to want *him*, not just to submitting out of a need for money, but because of some actual desire, even if it was just the desire for a night's fun, because even then the other could choose someone else. Do you understand? He was looking, I think, for approval, for vindication of his own self-perception.

"But of course there was far more to it than that. He also did it out of a sense of guilt, or perhaps fear, I'm not sure which, exactly. Something religious, though. I eventually came to learn that Emile was always a very devout man, and he went through life pained by his homosexual desires. He was doing nice by me as a way of sort of making up for all the immorality in his life. And me in particular, because I was the devil. Not that he ever thought I was literally the devil, of course, and he wasn't trying to appease me—nor did he think he could convert me with his kindness and save my soul. It wasn't about me at all. Like I said, his sudden need to burn me represented something dark within himself that frightened him. This was what I represented to him, what he feared and wanted to fix.

"I decided to stay in Paris. It was an adventure, I suppose, and I couldn't see any better future back home. As much as I wanted to return to the United States, it would have been as a fugitive, and I could never have the kind of life Emile was offering me.

"So I did my four years at Sorbonne—my degree, at least, is legitimate. Emile got me a part-time sales rep job to help pay the bills, and after I graduated, with a economics degree, he made me a manager.

"It didn't stop there, though. He kept promoting me, higher and higher in the company. Every few months I got a promotion, it seemed like. I don't know that I was a star performer, but I did well enough, and eventually found myself as one of the vice- presidents, working right under him, which I'm sure is where he wanted me.

"The last position I held there, as I'm sure you know, was as CEO. I was appointed to that position by the Board during a company reorganization that occurred shortly after Emile died. That was an unfortunate but entirely coincidental thing. He, his wife, and their two lovely children where killed in a freak accident on the Audubon. He'd actually made suggestions to board members to the effect that I was to be his successor as CEO in such an event, though how seriously he worried about his own demise I don't know. I don't think it was any particular preoccupation; I think he intended for me to stay with the company, working for him, for my entire life. Still, he said it, and it was done. In fact, I was actually surprised, after all he'd done for me, that I wasn't mentioned in his will. However, since all his heirs died with him, everything he had that the government didn't take went back into the company, so I got some of it anyway.

"Don't think I didn't see the hand of fate in his accident. Lucifer was taking care of me, I knew I'd have to repay him somehow. I thought it was my future to use my money and influence to spread the word, to make Satanism a real religion once again, something of that sort. I had no idea what was coming, I swear.

"But then, about two years into my CEO-ship, I heard about this most wonderful book, a best-seller work of fiction that spelled out the road map for the Apocalypse. I'm speaking, of course, of the first *Rapture* novel. I devoured it, maybe reading it half a dozen times. The chilling touch of destiny called to me from its pages. The Rapture was coming, and the Antichrist would take over. And I, I was literally Mr. 6-6-6! LeVay's Antichrist was a powerful businessman from Eastern Europe, and I was a powerful businessman pretending to be from Eastern Europe! There was more, much more: signs pointing the way for me, pointing me to my fate, and to my identity. I was the one he was writing about. I was the Antichrist.

"Now, I know there are also some differences, too. I know you don't think I'm vicious enough to be Antichrist material. I've given it a lot of thought, and it depends on who it is that chose me to the Antichrist. Was it God? Lucifer? Am I the literal Son of the Devil, and would I be the Antichrist even if I was just flipping hamburgers somewhere? I don't know, but I think there's some aspect of choice involved, That's why it has to be me, because I chose it, because I want to be the Antichrist, because I'm only too happy to give over my soul and play along.

"At least, that's what I think. So I immediately changed all my goals and began planning to position myself appropriately. I began studying up on the country from which I was supposedly from, and went there a couple of times to set things up. I prepared to retire from my position at Q-Com, and leave fabulously wealthy. I took up fencing.

"So you know how the rest of it goes. I resigned, 'returned' home a hero, made some obsequious gestures to the president, and got my UN posting. From there it was just a matter of waiting until the stars aligned and the Will of God played out as promised."

CHAPTER 29

"Oh, you want to know about the fencing, do you? It's quite simple, really. At the end of *Rapture*, the very end, the end of the whole series, everything culminates in the final battle between good and evil, the Battle of Armageddon. You probably could have guessed that, right? But at the climax of the battle, it becomes a way-cool one-on-one faceoff between Jesus Christ and the Antichrist. It's the ultimate duel, with Jesus wielding the Flaming Sword of Heaven, or something. That's what I'm waiting for. That's why I took up fencing and swordsmanship. To be ready to fight that duel on the last day, when the whole shebang comes to and end.

"Don't get me wrong, I'm not expecting to *win*. I don't win. I'm the bad guy here, I know that. I've read the story, I've read the Bible, I know how it ends. All the same, I can't wait, and I certainly promise to give it my best. That's why it has to be me who's the Antichrist. Who else would go along, knowing the end in advance? You think any ordinary psycho would do that? You think, if Hitler had known definitively in 1939 how things were going to turn out, he'd have gone ahead and launched the war? Of course not. It takes a special sort of person to do what I'm doing."

CHAPTER 30

One day, as Pope Perfect I stood on his balcony blessing the adoring crowds in St Peter's Square, he was shot by an assassin, a Palestinian who was promptly captured and confessed to killing the Pope in the name of Islam—and Sheik Yasin al-Tineri. This was followed shortly by a video posted on the Internet by the now fugitive former president/prime minister/et cetera, who admitted to organizing the assassination, because the Pope had to be eliminated due to being in league with Shahse, and threatened numerous others likewise enleagued in a rambling diatribe that declared yet another open holy war against the corrupted West.

Meanwhile, on another channel, a large crowd was gathered in the Old City of Jerusalem, surrounding a pair of derelict geezers wearing sandals and cloaks that looked like burlap sacks. The thickly-bearded geezers were screaming at the crowd, quoting from the Bible, repeating the words in several different languages: "AND I BEHELD WHEN HE HAD OPENED THE SIXTH SEAL, AND, LO, THERE WAS A GREAT EARTHQUAKE; AND THE SUN BECAME BLACK AS SACKCLOTH OF HAIR, AND THE MOON BECAME AS BLOOD!"

"Humph," Shahse snorted from where he sat slouched on his sofa, watching with disdain, a can of cola in his hand. "This is news? I could have told them that."

"Revelations Six, verse 12," said Griffin, sitting on the other end of the sofa, taking a sip from his own canned beverage, his a beer.

"Oh, shut up."

"Many here are saying these are the 'Two Witnesses' of the Book of Revelations," said the on-scene anchor, when the camera switched back to her. "Divinely appointed figures sent at the time of the end of the world to warn people of the impending destruction."

"Oh, for crying out loud!" said Shahse, slamming his soda on the table next to a large folder and jumping up. "'Two Witnesses?' Come on, what is the matter with you people!"

"It seems they're taking you seriously," said Griffin, calmly. "You keeping telling them this is the Biblical Apocalypse, and now it looks like they're beginning to accept that. I should think you'd be pleased."

"Well, yeah," Shahse grumbled, sitting down again. He muted the television. "It's just that's not how it's supposed to happen." He shrugged. "I'm just a little surprised, that's all. I'm supposed to deceive people and get them damned, but how am I going to do that if they actually start to believe me?"

"I thought you didn't want to deceive people."

"I don't."

"So? This should be right up your alley, then. What were you expecting?"

"I don't know," he said, taking a swig of his soda. "To be honest I was hoping they'd all come willingly."

Griffin chuckled. "You're kidding. You were hoping people would damn themselves willingly? Who on earth would do such an idiotic thing? I mean," he quickly corrected himself, "I'm sure there'd be a few, obviously, but it would be a very tiny minority, you realize that, don't you?"

"Yeah, well. It's just this dream I have."

Griffin shifted easily and unnoticeably into his psychiatrist mode. "You haven't told me anything about your dreams, Jack. What happens in this one?"

"I meant a dream as in an idealized vision. My sleeping dreams always escape me when I wake up every morning. It's very frustrating, I tell you. All these years of imagining hell, and I've never once had a dream about it. You'd think my subconscious would just naturally generate one every once and a while, right? But no, not one!"

"Maybe there's a message in that. Maybe the devil is keeping it from you because you'd change your mind about going if you actually saw how horrible it really is."

Shahse glared at him. "I don't see how," he said simply. "I'm sure I'd be even more excited about it, then I am just imagining it." He picked up the remote and switched to the continuing coverage of the Pope's death. They watched wordless for a minute, then Shahse's phone range. He leaned over to where it stood on the end table, and answered. "Send her up," he said after a moment.

"Her?" said Griffin. Shahse ignored him to finish up his soda. He tossed the can across the room, landing a perfect three-pointer into a small wastebasket in the corner.

The elevator pinged and Agent Samantha Tenney stepped out. She was haggard, with dark circles under her eyes and her hair mussed. She had managed to put on her makeup, but it didn't cover her obvious distress.

"Sam," said Griffin, "What are you doing here?"

"What are you doing here?" she snapped.

"Sam, you look awful," said Shahse.

"Yeah, well, fuck you. I haven't slept in a week. Not since...." She let her words drop, but the meaning was clear. Not since Sarah had stolen her soul.

"Why not?" Shahse smiled. "Have you been having nightmares? That's so unfair."

"No, I haven't had any nightmares because I haven't had any sleep! Look," she pulled out her badge and dropped it on the table before him, like a sort of offering. "I quit. I refuse to work for you anymore."

"But you can't!" he said with alarm. "Not now; I need you!"

"Fuck you. Give me my soul back."

"No."

"Give it back, damn you!"

Shahse shrugged. "Okay, sure. In fact, I've got it right here in my pocket." He reached into his pocket and then withdrew his hand in a fist. He cupped it in his other hand, and held them up to eye level. The right index finger stuck up suddenly, and he wiggled it back and forth. "'I'm Sammy's soul,'" he said in a squeaky voice. "'Help me, help me!'"

Tenney unholstered her gun and pointed the barrel at his nose. "Give me my soul back, you little piece of shit."

Shahse slowly lowered his hands, and smiled anxiously. "Now, Agent Tenney, you know I'd love nothing more, but it doesn't work like that. I don't have your soul. I can't help you. I would if I could, but please, Sam—these aren't my rules."

She stared at him for a moment, then lowered her gun and, resigning herself with a sigh, reholstered it. Shahse sighed in relief.

"There must be something I can do," said asked desperately.

"Well, I don't have any ideas, but there might be some-one who does."

"Who?"

"The 'Two Witnesses,'" he said with a pleasant smile.

"The who?"

"Two old guys in Jerusalem," said Griffin. "Supposedly they're part of the prophecy and work directly for God."

"So you want me to go to Jerusalem?"

"Sure," said Shahse, picking up the folder on the table. "That's the assignment I have for you—both of you. Official government businesses, everything's been taken care of."

"You're sending me to Jerusalem?" asked Griffin, with a cocked eyebrow.

"Yeah, well, you're still a pretty good FBI agent, or at least you used to be. You both work for the CIA, now, by the way."

Griffin coughed. "Excuse me? You can't just do that."

"Sure I can. I can do just about anything. Honestly, it's only a simple lateral transfer."

"What's the assignment?" sighed Tenney, who had remained standing.

Shahse hands the folder up to her. "I want you two to go there and arrest Mr. al-Tineri. A Mossad mole is reporting he's staying in the city. The undercover agent contacted his CIA handlers, and the CIA informed me, because for the time being I'm getting the same briefings as the President. Larry set that up for me. In fact, my briefings are probably better because I ask follow-up questions, since I'm actually reading them, and somehow I think he hasn't quite remained as in touch."

"Okay, so, let the Israelis deal with him," said Griffin. "Or the Italians. Or the regular CIA, even. What do you need us for?"

Shahse looked from one to the other. "If anyone else gets to al-Tineri first he'll disappear down some security hole. I was hoping you guys would transport him here so I could...talk to him."

"Bring him around, you mean?"

"Well, now that Perfect's dead, I need a major religious figure to orchestrate the one-world faith the Bible says I'm supposed to create."

"Al-Tineri is hardly a major religious figure."

"He'll do," he said with a careless shrug. "And I really need to get the Muslims on my side."

Tenney chuckled acerbically. "Do you not even care that he killed the pope?"

"Well, sure I care," said Shahse, looking hurt. "But what can I do about that now? I have to go with things as they are. Look, take the folder, take your badge, and go meet this agent. Take a little side trip while you're there—I'd love to hear what these wack-jobs tell you. Now, please, go. I need you for this. Believe it or not, right now you two are about the only people I can trust. Your plane leaves at noon tomorrow."

CHAPTER 31

Because capitalism is voracious and because you can't keep a good industry down, some limited commercial flight service had resumed, conveniently enough for the story. Griffin and Tenney found themselves in first-class seats, aboard a sparsely populated direct transcontinental flight to Jerusalem.

Tenney sat restlessly in the window seat, staring into her reflection hovering in the darkness.

"I can't stand this," she said of her reflection. "Let's switch seats."

"We already did that," Griffin reminded her. "Just get some sleep."

"I told you, I can't! Now switch seats."

Griffin sighed and stood up, stepping into the aisle. Tenney stepped past him, and he sat down in the window seat.

"You could sit anywhere, you know," he motioned around the near-empty cabin. There was another couple up a few rows up and a guy a few down; that was it.

"No, no. I have to sit next to you," She put her hands on his armrest and leaned in closer. "I want to hear more about it."

"More about what?" he asked, wondering briefly if she was trying to be romantic.

"That demented little freak. Come on, dish. What's your diagnosis? What's he got?"

Griffin rolled his eyes. Okay, not romantic, but this was actually more along the lines of what he'd been expecting. "He hasn't 'got' anything. He's a perfectly normal, functioning human being. A little eccentric, sure, and I wouldn't want him babysitting my kids, if I had any, but still, within the boundaries of sanity."

"You must be kidding me! Come on! I mean, I didn't think he was bi-polar or schizophrenic or anything, necessarily, but there's got to be something pretty screwed up with him."

Griffin shrugged. "What can I say? He's a special circumstance. He's paranoid, certainly, except there really are people out to get him. He's egotistical, but he really is a significant person. Even that whole story about this French guy who just kept giving him things and promoting him for no good reason—if anyone else had told me that I'd have dismissed it out of hand, but with him, I don't know, it could be true. He didn't say he was hearing voices or anything like that, but if he had, even that wouldn't necessarily be symptomatic of anything. I could believe God or the devil literally spoke to him."

"But if he really is the Antichrist," Samantha Tenney insisted, "how can you accept anything he says seriously? It's his nature to lie!"

"I don't think he's a pathological liar. I've got a seventh sense about these things. He might have neglected to mention some details, but he wasn't making up stories."

"He's a thirty-some year old virgin. You don't see anything unusual with that?"

"He says he's following the dictates of traditional faith. He hasn't found the right person to marry, and no marriage, no sex. Can I fault him for that? Is our modern world such that chastity represents a mental illness?"

"Yeah."

Griffin smirked. "See, this is why you're going to hell."

She looked at him with disgust. "I am not going to—wait," she said, becoming confused, "Was that a joke?"

"No," he said, raising his eyebrows in protestations of innocence.

"I can't believe you're making jokes about this."

"Sorry," he said with a shrug. "Look, the fact that he's still unattached is a bit unusual, but again, it doesn't mean anything in and of itself. He doesn't have any noticeable social deficiencies, no sexual perversions—"

"How do you know? He's not a pederast because he said so?"

"He has normal sexual interests; his fantasies all involve adults."

"Uh-huh. And these are the fantasies he has about hell? He fantasies about people burning in hell, and oh, yeah, the man actually wants to go there himself, he wants to go to hell, and you don't think there's anything unusual about that?" she whispered fiercely. "You don't think that's pretty fucking demented?"

"It's an identity," said Griffin, shaking his head. "Adolescent interest in Satanism is unusual, but not anything overly peculiar. It's just a pose, typically. Most people simply grow out of it, but in Jack's case he got stuck with this image of himself, first among his friends in the Army, then with this French guy. It became a hook he needed, then it was literally burned into his skin, and now after so many years it's established itself so firmly he's convinced himself that this really is who he is, that he really wants to go to hell."

"And what, you don't think he doesn't?"

"No, of course not. Who would? Not subconsciously, at least. I mean, we could debate the philosophies of nihilism, how choosing self-destructive behaviors is a form of protest, a strike for freedom and the establishment of a true independent identity, essentially negating the self in order to affirm its individualism, or the psychological dynamics of masochism, which is usually a form of role-reversal sexual play, a game of female dominance and male submission, which, because it is a game, actually reinforces traditional roles of female subservience, or even the use of self-mutilation by individuals to create a feeling of being alive, of engaging in the world through the intense psychical sensation and awareness produced by pain, but I don't believe he thinks in terms of any such serious pretensions. That's why he could never find any other 'real' fellow believers, despite looking. It's not that he couldn't find them, it's just that they reminded him too much of what he was doing to himself. They made him too uncomfortable, meeting other people who also worshiped the devil and wanted to go to hell, because they forced him to confront his own indefensible reasons, so he denies their genuineness, along with anything that might bring him closer into alignment with them, such as sexual promiscuity."

"Then what about Sarah?"

"She's very much like him, certainly, but what especially draws his obsession is that while she wants to go to hell, too, she's not creepy or freaky about it. It's just something she's willing to do for what he sees as perfectly rational reasons. Her justifications render her safe in his eyes. She's similar enough to him to arouse his interest but different enough not to disturb his own uncertain self-image."

"So basically they're the perfect couple."

"Maybe, but I'd be wary about bringing them together," Griffin said, shaking his head. "She'd only encourage him even further." Plus, he thought, there were other considerations. He was beginning to believe that Sarah was more than just some girl. Shahse right now was focused on finding a world religious figure to promote some made-up world religion that would trick people into worshiping him. Whoever he found, though, would be more than just a staff member, or someone else to use. According to LeVay, and the Book of Revelations, just as God was represented as the Holy Trinity of Father, Son, and Holy Spirit, the powers of evil were represented by an Unholy Trinity, comprised of Satan, the Antichrist, and a third figure known as the "False Prophet," a sort of Anti-Holy Spirit. This was the person who would set up the new religion, and so far this person's identity was still a mystery.

Griffin knew all this not only from his own study but from the sermon preached by Reverend Trenton during the one service he'd attended at Christ Church, the previous Sunday. Trenton, screaming at the congregation, warned them about the danger of Shahse's fake religion, which would ensnare anyone stupid enough to believe something someone just randomly made up on the spot (i.e. most of the population) and damn them to hell. It was coming! Make no mistake! Ensnare it would!

Griffin had sat in the back with Tenney and quietly listened to Trenton's endlessly repetitive fulminations, an hour of the three hour worship service, which also included a lot of singing. A pretty blond girl sang a solo hymn, and as she did Tenney whispered, "That's her," into his ear, and that was about all the contact he had with Sarah. She was surrounded by people after the service, so he couldn't speak with her, and didn't have anything to say even if he could. From the tragic story he'd gleaned from Shahse, he sympathized with her, but he doubted he could do much to help her, at least not the way Shahse had asked him to. She already killed a man, and that was a line that couldn't be uncrossed, plus there was the fact that it was his business to study people like her, not make them feel better. She seemed awfully nice, though, at least from a distance.

He'd been less successful in avoiding Haversham at the church, who was very smug and practically sneering. He cornered Griffin at the door as he tried to make his escape.

"So what happened with those fingerprints?" he'd said, shouting over the din in the church's Fellowship Hall

"Negative," Griffin had replied, avoiding all discussion.

"Can I say I told you so, huh? And so now you're here looking for alternatives. Admit it, you were wrong."

"I'm not wrong. I'm just here out of curiosity."

"Interested in joining?"

"No," spat Griffin. He didn't like the way Haversham seemed to consider his presence a personal victory, and he certainly wasn't going to add to it by giving him the satisfaction of claiming a convert. He ended their conversation as quickly as he could manage, and slipped out alone.

In his sermon, Reverend Lars Trenton had been convinced that the False Prophet was Pope Perfect. But now Perfect was out of the picture, and Griffin didn't seriously think al-Tineri was up to the job. But he had growing suspicions about Sarah.

Yes, Sarah. It made sense. As a minister's daughter, she knew all sorts of theological arguments. She knew how to talk the talk. She's already stolen one person's soul—Tenney's—and she was not only devoted to Shahse but had proven herself willing to do the dirty work he shied away from. The only concern was that she wasn't famous, but Griffin thought that the idea of two members of the Unholy Trinity being a couple made more sense, was more Trinity-like, than them just being any two independent people, and hence made up for that defect. Certainly, if she and Shahse did marry, as Griffin guessed was inevitable, she would become famous easily enough.

"What do you mean, 'further?'" asked Tenney, rousing him from his thoughts. "I thought everything was preplanned, but now you're making it sound as thought we could do something about it."

"That's true," said Griffin, turning to the window, and his dim reflection hanging above the invisible ocean. "We'll just have to see."

CHAPTER 32

They landed in Jerusalem in the early morning, and took a taxi to the Old City. Griffin carried the folder Shahse had given them; besides that, they had with them only their badges and their guns. They had been instructed not to bring any luggage, or really anything they didn't absolutely need and weren't prepared to carry with them everywhere, nor had hotel rooms been booked for them; apparently Shahse expected them to complete their mission in a single day. And it was entirely possible they could, assuming they could find the undercover agent quickly enough and that he was as on the ball as had been promised. Finding the "Two Witnesses" would be the most straightforward part, because assorted dedicated, curious, or otherwise amused people were monitoring and recording their words and movements for internet broadcast, so they had a location before they even got off the plane. Not to mention, the two had gathered a fair crowd about them, even at this time of day, so they found them almost immediately, standing on a dusty street corner, proselytizing doom and gloom in their booming voices.

"FOR THE GREAT DAY OF HIS WRATH IS COME; AND WHO SHALL BE ABLE TO STAND?" they declaimed thunderously.

"Another quote from Revelations, I suppose," Griffin said to Tenney.

"You'd think there wasn't anything else in the whole Bible," she replied. "So what now?"

Griffin raised his authoritative voice: "Excuse me," he called out to the two, and pushed his way through the crowd until he was in front, with Tenney surreptitiously following. He pulled out his badge and held it up. "Agent Griffin, CIA. This is my partner, Agent Tenney." In a quieter, languid tone, he added "We work for Mr. Shahse."

This brought sudden, frightened gapes from the surrounding company, but he disregarded them. His only concern was for the direct attention of the two, and he fully expected his admission would prove a useful hook for engaging them; he wasn't disappointed. One of them turned and stared at him, his eyes wide and blazing, windows to a hell fiercer than any Shahse could envision in his wildest fantasies. Griffin involuntary shuddered; whether owing to divine revelation or utter insanity, there was indeed something otherworldly about these two. No wonder they engendered such interest. "THE ADVERSARY THE DEVIL, AS A ROARING LION, WALKETH ABOUT, SEEKING WHOM HE MAY TO DEVOUR!"

"Right," said Griffin. "Anyway, he just wants to know who you guys are and what's going on."

"HE KNOWS," said the one, his glare fixed, as though he wished to stare him into submission.

"Now that doesn't sound like a Bible quote," said Griffin, arching an eyebrow in surprise. "But I'm glad to see you can do without them. Maybe next you could just tell me straight out what the deal is."

"GOD HAS CALLED US TO PROCLAIM HIS MESSAGE AND DENOUNCE THE EVIL ONE, AND HE HAS GRANTED US THE MIRACULOUS ABILITY TO RECITE SCRIPTURE IN A VERY LOUD VOICE!"

"I see that, yes."

"What about me?" exclaimed Tenney suddenly, stepping forward and interrupting their contest. "What does God say about me? I've been praying very hard and asking for forgiveness, I really have, I'm really sorry, I didn't mean it, she tricked me, I know it was wrong, but please I'm begging—"

"Sam," said Griffin, putting a hand to her shoulder and stopping her short.

"Right," she said, and asked the man, in an ever-so-slightly calmer tone, "So can God forgive me?"

He turned to her and shouted, "ALL SINS SHALL BE FORGIVEN UNTO THE SONS OF MEN, BUT HE THAT SHALL BLASPHEME AGAINST THE HOLY GHOST HATH NEVER FORGIVENESS, BUT IS IN DANGER OF ETERNAL DAMNATION!"

"What!" she cried out.

"I think that's a 'no." said Griffin.

"What!" she screamed again. "How can you say that?"

"THEN SHALL HE SAY, 'DEPART FROM ME, YE CURSED, INTO EVERLASTING FIRE, PREPARED FOR THE DEVIL AND HIS ANGELS!'"

"WHAT!" she shouted, finally reaching an equal decibel in her despondency.

"Okay, I think that's enough," said Griffin, holding her by the shoulders and trying to pull her away. She was too weak to resist, and came easily. The immediate crowd withdrew as far as they could, avoiding them as though they were plague-stricken, which perhaps they were, in a sense.

"WHORE OF SATAN!" the one shouted after them, which didn't quite sound to Griffin like a Bible quote, either, but then again what did he know. He dragged Tenney as far as a block away, carrying her entire weight slumped against his body, as she was too overcome to move on her own. She sobbed into his neck until he could take no more and hefted her against the side of a building, where she promptly slid do to the ground. He sat down on the sidewalk next to her.

"How could this happen?" she bawled. "Oh God, it's so unfair! What have I ever done to deserve this?" Griffin said nothing; he could think of nothing to say. Consoling the grief-stricken was not his area of expertise.

Suddenly she ceased her lament and jumped up. He rose, hesitantly, and carefully examined her. Her hands had balled into fists, her breath was short but heavy, like a snorting horse, and the veins on her neck pulsed visibly. He caught the glint of rage in her eyes.

"If that's the way it's going to be…," she muttered.

"Sam?"

Her eyes flickered to him, and she turned slightly. As she did, she raised her hand up and under her jacket, going for her gun. He immediately reached for his own, checking her actions. They stood there, immobile, their hands on the grips of their weapons, watching each other intently, waiting for the other to move.

"Sam," said Griffin cautiously, "what are we doing?"

Before she could answer, a short man in a white shirt and trousers stepped out of the flow of pedestrian traffic that passed them by and walked up to them. "Hello!" he called as he approached. They both warily turned towards him. "I hope I am not interrupting anything," he said in thickly accented English. He came right up to them, and offered his hand, saying, "I am Khaled Haneef."

They glanced at each other, both instantly recognizing the name from the papers Shahse had given them; it was the name of the Mossad agent they were supposed to meet. But it seemed too much a coincidence to just run into him on the street, so Griffin said, "What of it?"

Haneef smiled, seeming aware of the difficulty. He leaned in and said in a hushed whisper, "And I believe you are with the CIA?"

Which proved nothing, thought Griffin, since he had announced it amidst an entire crowd only a block away.

"I was told to meet you here and to escort you to see Sheik al-Tineri," he continued, cinching the matter.

"Who told you we'd be here?"

"My handlers. In Mossad."

"And how did they know to expect us?"

Haneef only shrugged. "How should I know?"

Shahse must have told someone they were coming, and that their first stop would be to check in on the Two Witnesses, which is where Haneef had obviously tracked them from. Griffin looked at Tenney. "Looks like he's not as isolated as he pretends."

"Who the fuck cares?" she said, evincing great irritation. "Let's just go and get this over with."

CHAPTER 33

It turned out that Sheik Yassin al-Tineri was holed up in an executive suite of the five-star King Solomon Hotel, in downtown Jerusalem, which struck Griffin as odd behavior for the world's most wanted terrorist. Mossad clearly knew where he was. Haneef easily led them there, through the front door and right up to his room. So why hadn't anyone arrested him yet?

"Oh, that is easy," Haneef told them, as the approached the room. "Everyone is waiting for him to take out the main target. Then they'll arrest him. Until then he's more valuable left free."

"Main target?" asked Griffin. "You mean Ambassador Shahse?"

"Sure, sure, the weirdo who thinks he is the devil." Haneef smiled at them. "Naturally he is the greatest target. I hear the Sheik already has an operation underway, though I doubt it."

"Why?"

"Simple. Why should the Sheik risk all his privileges? Once the devil is dead he is no long needed, so there is nothing to prevent him from being assassinated himself, yes?"

Haneef knocked on the door, and a burly man in a suit opened it. He asked no questions, just waved them in. With his other hand, he held an AK-47 to his side. Still, Griffin thought it careless, and that al-Tineri must be extremely confident in the protection his trump card afforded him.

There was another man in a suit in the sitting room, standing at the window, also holding an AK-47. Haneef exchanged a few words with him in Arabic, then turned to the agents and said, "It seems the Sheik is just now taking a bath. We will have to come back later."

Griffin figured what worked once would work again, and said to him, "Tell them we work directly for Mr. Shahse."

Haneef gave him a worried glance, but repeated the message. The bodyguard laughed and left the room. There was more laughter from behind the door, then he reappeared and spoke with Haneef, smiling the whole time.

"The Sheik will see you," translated Haneef, humbled and perhaps a bit frightened. He led them through the door into the bedroom, which contained a canopied, king-size bed, and then into another room which turned out not to be a bathroom but a hot tub room. The hot tub, large enough for at least four people, was recessed into white marble, and the floor surrounded it with white and gold tiles. It was full blast, the water bubbling energetically and filling the room with steam. Al-Tineri, relaxing comfortably by himself, smiled and nodded to them as they entered. It was a bit startling to come face to face with such a famous person, and to find him sitting before you in all his naked splendor (not that they could see said splendor, as it was appropriately hidden by the bubbles).

"*Salaam alaykum!*" he called out. "You will excuse me for not arising, but it would not be decent in the presence of the lady," he said, motioning at Tenney. "Would you like some chairs brought in?"

"No thank you," said Griffin, eyeing him suspiciously.

"Ah, then this will not be a long conversation, then? Pity," said al-Tineri, who then dismissed Haneef with a curt wave, and he complied without reluctance, briefly nodding to them. "So tell me, my friends, what message, what *brief* message, has the esteemed *shaaz* sent you half-way around the world to deliver?"

"Actually, he wants to talk to you in person. He sent us here to escort you to America."

"Is that so?" al-Tineri chuckled, his eyes gleaming. He seemed to be enjoying himself immensely, far more than Griffin thought the situation warranted. "I do not believe I shall be able to comply with his request. I know his game, and there is nothing he can do to merit my support. In fact, there is nothing he can do even to redeem his life from the fate that awaits him."

"Right. It's not a request. If you won't come willingly, we have a warrant for your arrest." Griffin opened the folder and pulled out a copy of an international arrest warrant issued by INTERPOL, which Shahse or the CIA or whoever had helpfully included along with their other material.

Al-Tineri simply laughed. And loudly, too, so his body shook, sending ripples through the water. "My friends," he said, "I understood that 'escort' was a euphemism, but I am most certainly not going anywhere with you."

With that, Tenney reached into her jacket and withdrew her pistol. She held it up to ensure he saw it, then lowered her arm and held it to her side. Griffin gave an absent moment's thought as to how composed she was, how much she'd improved since earlier. He replaced the warrant in the folder, but made no move for his own gun.

"Now be honest, my friends, how far do you think you will get in this fashion? Will you drag me past my friends out front, when there are only two of you? And even if you did, do you think it will be so easy to take me out of this country? Do you expect to simply bring me to an airport and walk aboard a plane?"

"The Israelis are protecting you," an impassive Griffin said.

"Protecting?" he said, amused. "No, they would just as readily imprison me as not. And indeed, you're friend's 'arrest' will surely be more congenial then theirs. It is about *credit*. They will not let you, and *him*, take credit for my capture."

"Please. Of course they're protecting you. They all know you're here. *You* know they know you're here. You're hiding out in the most posh hotel in Jerusalem, yet they don't come and arrest you. They want you free so you can assassinate Mr. Shahse."

Al-Tineri shifted about, finally rising himself to a fully upright sitting position. "This man is insane. Everyone on earth hates him. Prime Minister Heifetz and I are in complete agreement on the threat he poses and the need to contain this threat."

"Now who's using euphemisms?"

Al-Tineri smiled and nodded. "Eliminate, then. It will not be long now. Indeed, I am surprised he has not been killed already. Yet your president protects him. I do not understand it at all. And you. Here you are, bragging of your connection to him, braving the crowds at the risk of your own lives. Why? What hold does he have?"

Before Griffin could answer, Tenney stepped up to the edge of the tub and raised her gun. "Okay, that's enough. You're under arrest, so let's just get going."

Al-Tineri snickered. "I do believe I have already explained that I am not going anywhere."

Tenney leaned in a little closer, and said in a soft, conspiratorial tone, "You know what he really wants from you, don't you?"

"Of course. He wants my public support, which is to say he wants to marginalize my people. He thinks he can neatly divide the world, but my continued opposition intrudes upon his fantasy."

Tenney smiled faintly. "Oh no, he just wants you not to kill him, that's all. He doesn't care about your positions, or your opposition, and he doesn't care what you do to anybody else. In fact, I thought he seemed terribly callous about the Pope. So just promise you won't kill him. Just...." Here she paused and licked her lips. "Just say that you're loyal to him."

"My friend," he said after a moment, "I am loyal to none but Allah."

Tenney's smile disappeared and she became tense. She leaned in even closer and placed the barrel of her gun against his head. "Say it, say you'll be loyal to Sei Shahse, or I'll have no choice."

"Stop it, Sam," said Griffin.

She ignored him. "Say it right now," she said, shaking the gun a little for emphasis.

Al-Tineri, though, was convinced she would never shoot him, because with his bodyguards in the next room, doing so would cost her her own life. So he remained indifferent. They stared at each other for a moment, then Tenney suddenly reached past him and seized a thick towel sitting on the edge of the hot tub, one of the hotel's thick white cotton towels, with its name emblazoned on the front. She held the towel against the barrel of the gun and fired.

The towel only partially muffled the sound. There was a thud of footsteps as the bodyguards rushed to the door, and Tenney turned to face them as the barged in. She was ready, and fired past Griffin, shooting them both as they came through the door, before they could even raise their guns. As soon as they were down, she stepped over them and back out into the sitting room.

Griffin was stunned. He couldn't believe what he'd just witnessed, but he looked again, and there al-Tineri, slumped down with a bullet through his neck, gurgling blood into the churning water. Everything had taken place before he had any chance to react, and even now he could only slowly turn and follow Tenney.

In the front parlor, he found her bearing down on Khaled Haneef, who had been waiting for them.

"What have you done?" he shouted, tears in his eyes. His hands were raised.

"Get down," Tenney said. "On your knees"

Griffin pulled out his own gun and pointed it at Tenney's head.

Tenney turned her head to look him in the eyes, and smiled. Then she turned back to Haneef. "Do it or I'll shoot."

"Get out," Griffin said to Haneef. Haneef turned and ran for the door, and just as he reached it Tenney shot him in the back. He cried out and fell, clutching at the doorknob a moment before collapsing to the floor.

"What the fuck," said Griffin.

"You're not going to shoot me," said Tenney, lowering her gun and turning to him. Griffin could only shake his head, still having a hard time comprehending. Before he could say anything, he heard a pounding in the hallway, and the door suddenly burst open. In poured half a dozen police officers, their guns raised. Obviously they'd had al-Tineri under watch the whole time, and were responding to the gunshots. They were shouting in Hebrew, but Griffin and Tenney got their meaning. They dropped their guns and raised their hands.

CHAPTER 34

The detective, or officer, or whatever he was, who sat across the metal table from him was in his late fifties, balding, and had a bit of a paunch, but was still hard muscled. Griffin pegged him as career military, probably a former officer. He was leaning back, slouching to one side, trying to affect a careless, cynical attitude, but he was having a tough time of it. He kept shifting uncomfortably, arching his back. Still, he kept a remorseless eye on Griffin.

"You have no jurisdiction here," said the man in a gravelly, heavily accented voice that radiated scorn.

"One more time," said Griffin. "We are agents of the United States government."

"The CIA is not a law enforcement agency."

"We have a legitimate, international warrant for Mr. al-Tineri's arrest."

"Shooting a man in his bath tub is not an arrest."

"Well...he had armed guards."

The officer shifted around in his seat again, and sniggered. "Your actions were not justified, and you know this. You two are nothing but assassins."

Griffin leaned forward. "And you people were protecting an international terrorist, who murdered the *pope*, for God's sakes. But you have your own little assassination plot going, don't you?"

The man smiled coldly and shook his head. "By killing him, all you have done is to make him a martyr for his cause. Tomorrow there will be a hundred more just like him, murdering in his name."

Griffin saw he wasn't going to get anywhere; he wondered if he and Tenney were being set up for something. Of course the authorities couldn't very well hide the fact of al-Tineri's death, but at first he had thought it was something they would celebrate, trying to take credit for themselves. Now he believed they'd attribute it entirely to Shahse and indirectly denounce him for it as a means of developing, or at this point, furthering their common cause with the Arabs.

"It's ironic, isn't it," Griffin said. "You and the Arabs working together, united in your mutual hatred for Mr. Shahse. It looks like he brought peace to the Middle East, after all."

The man's smile only hardened.

Fortunately for the pair, however, Tenney was having a much better time with things in another room. Her interrogator was a nervous young man, inexperienced, and awed by her connection to Shahse. Here, it was she who sat back with a casual air, in complete control, while the young man squirmed.

"Do you really know him?"

"You bet I do. Would you like me to introduce you?"

"No!" he said, horrified.

She smiled sweetly. "You know he's going to be wondering whatever happened to us. I should really let him know where we are."

The man shook his head, alarmed.

"Well, I am entitled to a phone call, aren't I? You wouldn't want him to have to come all the way out here, looking for us?'

He shook his head again. It was so wobbly it could have fallen off at any moment. "I-i-is he really the d-d-devil?"

Tenney straightened up and leaned as far across the table as she could. Staring straight into the man's eyes, she cooed, "Oh yes. And he will suck your soul out just like sipping soda through a straw. I've seen it."

She got her phone call.

CHAPTER 35

Jerusalem and Washington were seven hours apart, so while it was late in the evening when Shahse got the call from Tenney, he was still awake. In fact, he was still in his office, surfing through various news outlets online to check up on the day's events, and was not at all sorry to be interrupted, especially to learn about the mission he'd sent his two favorite agents on. Unfortunately, this good feeling did not last long.

"Well, he refused to come with us, and he had guards with sub-machine guns, so to make a long story short he's dead and we're in jail."

Shahse couldn't say anything for a moment.

"Hello?"

"You killed him? He's dead?"

"Afraid so."

"How could you? I gave you explicit instructions to bring him back here alive."

"Oh, shut up," she said, which surprised him again. "What, you think he's some two-bit street thug we could just go and pick up? Look, master, things just don't work like that in the real world, and besides what's done is done, okay, so forget about it, and just get us out of here."

"Well, I—" he stopped short realizing what she said. "Did you just call me master?"

"Yeah."

"Oh. So, I take it things didn't go too well with the two—"

"No, it didn't."

"Oh. I'm sorry."

"Look, this has been a really shitty trip for me all around, okay, so I'd appreciate it if you'd just get us the hell out of here."

"Yeah, sure, no problem. I'll call some people, and you'll be free in an hour. But listen - She cut him off by hanging up the phone.

CHAPTER 36

Despite the rude treatment, Shahse proved better than his word, for in an hour they were not only freed from police custody, they were already in their seats on the plane awaiting the return flight. Not twenty minutes after Tenney hung up, the police officers abruptly ended their interrogations, took them out to a police car, drove them to the airport, and personally escorted them onto the plane, walking them right up to their first-class seats. Before leaving, the police sternly admonished them to never, ever, *ever*, return to the Holy Land. Griffin did not think it would be possible to abide by this directive, since there would inevitably be so many prophecy-related events happening here, in which they could not help but to be involved given their close association with Shahse, as well as their status as main characters in the story.

Tenney, sitting in the window seat, leaned back comfortably and yawned. "When we get back," she said breezily, "the first thing we have to do is go over to that church. I want to have a chat with that little bitch."

"You can't kill her," said Griffin, sitting tensely. He was disturbed by Tenney's new, casual air, disregarding of what she'd done. "I still can't believe you shot all those other people. You told me you'd never killed anyone, and then you go and blow away four people all at once, and you're not even fazed. I don't understand how that's possible."

"Yeah, well," she shrugged. "It didn't mean anything. It was like a video game or something. I guess it's not as traumatic as I thought it would be."

"No, I don't think that's it."

"Well, then I guess I'm really screwed over, aren't I? Now do you understand why I want especially to see that bitch? And Jack can't do a thing about it. Even if I did whack her, it's not like he'd kill me for it."

"I wouldn't press your luck on that. Anyway, he could still put you in jail."

She laughed, clear and sweet. "Yeah, whatever. Don't worry, I'm not going to kill her. Not yet, anyway. I just want to have a talk with her. Right in front of the whole congregation,." She yawned again, and within a few minutes she was soundly asleep.

A stewardess appeared by his side. "Would you like me to get you a pillow, sir?" she said with a bubbly cheerfulness that Griffin, pondering the desolation of the world, thought inappropriate.

"You know what I would like?" he said, turning to her, his eyes becoming sharp and bright, his voice taking on a heavy timbre. "I would like the protection and power of God by my side, as I stride forth into the raging maw of the typhoon, the epicenter of the dark forces which will make the Vale of Tears a torrential river, bursting through the fragile levees of normalcy that we've foolishly built up to protect our fleeting lives, sweeping away in its horrendous floodwaters all that we cherish and entrust our profoundest dreams and hopes to."

The stewardess blinked at him.

"A pillow would be fine, too, thanks" he said, his voice normal again.

As she stumbled away in a daze, Griffin checked his watch and calculated how long the flight would take, factoring in the time zone changes. Tenney was right; they would arrive just in time to make the morning church service.

It was Sunday.

And we know what that means.

CHAPTER 37

President Ruben was sitting cross-legged at the foot of his four-poster, king-sized bed in the White House bedroom. He was wearing his silk, navy-blue White House pajamas, with the seal on the right breast pocket. He sat watching a 13-inch television that was on a stand and had been rolled right up to the bed, because he'd been staring at it pretty hard the last few days. At the moment, he was watching a news broadcast concerning the Pope Perfect assassination and funeral, a topic he'd obsessed over from the moment he'd learned of it.

Vice President Baines was with him, sitting only a few feet away on a chair that he'd pulled over. His hands rested on his knees, and in one he held a piece of paper, and in the other a fountain pen.

"You know you'll be next," he said to Ruben absently.

"I know."

"Really, it's the only way to protect yourself. Don't think hiding in here is going to stop them."

"I know."

"And you've become entirely ineffective as a leader. I'm sorry but it's the truth. You're letting the country down just when it needs you the most. There's no telling the damage your absence is inflicting. It may be almost as bad as the damage your presence inflicted."

"Okay, I get it," Ruben said, finally expressing some irritation. He reached out and Baines handed him the paper, but didn't look at it.

"Aren't you worried they'll come after you?" Ruben asked blandly, simply to delay the moment.

"No," said Baines. "I believe I can undo the damage you've caused, and bring everyone into a mutually beneficial agreement."

Ruben looked dully at the television for a minute, then finally down at the paper. It was a short, single-paragraph letter, printed on White House stationary. It said:

I, Lawrence Ruben, hereby resign my position as President of the United States, effective immediately.

He put the paper down on his lap.

"It's inevitable, whether you go willingly or not," said Baines. "The secretaries are all in agreement on this."

Ruben nodded slowly, miserably. Baines was referring to the 25th Amendment, which stipulated that if the vice president and a majority of the cabinet secretaries declared that the president was unable to perform his duties or was otherwise unfit for office, he would be removed and the vice president would become acting president. Ruben completely believed him that it was about to happen, and didn't want to allow it. He felt shamed enough not to want to suffer the humiliation of being forced from office, and would prefer the dignity, limited as it was, of a voluntary departure.

He reached out and took the pen, an official White House pen with the seal printed on it, and stood up. Using the top of the television as a table, he quickly scrawled his signature across the paper, and then quickly handed it back to Baines. He sat down on the bed again, clutching the pen like a sword.

Baines took the paper with a broad smile and began laughing. After having waited so long, and been thwarted so often by the unkind political process, he had finally achieved his dream of becoming president, and though it was under unfortunate circumstances, he couldn't help but be pleased. Fortunately, his laughter was a quiet chuckle, not a villainous cackle, though it did little to calm Ruben. He was feeling queasy, and could not help thinking that Baines, with his dark hair and beard, looked rather sinister. His grip on the pen tightened, as he silently prayed this would not prove to be yet another mistake for which he would have to repent.

CHAPTER 38

Shahse was pacing around his penthouse suite, anxiously swinging his broadsword in little circles as he did. He repeatedly managed to find himself near a window, and paused each time to peek outside. Each time he did, he felt the need to check his watch, and did so in a quick, fidgety manner. The entire sky outside was a mass of grey-black thunderclouds, and ominous booming could be heard in the distance. But this was so much more than just another storm.

Once, he saw the moon through a break in the clouds, and it was red.

He was so excited about this, because he was certain it was an omen, and not just any old omen, but the initial sign of the next Biblical doomsday disaster described in Revelations, the one that comes after the Four Horsemen of the Apocalypse, and unlike that one, this he'd actually get to see. This was a big one.

It involved several calamities of unspeakable horror that would absolutely overwhelm people everywhere with fear and dread, but Shahse couldn't wait. (Actually, what bothered him in the back of his mind was the awareness that afterwards, he would be required to make yet another stirringly emotional and inspiring speech about the need for the whole world to band together amidst these trying time and forge a new world-wide unity and lasting peace to help build a better world, blah-blah-blah).

This was the famous "sun as black as sackcloth and the moon like blood" verse, the one most oft-quoted by preachers trying to terrify their listeners with warnings of The End.

He looked out the window again. Sun black as sackcloth? Well, it was past sunrise, but thanks to those clouds the glowing yellow ball was still nowhere to be seen, so that was a check.

Moon like blood? There it was, a middling red, a little on the orange side perhaps, but it was definitely red. So check and double-check!

What else? This one was a doozy. According to the Bible, all the following would occur:

There would be a massive, world-wide earthquake.

The stars (well, "stars") would fall to the earth.

The "sky" would disappear (he put sky in quotes here too, because if the actual sky disappeared, everyone would instantly suffocate, and he had his doubts about whether or not that would be a wise move on God's part; of course we all know that "God's wisdom is not man's wisdom," but he thought this instance might be the rare exception where the two strangely coincided).

The massive, world-wide earthquake would cause mountains to collapse and islands to sink into the sea (which led him to wonder how God came down on Australia as small continent or big island debate; all he could say was that he was glad he wasn't there).

Shahse knew all this less from the Bible than from his copy of *Rapture, Volume 2*, which he wanted to look through again to remind himself of all the delicious details, but resisted mightily because he was expecting to have to leave any minute. Stepping lightly, he went back to the living room and turned on the television to check the news. What had woken him up this morning was a phone call from the White House, summoning him to a special audience with the president, and now he was just waiting for the limousine to arrive. He assumed the invitation was related to this unnatural phenomenon, which surely everyone on earth could see. Naturally they'd want him on hand. The only thing he wondered about was whether he was being asked to be the government's spokesperson, or whether the weather had been enough to finally dislodge Ruben from his self-imposed exile, and he genuinely wanted some advice, or assurance, or some similar thing Shahse couldn't possibly provide.

On the screen, the anchor spoke in his usual impassive drone. "If you're just joining us, a massive storm front has covered the Eastern seaboard." They displayed a weather map to illustrate this, which disappointed Shahse in that it, in fact, did not cover the entire globe. But still! It was big, no denying that! The program cut back to the anchor. "Joining me now to discuss these unusual atmospheric conditions is Dr. Eugene Efflebert, Nobel Prize-winning professor of physics at UCLA. Dr. Efflebert, thank you for being here."

The camera turned to the left for a close-up of the esteemed scientist. "Always a pleasure, Bob," he said, nodding his head.

"Dr. Efflebert, tells us about this extreme storm that's brewing."

"Bob, frankly, it's just a big storm. But on the other hand, it's clearly another sign of the approaching alien attack. As I've been warning people for weeks, an invasion by extra-terrestrial beings is imminent. A vast armada of star ships may be approaching our planet at this very moment, traveling at speeds close to that of light. Now, if you'll look at these photographs I've obtained—" Frowning, Shahse clicked the set off.

Finally his phone rang, and the guard downstairs announced his limo. He laid the sword down carefully on the coffee table and took the elevator down. He admired the sky as he walked to the car, and as the driver, a stocky, black clothed Secret Service agent, opened the door for him, he commented, "Nasty weather, huh sir?"

"Oh, you don't know the half of it." There was a loud crash somewhere not too far off, and they both jumped.

At the White House, he was met by two more Secret Service agents, one of whom he recognized as Agent Alexander, from the plane. As always, they were the utmost professionals and displayed no emotions, but Shahse had the distinct impression that the second fellow, at least, was afraid of him, judging by the way he held back as they walked about. The two escorted him through the West Wing and into the Oval Office, where Shahse was disappointed, though not entirely surprised, to see Preston Baines once again sitting behind the president's desk. The two agents led him into the room, and then, strangely, did not depart. Instead they took up positions a little to the right of the desk, and stood impassively.

Baines smiled a toothy grin. "So once again, you grace us with your presence, Ambassador Shahse." He held up a finger. "Don't bother taking a seat; you won't be here long."

"I was told the President wanted to see me," he replied expectantly.

"And so I do."

Shahse grinned. "Excuse me?"

Baines leaned back comfortably. "Lawrence Ruben resigned a few hours ago. I am president now."

"Oh! I see."

"I've spoken to the Speaker of the House and several cabinet secretaries since becoming president, but you're the first official I've met with, for one simple reason: to put you in your place. As I promised, my administration will take a very different attitude towards you and your little games."

He was going to try something, Shahse knew, a knot forming in his stomach. "I'm not playing any games."

"You might have fooled Larry, but I see through your charade. Of course, I must admire your audacity. You've managed to pull off the single largest scam in history. You should be proud, even if it is about to unravel."

"What are you talking about?" He pointed to the window. "Haven't you looked outside? It's Revelations Six-Twelve! The sun is black as sackcloth and the moon has become red like blood!"

Baines laughed heartily. "Some bad weather is your idea of the Apocalypse? Maybe it never rains back over in the Old Country, but on this side of the Atlantic we've been known to get a storm or two."

"Haven't you seen the moon? It's red! Like blood!"

"A perfectly natural phenomenon, rare but hardly unique, caused by a high concentration of dust in the atmosphere. The moon's light, filtered through it, appears darker than usual, sometimes even taking on a reddish tint. Nothing more."

Shahse was getting confused. He shook his head. "But what about the Rapture? Surely you haven't forgotten that? Millions of people instantly vanished in a flash of light! You can't tell me that's a natural phenomenon!"

Baines sighed, as if explaining these things bored him. "It is a small mind indeed that decides, merely because we don't have an explanation for something right this instant, that no explanation is possible and therefore it must be the work of God."

"Don't tell me you think it's the aliens, too?"

Baines shrugged. "Not particularly, but one never knows. There's no reason to rule it out."

Shahse couldn't believe what he was hearing. "What are you, some kind of atheist? How can you say things like that? The world is ending right before our eyes!" He pointed out the window again. "I mean, just look!"

Baines turned to Alexander and smiled. "I find it curious," he said, "that the self-proclaimed Antichrist thinks I need more faith. Don't you find that odd?"

"Yes, sir. Although," he answered uncomfortably, "you should have more faith. Sir."

Baines shook his head. "You too? Wonderful." He turned back to Shahse. "Anyway, we're done. And you're through. I'm placing you under arrest."

"For what?" he demanded.

"Oh, I'm sure there is any number of charges I could select from. Be honest, now, you know how true that is." He showed his teeth again. "We'll start immigration fraud, for one. What do you say to that, Private Snell?"

Shahse was stunned. He took several steps back. "You have been spying on me!" he cried.

"Well, of course I—we—have. We've heard every word, and I must say, Mr. Snell, you're an absurd, creepy little man."

"I am the Antichrist!" he shouted. "I've come to conquer the world in fulfillment of prophecy! If you touch me, you'll only be interfering with the Will of God!"

But Baines, who had been up all night, first coaxing Ruben out of office, then sliding himself into it, making all the arrangements and making sure the resignation letter got to the right people to make it all official, was too tired to bother with Shahse anymore. He motioned to the two agents, saying, "Get him out of here."

Right then, they noticed a rumbling sound, and it filled the air, getting louder and louder within the space of a few moments. The ground began to shake. Baines stood up suddenly, and Alexander, acting on his instinct to protect the president, stepped towards him, while the other agent cowardly moved away. An instant later, the whole room seemed to explode, and Shahse was thrown back clear across the room.

Fortunately, he managed to avoid hitting his head on anything, and jumped up immediately. He ran to the door but stopped there to look back, and saw that the whole opposite half of the room was destroyed. The ceiling and walls had caved in, the furniture was smashed to kindling, and in the center of it all, right where the president's desk had been, was a gaping hole. He recognized it as a meteor strike. Obviously it was part of the prophecy, the "stars" that were to fall to the earth being in actuality nothing but meteorites, just as shooting stars have always been, of course, of course.

What did surprise him was that it had happened right in front of him. He'd thought he was safe from all harm, but that had been awfully close. Although, he *was* still safe, so he could hardly argue on that point. Baines, however....

Baines was gone. President Baines had been crushed beneath the meteor, along with Agent Alexander. The other agent had survived and was lying on the ground a few feet away.

Shahse left his position by the door and cautiously walked around the room, making his way to the agent to check if he needed help. He simply could not comprehend how Baines had ceased to exist, just like that. He didn't know how to react, what to say. Dimly he realized that this was supposed to be a global plague, so if this had happened here, just think of the tremendous damage that was being wrecked elsewhere.

It was way freaking cool.

The remaining agent crawled through the debris until he saw what was left of an overturned chair, one of those upholstered green armchairs that Shahse never liked, and lifted himself up to a kneeling position. He looked around at the destruction, terrified, and began to sob when he noticed Shahse approaching.

"Please don't kill me!" he begged, folding his hands together and shaking them in supplication. He looked up to Shahse from his position on the floor, tears in his eyes. "Please, I'll do anything you want, just please don't kill me!"

"I'm not going to kill you," Shashe said weakly. Did the agent think he had done this?

"Please, Lord, don't hurt me! I beg you! You're a god, and I'll do anything!"

Shahse felt queasy and started walking backwards, towards the door, eager to escape. Did the fool realize what he was doing? He was damning his immortal soul, and Shahse couldn't bear to listen anymore. He turned and ran to the door and flung it open.

He stopped short immediately. Two dozen other White House employees, advisers, interns, guards, and the like filled the hall, drawn by the explosion. Looking past Shahse they could see the smashed, smoking office, and the one pitiful agent crawling about, weeping. One woman screamed, and they all started screaming, or shouting, or even crying. Shahse stepped out into the crowd, and almost all of them fell to the ground. A few maintained enough presence of mind to turn and run, but most became like the agent still in the Oval Office, desperately pleading with him not to kill them.

"Spare me!"

"Anything! I'll do anything!"

"My Lord!"

"Please, oh please!"

Shahse was now officially more freaked out than he'd ever been in his whole life. All these people.…He ran through them, pushing them aside, right and left, and kept running until he was back at the front door. An agent was standing there, cowering away from his approach. He grabbed him by the shoulder.

"Don't hurt me!" the agent cried out.

"My car! Get me a car!" said Shahse.

"Anything! Anything! Just don't kill me!" the agent scuttled away bawling.

Shahse opened the door himself and walked up to a limousine just as it pulled up. He opened the back door and jumped in before it had even come to a complete stop. "Take me to Christ Church!" He yelled at the driver, a dark haired young man with a startled look on his face. "Herndon, Virginia," Shahse added, "I'll direct you. Just go!"

The car sped away, and as it did another tremendous explosion sounded somewhere else in the city, not too far away.

Shahse had only one thought on his mind: Sarah Trenton. He needed to see her again, right away. It wasn't so much fear that a similar disaster could strike her—he couldn't allow himself to think about that possibility—but rather a longing for the comfort of her presence, and an overpowering sense that he needed to be with her, that everything would be alright if only she were by his side.

CHAPTER 39

Unlike in most churches, the vestibule of the sanctuary of Christ Church did not open up directly to the outside, but to the foyer of the overarching building, so Shahse was surprised to find himself in a wide, empty room when he burst through the front doors. What was in front of him, though, was the internal front wall of the church's main office. He could see through the large window that there was someone inside, so he went straight in.

A young lady, unfortunately not Sarah, was standing with her back to Shahse, fiddling with some papers on a table up against the far wall. She turned at the sound of the door, but stopped short when she saw Shahse.

"Hi," he said with some cheerfulness. He'd escaped the frantic feeling he'd been possessed of at the White House. "I'm looking for the sanctuary."

The young lady stared for a moment, finally stammering out, "You're...you're... you're—that guy!"

"Yes, Sei Shahse, thanks for watching," he nodded. "Now, could you tell me where the sanctuary is?"

The lady started to cry.

"Really, maybe you could just point me in a general direction?"

She blubbered on, her cheeks flushed a scarlet red, "You're the devil, you're the devil, please don't kill me, in the name of Jesus don't kill me!"

"Look now, I just want to know where the sanctuary is." He stepped up to her, meaning to giver her a shake and tell her to get a grip on herself, but she shrieked at his approach and fell to the ground in a faint.

Shahse stopped in shock, then bent down to check her pulse. Ascertaining that she was still alive, he stood up and muttered, "Okay, I'll guess I'll go find it myself."

As he turned, he saw the double doors through the office window. "Oh, there it is!"

As he approached he could hear the sounds of Reverend Trenton's booming preacher's voice, as he exhorted his listeners to beware the wiles of Satan. He opened the door a crack and stood behind it, allowing himself to listen for a minute, to get a sense of the man, before making his appearance, which he reasonably suspected would cause a disruption.

"For we," Trenton was saying, "have the everlasting victory over evil and the power of Satan! Victory! In Ephesians 6, Paul says to the church, put on the whole armor of God and fight the good fight of faith. That means the last picture of the church was to be of a militant church, taking a stand against evil! A hard, true stand, the only hope of our escape! Never giving in, never giving ground, never condescending to that which is in the least impure and unholy! There is no victory without a fight! There is no glory without some cost! You must persevere absolutely! You must give All for Christ! Every thought, word, and deed must be beaten into submission to His Will and His Name! For as it says in the First Epistle of Peter, 'The Devil prowls about like a roaring lion, seeking whom he may to devour!' He is vicious and monstrous, and you can never have the slightest dealings with him! How anyone could be so foolish as to listen to his lies is beyond me. How could anyone question God? How could anyone be less than happy to endure the wonderful world He has created? We must listen only to God! Anything, any thought or feeling that causes you to compromise with the holiness of God must be cut off and abandoned! The Bible says for this cause Christ came into the world, to destroy the works of the Devil. Jesus said, 'He that is not for me is against me.' James writes, 'The friend of the world is the enemy of God.' If you care about anything in the world, you are the enemy of God, and he surely brings his vengeance upon you, for we are living in the last days, when the Just and well-deserved Judgment is coming for the corrupt, God-hating world! So whose side are you on?"

There was some cheering from the crowd, and amidst this, Shahse, highly entertained, slipped in. Instantly he was noticed, and a commotion ensued as he'd expected. People nearest him cried out and pushed themselves further down the pews and away from him. Trenton stopped short and stood on the stage a moment, dumbstruck.

"Hi, everybody!" said Shahse, as all eyes focused on him.

The people murmured in response, so he tried again. "Come on, you can to better than that. Hi, everybody!"

"Hi, Mr. Shahse!" they replied in loud unison.

"There you go," he said, beaming. He glanced around, looking over the audience but mainly searching for Sarah, until he noticed her sitting with the choir, in the back, on the right side and perpendicular to the altar. She sat, staring at him in astonishment, in the front position closest to the altar, wearing as did all the others a pure white robe. He felt immediately relieved to see she was unharmed and apparently undiscovered, and amused, too. The *choir*, for heaven's sake!

Haversham was sitting in the back, but on the far end of the aisle. Realizing the opportunity he dreamed of was now at hand, he reached into his pocket for his pistol, only to find it wasn't there. How stupid he'd been, not to take his gun with him into church!

"You! What are you doing here?" Trenton screamed at Shahse from the stage, finally recovering himself.

Shahse started walking forward. People jumped away from him as he passed them, and Haversham used the cover of the commotion to quietly get up and slip out a side door, to go find a weapon. "Oh," Shahse said directly to Trenton, "I was just in the neighborhood, and wanted to stop by to ask your opinion on something."

"How dare you defile the House of God!" Trenton's veins were popping.

"I'm sorry?" He stood right in front of the stage, looking up at Trenton in perfect sincerity. "I thought everyone was welcome in church?"

"Get out! Get out!" said Trenton, making the sign of the cross with his fingers. "I command you, in the Name of Jesus, be gone, you accursed demon!"

Shahse widened his eyes and glanced innocently around at the audience. People were riveted to their seats, struck dumb, but out of the corner of his eye he saw Sarah with her hand over her mouth trying in vain to suppress a grin.

Trenton didn't appreciate the mockery, and grabbed the heavy brass cross from the altar and waved it around, holding it high as he approached Shashe, who didn't budge. When Trenton had stepped down the two stairs from the altar to the sanctuary, Shahse reached out and touched his shoulder. Trenton screamed and ran back up to the altar.

"Get out!" he yelled again.

"Not until I've asked my question."

Trenton stood still for a moment, shocked that Shashe wanted to *ask* something. "What is it?" he said hesitantly after a moment.

"Well, as you may have noticed, the sun has darkened, the moon has turned red, and humongous meteors are crashing all around us. It's obviously the fulfillment of Revelations 6:12, except for the part about the massive earthquake. I thought that was supposed to happen first, yet it clearly hasn't. I don't understand how that can be, and I'm hoping you have an answer."

Trenton took a moment to respond, as he was knocked even deeper into shock than he had been. "You know about prophecy?" he said at last. "You understand what's going on?"

"Of course I do!" Shahse smiled ingenuously. "You didn't know that I knew? I thought you guys were listening in on all my conversations."

Now Trenton was too shocked to speak at all. Shahse didn't think it was a case of them not getting the information, because he knew it was out there. Baines certainly seemed to have heard it in full. But if Trenton had listened in as well, he may not have been able to take it all seriously. Or no, on second thought, Trenton was likely simply shocked at being found out, at the mere fact that he knew what they were doing.

"You're not going to tell me?" he prodded.

Trenton regained his senses, and then went further, steeling himself for another condemnation against evil. He replaced the cross on the altar and came around to face Shahse directly, standing only a few feet away.

"You will be defeated," he said sternly, but calmly.

"Well, yes, I am aware of that."

"You are nothing. You are a murderer and a liar, a child of evil, and you and all your works will come to naught. You may think you are a mighty man now, but it is we, the people of God, who will triumph and rule for eternity with Christ, while you will be crushed and utterly forgotten."

Shahse smiled faintly. "I disagree."

"You think you will defeat God Almighty?" said Trenton, his voice rising.

"I didn't say that, exactly."

"No, of course not. You can't! God shall triumph. We will live forever in His all-encompassing love, and He will be forever triumphant over you!"

"Well now."

"How dare you mock," said Trenton coldly. "You will be thrown into hell and punished for your sinful ungodliness for all eternity. You are nothing. Nothing!"

"Yes, well," Shahse said with a little shrug. "As I said, I disagree. I just think that I must actually be very significant in the grand scheme of things indeed, if little old me can do anything to hurt the omnipotent divine creator of the universe, let alone something that upsets God so much that he can never, ever, ever get over it and has to punish me for all eternity. What was it Confucius said? 'If you can't control you anger, your anger will control you.' Something like that."

"How dare you!" shrieked Trenton. "How dare you!"

"I'm just saying."

"That's not it at all!" shouted Trenton. "It's about Justice! Perfect Justice!"

"Justice? You think anyone deserves to burn for all eternity?"

"Yes!"

Shahse grinned broadly. "Cool," he said. He turned to the audience. "Well, I think I've stayed long enough. *Au revoir!*" He waved to them all around, and then started to walk back down the aisle.

Abruptly he stopped, and turned around again. "Oh, yes, one more thing," he said, this time speaking to the audience, giving them a quick sweep with his eyes. "If anyone wants to come with me, they're more than welcome."

Of course he'd said this for Sarah's benefit, to let her know it was okay to reveal her true feelings now, because he would take care of her. He noticed her sitting bolt upright, perhaps wanting to come but being unable to do so in front of all these people.

"No one here will ever go with you! These are good, decent people—they would never be on your side!" said Trenton.

"All right then." He gave Sarah another few seconds, but she remained stuck in her chair. She looked frightened and miserable, though, and he decided she wanted to go, but he needed to give her a more direct push.

He turned around, took a few steps in the direction of the door, then stopped again. "Hey, before I go, can I just say a word to Sarah?"

"What?" asked Trenton sharply.

"Yeah, Sarah. Your daughter. We met on the plane; I'm sure you know all about that." He motioned to her. "Come on down, Sarah."

"Stay where you are!" Trenton said to her before she had a chance to stand up. She hesitated a moment, then got up anyway, and slowly walked their way. Shahse felt a cheer in his heart as he watched her approach. The robe she wore looked a size too big for her. The sleeves came down to her fingers, and the hem was barely above the floor. It was zipped up right to her neckline, so none of her other clothes could be seen. She might have been naked under the robe, a thought which delighted Shahse.

Trenton went right up to her and caught her before she got more than a few paces. "What are you doing?" he said. "Get back in your seat!"

"But Daddy," she said quietly.

"No! Now get back over there."

"But I want to hear what he has to say." She tried to move forward again, but he held her stationary.

Shashe saw that the situation needed even more intervention. He bounded up the two steps to the stage, and went right over to the two of them.

"Get out of here!" Trenton said to him.

Shahse ignored him. "Sarah, I realize I was wrong to let you go. I want you to know how much I care about you. I came here on the spur of the moment, so I don't have a ring, but Sarah," he said, getting down on one knee, "will you marry me?"

The audience collectively inhaled. Trenton blinked rapidly several times, unable to understand what he was hearing. Sarah, though, smiled with enormous delight and took his hand.

"Yes!" she said. "Yes! I will!"

"Aww," said the audience, while applauding.

"What!" said Trenton, his face reddening. "How, how, how could you!" he demanded, speaking to both of them. Shahse stood up, and he and Sarah, laughing with giddiness, ran off the stage and up the aisle.

"Stop them!" shouted Trenton. "Don't let them get away!" Shahse and Sarah continued unconcerned, because hadn't these people just a moment ago been trembling in fear of him? Yet Trenton kept shouting. "For heaven's sakes stop them! He can't hurt you. God will protect you!"

And the people believed that, for several of them suddenly took up positions at the end of the aisle, blocking their escape. Shahse stopped, awestruck. More people, men and women both, got up to join those standing guard.

"What gives?" said Shahse, looking around at them. They were still scared, he could see the fear in their eyes, but now they were summoning all their courage to stand firm against him and his cruel tyranny (which still hadn't started, but that was no reason to pass up an excellent opportunity to stand firm against it).

"You can't stop me," he said. "I'm the Antichrist, et cetera. Remember? Aren't you afraid of me?" They ignored him. More people began to stand up, and they started to move in closer to where he stood.

Shahse, as always, was unconcerned about his own safety, but he was worried about Sarah. Now that her true loyalties were revealed, there was no telling what they might do to get her to repent once they got their hands on her. The only recourse seemed to be going back to the stage, and trying to escape out the back way, but how were they going to get there from where they stood?

"You have a gun?" Sarah whispered to him.

"No."

"A cellphone?"

"Sure," he said, pulling it out of his pocket and slipping it to her. "But what good's that going to do?" His only thought was that she might use the camera feature to set off a flash, momentarily blinding the people, giving them a second to run back down the aisle. But how would that work against all of them?

She took the phone, flipped it open, and quickly punched in a number.

"Who are you going to call?" asked Shahse, watching in perplexity. "I don't think anybody's going to rescue us."

"I'm calling my own phone, which I left in the bunker downstairs." She looked up at the crowd, straight in their eyes, and stared them down. She spoke loud enough so that everyone could hear. "Guess what I've been doing in my spare time, when I'm down there all alone? I've been a bad girl. I've wired all your explosives together, and connected my phone to a detonator. All I have to do is press 'dial,' and this whole building blows sky high."

As expected, the audience erupted in panic at this, and people began screaming and darting for the exits in all directions. The aisle filled up as people pushed and shoved each other aside in a sudden desperation to escape. Sarah grabbed Shahse's hand, and pulled him through the crowd in the opposite direction. The managed to climb onto the stage, where they rushed past Trenton, who had been shocked into immobility, and could only stare hopelessly at them as they slipped through a back door. Sarah led him down a hall, past the choir's practice room, as well as several others, and finally through another door that led outside, where the sky was still filled with black clouds. They slowed down their pace as they fled the building, until finally they stopped in the middle of the parking lot, and faced each other.

"We did it!" she said.

"Yeah, that was great. But, um, did you really wire up all the explosives?"

She laughed. Other people ran past them, hurrying to their cars, apparently no longer concerned about keeping them from fleeing. "No," she said. "Not that I didn't think of it, all alone down there in those dark empty nights, but no."

"Oh, that's good," Shahse said with a small sigh of relief.

"Don't tell me *you're* scared?"

"Not at all. It's just that I can't condone that sort of thing, and I'm glad you weren't really planning on blowing up a church. That wouldn't be right."

"No, of course not," she quickly agreed.

"Though, admittedly, it would be pretty cool."

She took his head in her hands, and pulled him down to her. They kissed hard on the lips, and kept kissing even when he thought the moment over and tried to pull away. This only caused her to pull him closer, and she slipped her tongue into his mouth, to brush against his teeth and play with his own. They stood like this for a full minute, right in the middle of the parking lot, as cars whizzed by them in a desperate escape.

Finally they ran out of oxygen and had to separate. Sarah looked up at him with a gleam in her eyes. "Are we really going to get married?" she said, panting. She couldn't wait until they were together, as they belonged. She was filled with excitement at finally being with the man she loved, and the glorious promise their future together, short as it would be (what with the world ending and all that). And she was so eager to tell him of all the things that had happened while they'd been separated, principally about that nice young man she'd converted, and how he'd come back the next day with his boyfriend, whom she spoke to and also converted, and how the pair had gone off and converted a whole bunch of their sympathetic friends, and how it just kept spreading, so that without even realizing it, Shahse already had a sizable following of devout Antichristians (Shaheians?), all headed straight for hell. He would be so proud of her.

"You bet."

"Very soon?"

"As soon as possible. It might be a week or two, because things are going to be pretty chaotic for a while, once that earthquake hits. Speaking of which, I never did get an answer to my question. I don't suppose you know?"

She shook her head. "Sorry. But we'll figure it out later. Right now we have to get out of here, before anyone else tries to stop us."

"Too late," said Haversham, who they suddenly realized was standing only a few feet away, his gun aimed at Shahse's head. It hadn't been in his car, and he was a mile up the road before remembering all the guns in the church basement, where he'd just been, in ignorance of everything going on above; but whatever, it was beside the point, as far as he was concerned. They turned to face him, and Sarah put her hand on Shahse's shoulder.

"At last!" he said, grinning rather fiendishly. "I've been waiting for this."

"You can't!" cried Sarah, stepping in front of Shahse and shielding his body. "You can't kill him. He's the Antichrist, et cetera."

Haversham twisted his mouth in disgust. "Oh, not you too, Sarah. You know I don't believe in that shit. I don't believe anything's inevitable. The future is ours and ours alone to summon from the innumerable formless possibilities into the one solid reality."

Shahse laughed.

"You're a fool," said Sarah. "But besides all that, I won't let you kill him."

"Why not? What's going on now?"

"I won't let you kill him. We're in love."

Haversham lowered his gun, but only partly. "In love?" He shook his head. "Sarah, I don't know what he told you, but he's lying. He's a manipulator. He's evil. He has to be destroyed. Now, please get out of the way. Because I will shoot you if I have to, to get to him."

"You will? You'd shoot me, without even offering me a chance to repent of my evil ways and come to know the Lord?" she mocked. "That's so un-Christian of you."

Haversham puzzled over that a moment, thinking of an appropriately biting quip, was unsuccessful, and decided just to shoot them. But just as he prepared to pull the trigger, they heard a low thunderous rumbling sound, coming from all directions, and suddenly the ground started to vibrate. They could feel the vibrations running up their feet into their bodies, and they swayed along with everyone and everything else in the vicinity, until they could balance themselves no longer, and fell to the earth. The violent shaking lasted several more seconds before it finally subsided.

The earthquake! Shahse was delighted that it had happened, just as it was supposed to, just as the prophecy had foretold, but before he could say anything, or even move, the church building exploded.

The quake had torn the building apart, loosening the electrical wires, which fell into, and set off, the massive numbers of explosive chemicals being stored in the basement. A chain reaction set them all off nearly simultaneously, and the resulting blast blew the walls flat and sent the roof flying in a million directions. A fireball roared out, smashing and burning the few cars still left in the parking lot.

Shahse, Sarah, and Haversham were all close enough to the ground that the incendiary heatwave passed right over them, harmlessly. After things settled down, they slowly sat up.

"Oh, wow," said Sarah. "That was so cool!"

"It was, wasn't it?" said Shahse, taking her hand as the stood up together. They looked at each other and grinned. "Now let's get out of here." Together, they raced across the lot to where Shahse's limousine was parked, a bit charred looking but evidently unharmed. The road surface had some new cracks in it, but its pavement was made out of recycled tires, so it had been rubbery enough to withstand the shaking for the most part. Glancing at it, Shahse thought the quake hadn't been that bad after all, but then he remembered Washington wasn't anywhere near a fault line, so it was understandable the effects had been muted here. But just think how intense it must have been elsewhere, especially at places that *were* on fault lines. The western half of California must have finally broken off and sunk into the Pacific, causing untold millions of deaths, which was awful beyond the scope of imagining, but was also, for that very reason, pretty freaking cool.

Haversham stood up and watched them go. He was furious at them for escaping, and was inclined to run after them, but he could hear someone shouting for help in the distance. He turned and looked at the burning ruins of the church, and knew the most responsible thing to do was to go through the wreckage and search for survivors and other victims who needed his aid. Shahse could wait until another day. After all, Haversham knew where he lived.

At the limo, the pair found the driver kneeling in prayer, with his forehead touching the ground. He was sobbing quietly as he did.

"Hey, come one, we have to get out of here," said Shahse. He opened the back door and held it for Sarah, before sliding in himself and slamming it shut.

The chauffer got in behind the wheel and sat there a moment in silence.

"Hey, let's go," said Shahse.

"It is true, isn't it," the man said evenly, without moving. "You are responsible for all of this. They said you were the devil, and I was not sure, but now I see the truth. Now I see what I must do." He turned around in his seat and looked at them through the small open window in the panel that separated the front seat from the back. He was a young Arab, and he was holding a gun.

"Sheik al-Tineri ordered me to kill you," he said, sounding frightened and morose. "He sends his greeting." He raised his gun, then lowered it. Then he raised it again, but could not pull the trigger.

"Well, shoot me already," said Shahse with a bored sigh. This was getting very annoying.

The chauffer held the gun steady at Shashe a moment longer, then abruptly swung it to Sarah and fired. She jerked back against the seat with a shocked yell.

"Sarah!" said Shahse, grabbing her.

There was a gaping hole in her upper chest, and blood was soaking her gown in a pattern spreading out and down. She looked up at

Shahse, and he could see fear in her eyes for a brief moment, before they went dark and her body became limp.

"Sarah! No! Oh, God, no!" said Shahse, beginning to sob. He cradled her and repeated her name over and over. He hardly noticed the click when chauffer pulled back the hammer of his pistol and held it to Shahse's head.

He could sense the gun and turned. The youth looked more certain than he had a moment ago, as if killing one person had steeled his nerves to kill the second. But behind him, Shahse could see a figure moving outside the car. The figure opened the driver's door, and another gun appeared. The chauffer saw the gun and tried to turn to shoot the intruder, but he had to pull his arm through the window between the front and back seat, which delayed him, fatally so. The figure fired, and the chauffer fell across the front seat, dead.

Shashe watched as the figure moved around to the back of the car and opened the door.

"Jack? Are you okay?" said Griffin, leaning in.

"She's dead," was all he could say.

"Come on, Jack, let's get you back home." He reached in and took Shahse by the arm and pulled him out. Shahse went, but only very reluctantly. "Sarah," he moaned repeatedly. When Griffin had extracted him from the car and got him standing, he had to help him walk as they crossed the short distance to his own car. Tenney was standing next to the open driver's side door.

"What happened?" she asked.

"She's dead," said Shahse.

"Sarah's dead?" asked Tenney, lightning up.

"Shut up," said Griffin. "Just get in." He opened the back door and maneuvered Shahse into it, then shut the door and went around to the passenger side and got in.

Tenney started the car. "Well, it serves her right," she said.

"It's not fair," moaned Shahse from the back. "How could God allow this to happen?"

"Gee, I wonder," said Tenney.

"Just drive," said Griffin.

CHAPTER 40

Most of the people had stormed out of the church together in the panic, so almost nobody was still inside when it exploded. Reverend Digby and a few of the other ministers who had nowhere else to go had hung around close enough to the building to sustain some minor injuries, which Haversham easily treated. Reverend Trenton, though, was missing and presumed dead until someone saw him at the far side of the parking lot, by the deserted limousine.

Haversham went to check on him, and found him sitting in the back seat by the open driver's side door, weeping and cradling Sarah's bloody corpse in his lap. He hesitated to approach, but decided he should say something.

He stood next to Trenton and said, "Hey." Trenton didn't answer, just sat stroking Sarah's hair. Lying down like that, with her eyes closed, she appeared rather peaceful.

"Everybody got out," said Haversham. "No major injuries, but the building's a total loss. All our computers and supplies and weapons, everything's gone. Well, except for a few guns we were keeping in the tool shed."

"My baby is dead," said Trenton.

"I'm sorry."

"She's dead and her soul is lost, lost forever!" he wailed.

Haversham didn't think it was appropriate to even acknowledge having heard that, so he kept silent, his face passive and calm.

"This is all *his* fault," said Trenton. "That monster. He's a destroyer and a deceiver and he's ruined *everything.*"

Haversham looked down at him with all sympathy, and knew what he was going to say as well as he knew it was wrong to say it. Now wasn't the time. He should just leave the poor man to his grief, and worry about how they were going to rebuild their mission later. But mere resistance was clearly no longer enough; it would only result in more heartache and loss. There was only one thing left to do. What were they all doing here, if not for this?

"So," he said carefully, "what do you want to do about it?"

Finally, Trenton looked up at him, his teeth bared in an intense grimace. "Let's go get him."

Haversham nodded. "About time."

CHAPTER 41

Tenney and Griffin drove Shahse back to his office tower in Tysons Corner. The ride there was strangely smooth. The roads were cracked in places, there were numerous potholes, and an overpass had collapsed, but the damage was surprising light, given the enormity of the world-shattering earthquake that had just occurred. But then again, with no fault lines in the area, it was enough to suggest the limitless extent of the quake's power. Shahse, world leader that he was supposed to be, wasn't taking any notice of the damages during the trip. He just in the back seat, moaning, and occasionally mumbling some pitiful lament about Sarah.

Shahse's tower was still standing, and looked unscathed. They hustled him inside and up the elevator, which, thanks to the building's back-up generators, was in perfect working order, and into his penthouse, where he collapsed on the sofa.

"I can't believe she's dead," he whimpered.

"Oh, what is your problem?" said Tenney. "Come on Jack, think of it this way: she's in a worse place now."

Shahse looked up at her, a scowl on his face.

"And isn't that what she wanted?" she pressed on. "She wanted to go to hell, and now she's there. You should be happy for her. Even though I'm sure *she's* not very happy." She glanced at Griffin with a smile. "Yes, burning in hell. But you like that idea, don't you? It turns you on, doesn't it, you sick freak."

"It's not like that," Shahse said, with his grief slowly giving way to a rising anger.

"Oh, please. We all know you're one fucked up little bastard."

"Leave the poor man alone," said Griffin. He was standing by the far wall with his arms crossed, observing them.

Tenney turned her head to face him. "Excuse me? The 'poor man?' Millions of innocent people are probably dead from that earthquake, and this guy's all weepy over the one single person who actually deserved it."

"Stop it," said Shahse. Impulsively, he reached for his broadsword where he'd left it, on the table, only to find it missing. But no, after a second he noticed that it was only on the floor; it must have slid off during the quake. He bent down and grabbed the hilt, gave it a swing, then stood and pointed the tip at Tenney. She looked at it and smirked.

"Is that supposed to scare me?"

"I'd be careful, if I were you," said Griffin. "He's very good with that. I've watched him practicing. He'll take your head off before you can blink."

"No he won't. Come on, it's a *sword*. It's not like it's going to go off accidentally."

Shahse glanced at the sword and gave a start, as though he was surprised to realize he was holding it. He tilted it back and forth for a few seconds, watching the light glint off it. "I bet that's it," he said quietly. "I bet that's why she died. To get me enraged. God's trying to provoke me to kill someone. Or maybe it's the devil. Or both of them, even. They're trying to push me over the edge, turn me into the murderer everyone wants the Antichrist to be."

Griffin and Tenney exchanged concerned glances. "You don't want to do that, Jack," said Griffin.

"No, I don't," he replied, with a sad shake of his head. He sat down on the sofa again, and placed the sword back onto the table. "Maybe I'm going about this the wrong way."

"There's a right way to destroy the world?" asked Tenney.

"Maybe I don't want to be the Antichrist any longer," he said. "It's not fun anymore. Maybe I should get out. I can change my mind if I want. I still have free will, right? If I chose to be the Antichrist, I can choose to not to be."

"I think it may be too late for that, Jack," said Griffin.

"No, it can't be too late. Just because Sam Tenney can't repent doesn't mean I'm stuck. If my being the Antichrist in the first place is dependent upon my free will choice, then I can rescind that choice at any time. I have to always retain my free will, because if I don't have free will, I'm not responsible for my actions, and what kind of a mess is that?"

"But I can lose my free will?" asked Tenney, confused.

"Well, yeah. You're just a bit player. I'm the one holding everything together. God needs me and my eager willingness. I just have to stop all that, stop playing along, stop doing what I'm doing."

"How?" asked Griffin. "I thought you weren't doing anything in the first place. Stuff just happens to you, remember? Your life is one coincidence after another."

"You're right." Shahse hummed thoughtfully and looked up at him. "This requires drastic action. I may have to kill myself."

CHAPTER 42

Having sped all the way over, doing untold damage to his beautiful, shiny green Hummer by bouncing through potholes and slamming past debris, Reverend Trenton pulled up sharply to the guard booth in front of Shahse's office tower, with Haversham riding shotgun. The lone guard stepped out and came over to the car. Scowling, Trenton rolled down the window as the guard leaned down and said, "I'm sorry sir, this is a restricted area—"

Without a word, Trenton raised the pistol he was holding in his lap and fired into the guard's face.

Haversham was taken aback but was careful not to say anything. Trenton floored the gas, driving over the spikes in the road and shredding his tires as he smashed through the gate.

The car crawled around to the building's front entrance. Trenton turned the engine off and jumped out. A guard stepped out of one of the double doors and Trenton blew him away before he had a chance to react.

Haversham got out slowly and unholstered his own weapon as he followed behind Trenton into the building.

Inside was a spacious, well lit, potted plant-filled lobby blocked by a metal detector and two guards. Before either could react, Trenton reached under his jacket with his left hand and pulled out a second gun, and raised both his arms and shot the guards simultaneously.

He walked through the metal detector, which beeped noisily, and continued apace up the foyer. A side door opened, and two more guards stepped into the hall. Again, Trenton shot them both simultaneously, hitting them dead center. He'd been doing target practice in the parking lot at the church in his spare time, sometime with Sarah, sometimes with Reverend Digby, but most often alone.

Haversham walked through the metal detector and glanced down at the guards sprawled on the floor. He was surprised to notice that none of them were carrying guns, just batons. He looked up in time to see Trenton blow away the guy sitting with raised hands, begging for mercy, at the desk next to the elevators.

Trenton stood tapping his foot impatiently as he waited for the elevator. It opened just as Haversham caught up with him, and he got in. He looked over the numbers and noticed the PH button next to a keyhole.

"Get his key," he shouted to Haversham, who already knew about the key from his previous trip and was now pushing the last guard, who was actually still alive and slumped over the desk, breathing with raspy labor through the ragged, gaping hole in his chest but otherwise couldn't move, out of the way. Besides the key, he knew there was a simple button on the console that would give them access to the penthouse, and he pushed it before getting into the elevator. The PH button was now lit.

"Nice shooting," said Haversham.

"Thanks," said Trenton. "I've been practicing." He wasn't in the mood for talk, though, and didn't elaborate. As the elevator approached the penthouse and slowed to a stop, they cocked their guns in silence.

CHAPTER 43

They hadn't heard the shooting in the lobby, but Tenney and Griffin pulled out their weapons when the elevator unexpectedly chimed its arrival. It opened and Haversham and Trenton jumped out, ready to start firing, then stopped when they noticed who else was present. The four of them stared at each other across the room.

"Oh, it's you," said Griffin, mildly surprised. They all lowered their guns but held on to them. "What are you doing here?"

"What are we doing here? What are *you* doing here?" Haversham demanded.

"Are you here to try to kill me again?" sighed Shahse from the couch. "Didn't you learn anything from your last attempt?"

"You're going to pay for what you've done!" snapped Trenton, rattling his guns at Shahse.

"Oh, all right," said Shahse, who wearily got up and walked over to where they stood.

"Hey, Jack, don't forget your sword," said Tenney. "I want to see you slice off his head before he can blink."

"No, no." He waved his hand at her dismissively.

"Oh, come on, Jack," she said with a grin. "Please?"

He only shook his head, and Haversham asked, "Why are you calling him Jack?"

"Because that's my real name," said Shahse. "Don't you know that? Don't you know all my secrets? Honestly now, I thought you people had my place bugged from top to bottom and were listening in on all my conversations. Don't tell me after all this time that you weren't!"

"We were," said Haversham. "Or at least the Secret Service was. One of our members is an agent, and he was supplying us with transcripts through Captain Hiram Manly, but after he died there's been some problems, so we haven't gotten anything." He glanced at Trenton. "Right?"

"He was working with you, Samantha," said Trenton, looking over at her with perplexity, a newfound suspicion.

"Yeah, well, you caught me," she said causally. "I never passed them on."

"You?" said Haversham. "You were spying on us? For *him*?"

"Yeah, yeah. I was the spy all along. I told him about the bugs and all that."

"How could you?"

She shrugged. "Like I said, he already knew everything. I was just confirming. The only serious stuff I did was in what I neglected to tell you."

"Traitor!" shouted Trenton. "You're responsible for Hiram's death!"

Tenney shook her head with a chuckle. "Oh no, that was all Sarah."

"Liar!"

"No, it's true," said Shahse, who was still just standing there, waiting to be shot. "I mean, now that she's dead, there's no point keeping it a secret. In fact, I think she would have wanted you to know, just to rub it in. She killed your captain friend, all by herself."

"No, I don't believe that." His face was turning red as his every utterance became more empathetic.

"It's really true," said Tenney. "She also told me all about how Shahse stole her soul and turned her evil. And now she's burning in hell."

Trenton began to tremble. Haversham said, "It's all his fault, just like you said. Now here's your chance, so shoot him already."

Trenton raised the gun so that the barrel was level with Shahse's head. Very slowly he squeezed the trigger, straining as though it was a tremendous effort, but at the last moment he relaxed his grip. He held the pistol up for another few seconds before lowering it and saying, "I can't do it."

"What do you mean you can't do it!" Haversham exploded. "We came all this way, the man's destroyed everything you hold near and dear, and you can't do it? Your own daughter is burning in hell right now! Right now! And for all eternity! All eternity! And it's all his fault! Now shoot him, for God's sakes!"

"I can't," sighed Trenton. "It wouldn't be right."

"Why the fuck not?"

"He's unarmed. Killing is only justified when it's done in self-defense, but he's not threatening anyone. If I shoot him, it would be murder."

Now it was Haversham who was becoming red-faced and apoplectic. "What about all those guards downstairs? None of them had guns!"

"Well, I didn't know that. Who hires unarmed guards these days?"

"I didn't think I needed any protection," said Shahse. He blinked in disbelief. "You killed all those guys?" Those guys had been his friends, sort of, or at least they were among the very few people he was speaking to these days.

Trenton shrugged. "Besides, they were working for Satan."

"And he *is* Satan!" screamed Haversham.

"Technically, I'm only the son of Satan. There is a distinction, you know. Our Trinity doesn't work the same way as that other one."

"Shut the fuck up!"

"It wouldn't be right," Trenton continued. "Jesus calls upon us to forgive our enemies, and so I must forgive him, even for all he's done. 'Vengeance is sin, sayeth the Lord.'"

"How—" Haversham stammered a moment before calming down. "Okay then, fine, don't kill him for vengeance. Kill him to save the millions, no billions, of other lives he's going to destroy!"

"We can't do that," said Trenton, shaking his head.

Haversham lowered his gun and turned to Trenton. He looked him straight in the eyes and said, slowly and forcefully, "Let me tell you something. I am a cop. I have dedicated my life to stopping bad guys, and this right here is the biggest bad guy of them all. I did not come here, *again*, just to turn around and walk out the door, *again*, without doing what I came here to do. We have got to put an end to this, right here and right now!"

"Yes, but I mean we can't. Remember? He's the Antichrist, et cetera?"

With that, Haversham's frustration finally reached the boiling point. He screamed and shot Trenton in the abdomen. The reverend dropped his guns and staggered backwards several steps before collapsing. They all stared while Trenton bled out all over the carpet. He reached up, into the air, slowly opening and closing his hand, and tried to say something but could only gag. After a moment he finally lost the strength to do even these things, and his arm fell, and his body became still as the life left him.

"Well now," said Shahse, turning back to Haversham, "that was completely unnecc—"

Without a word, Haversham spun around and fired. Shahse was hit directly in his chest, and fell backward. Shocked that he'd actually done it, he looked down at Shahse's body, at the red blood slowly seeping out of the wound in his chest, right in the vicinity of his heart. He lay flat and unmoving, evidently dead in an instant.

Haversham looked up at Griffin and Tenney, grinning in awe at his own achievement. "I did it," he said. "I killed him. I killed him!"

"I thought that wasn't possible?" Tenney said to Griffin. She was puzzled, but nothing more. She thought she'd be pleased, but if not elated, that the antichrist was dead and her soul freed, but instead she felt only a slight sense of dread. She knew it would take a few minutes for it to sink in, before she could feel any true emotional response to Shahse's death. Until then, though, she was left with the unsettling awareness that Shashe wasn't supposed to die, which meant something must have gone very wrong.

Griffin also felt the same understanding. "It's not," he said in response to her question. To Haversham he said, "You shouldn't have been able to do that."

"Well, I did, and now the world is free. It's free from his insanity, from his careless cruelty, from this reckless obsession that the world is going to end."

"Well, it is still going to end, one way or another," said Griffin.

"Not on my watch," laughed Haversham. "I stopped the Antichrist!"

"Only the Christ can stop the Antichrist."

"Right, at Armageddon. Fuck that. We don't need that. I've stopped all that from happening. I've saved the world!"

"Only Jesus can save the world, which makes that blasphemy," said Griffin thoughtfully.

"Oh, get off it."

"Perhaps we've had it wrong the whole time, despite all the evidence to the contrary. Perhaps Jack never was the Antichrist, it was all some sad delusion on his part."

"Oh, no," said Haversham, already seeing where this was going.

"But *you*," said Griffin, pointing at him.

"Fuck you!" shouted Haversham, enraged again. "I just saved the whole fucking world, and suddenly *I'm* the bad guy? What the hell is the matter with you?" He gestured down at Shahse's body. "And did you forget already? He's 6-6-6!"

"At what does your name mean?"

Haversham, of course, sputtered in disbelieving frustration without answer, but Tenney did. "I know. He told me once, just in a sort of offhand, amusing way. 'Haversham' is an old Celtic name meaning 'goat herder.'"

"Of course," said Griffin, struck with revelation. "The goat is a pagan symbol. The Last Judgment parable of Matthew 25 plainly compares believers and those who do good works as sheep, while the wicked are referred to as goats. Jesus is the described as the Good Shepherd, and always associated with sheep, so it makes perfect sense that the Antichrist would be a herder of goats. Plus the Druids were Celtic."

Haversham just shook his head. "Oh, for the love of God," he said. "Don't make me shoot you, too."

"How about his first name?" said Tenney, mildly amused by the whole argument. A sense of comfort and pleasure at the death of Shahse was slowly creeping through her. If he wasn't the Antichrist, then her soul was hers again, and it might even be possible that she could find some way to get into heaven. "Did you ever hear what it was?"

"No, I never did. I've learned everyone else's first name, yet strangely enough Haversham's first name has never been mentioned, almost like it's a key piece of information that's been purposefully kept a secret the entire time in order to be revealed at the critical moment of our adventure."

"Yeah," said Tenney, trading quick glances with Haversham. "Anyway, his first name's Nicholas."

Griffin sucked in a deep breath. "Of course! That settles it!"

"Oh, for God's sakes," said Haversham, thoroughly disgusted. His raised his gun at Griffin. Griffin reacted instinctually, raising his own gun at him. They fired simultaneously, the double blast reinforcing each other to echo in the penthouse with a percussion greater than two separate blasts. The wall next to Griffin exploded with the impact of Haversham's bullet, while Griffin's found its mark. Haversham fell backwards, and Tenney screamed. She rushed across the room and knelt down at this side, driven by an impulsive concern for her former partner, the man with whom she spent thousands of hours investigating crimes and interrogating suspects and chatting aimlessly long into the night as they waited in quiet stakeouts. There was a bullet hole right in his forehead; Griffin's aim had been perfect, and he'd died instantly.

She felt tears welling in her eyes. "He's dead! How could you!" she shouted at Griffin.

"Well, I had to," said Griffin, unruffled. "He was going to kill me." He shrugged. "Besides, he's evil. He's the Antichrist."

"If he's the fucking Antichrist," screamed Tenney in outrage, "then how did you kill him?"

Griffin felt a shock so intense it was almost a physical sensation. "I don't know. You're right, I shouldn't have been able to do that. Unless he wasn't the Antichrist. But that can only mean..." For the first time in his life, he was afraid, truly and deeply afraid, an existential terror that beat on his chest and tore at his mind like a wild animal. "That can only mean that *I'm* the Antichrist."

"What?" said Tenney.

"It all makes perfect sense," said Griffin, now visibly shivering. "I'm so morbidly obsessed with evil and violence and the dark mysteries of the human soul. I wanted to know the heart of evil. And I keep having these disturbing fugues (a dissociative disorder characterized by an episode in which an individual forgets his past, assumes a partial or complete new identity, and travels away from home or work, in some cases taking up a new name, occupation, and lifestyle). And my name is Lucious, which sounds sort of like Lucifer, so it must be a sign of evil!" he stared at Tenney with a wild, wretched look that was completely unrecognizable in him.

"But," she said weakly.

"I'm pure evil!" he cried. "I have to stop myself!" Despairingly, he stuck the barrel of his gun into his mouth, and pulled the trigger.

Tenney shrieked again as his brains splattered across the wall behind him, and his body collapsed to the floor. She shivered violently and looked about at the death that now filled the room. But in that quiet mess, the main question, the most basic elemental question, was what frightened her most. Who was the Antichrist? If it wasn't Shahse, and it wasn't Haversham, and it wasn't Griffin, or for that matter Baines or al-Tineri or Pope Perfect or Sarah, or even Reverend Trenton for that matter, since they were all dead, then just who was it? There was only one person left.

"Shit," she said, "I don't want to be the Antichrist, either." And so she pulled out her gun and put it to her head, and blew her own brains out.

She slumped to the floor, and for a minute there was a stillness so complete that chirping birds outside could be heard, then Shahse opened his eyes and sat up.

Painfully he stood to his feet. He opened his jacket and reached within to the spot where the bullet had hit, and pulled out the book he'd been keeping in his inside breast pocket. An old single serving packet of ketchup that had been in there was stuck to the back of the book, right where the bullet had passed through. He turned the book over, and saw its cover was undamaged, the bullet having lodged somewhere in the middle.

The book was the pocket-sized Holy Bible. "Why was I even carrying this with me?" Shahse exclaimed angrily, shaking the book, then tossing it across the room.

He observed all the dead bodies strewn about his living room, and all the blood and guts and brain on the floors and walls. It was ghastly, and very disgusting. He clearly wasn't going to be living here anymore.

As he took in each body, he couldn't help thinking of what had become of them in the next world. Trenton had killed a bunch of innocent people, which is normally pretty damning, but then again he seemed to have come to his senses at the end. But on the third hand, he hadn't repented and said the Sinner's Prayer, so it didn't matter. He was screwed.

Haversham had killed a minister and tried to kill two other people, plus he'd tried to interfere with God's plans by saving the world, so he was definitely going to hell.

Griffin had committed suicide, and we all know what that means.

Shahse considered each of them, now burning in the unquenchable fires of hell, and felt sick. It was so awful, so horrendous. And then there was Tenney. There was no question where she was going to end up. He could imagine it vividly, her, naked body, bobbing up and down in the Lake of Fire, screaming and thrashing about as she did. It was just a terrible, terrible, terrible thing, too terrible to even think about thinking about. He did anyway; he couldn't help it, and it gave him chills, set his hairs on end, raised goosebumps all over his body, and sent a cold tingly feeling running down his spine.

The feeling brought a slight smile to his lips. "Mmm, tingly," he said.

THE END

DON'T MISS THE INEVITABLE SECOND VOLUME:

Rapture: Or, The World Continues to End

ABOUT THE AUTHOR

W. JASON PETRUZZI

Jason Petruzzi was born in New Rochelle, New York in 1977, and within days was diagnosed with complex congenital heart disease. In spite of these severe life-long physical limitations, he maintained a cheerful disposition and intellectual curiosity.

After a family move to Northern Virginia, Jason graduated HS in 1995 and worked as a Fairfax County administrative assistant, beginning in 1996. He later earned a B.A. degree in English from George Mason University in 2006, and an M.A. degree in Library & Information Studies from Florida State University in 2011.

Jason had just begun his 19th year of service with Fairfax County when he was seriously injured in a car accident (due to a critical malfunction of his vehicle). After a week in intensive Cardiac Care, he died in 2014 at the age of 37.

Capitalizing on his intellectual strengths, Jason spent much of his free-time creating and writing several novels, poems and short-stories. His own life-long struggles gave him insight into the courage, kindness and compassion for others. Knowing full well how fragile his health was, he left a note to his parents asking for help getting his works published, should he not be able to do it himself.

"Rapture: Or, Satan Wins Again" was created as the result of Jason's deep interest in religious writings and the afterlife, while his first novel, "Dawn of All Things" demonstrates the need to be accepted for all that you are.

www.ingramcontent.com/pod-product-compliance
Lightning Source LLC
Chambersburg PA
CBHW071449170626
46811CB00007B/2520